FOUND DEAD

NATALIE D. RICHARDS

Published by Sourcebooks Fire, an imprint of Sourcebooks
P.O. Box 4410, Naperville, Illinois 60567–4410
(630) 961-3900
sourcebooks.com

Cataloging-in-Publication Data is on file with the Library of Congress.

Printed and bound in the United States of America.
WOZ 10 9 8 7 6 5 4 3 2 1

To Tiffany

Wishing you all the light and
goodness this world can hold

**FOUR FOUND DEAD IN APPARENT
MALL KILLING SPREE**

SANDUSKY, Ohio (AP)—April 8, 2023. Three teens and one adult were found dead after a nine-hour entrapment in the former Riverview Fashionplace shopping mall. Details of the evening are still under investigation. The Sandusky Police Department provided no comment at this time.

I spend a lot of time thinking how that night was supposed to go. We were going to thank the customers who watched the last movie. We would eat one last handful of popcorn and lock the doors for a final time. Then we'd caravan to the IHOP for pancakes and stories and memories.

Now I just want to forget.

Who'd want to remember the night half of us died?

CHAPTER 1

I'LL *NEVER* LOCK THESE DOORS AGAIN. MAYBE THAT'S why I linger at the thick glass, watching the stragglers make their way through the parking lot. They file to their vehicles in pairs and threesomes. Headlights bloom to life; cars reverse and dart. It's an abstract automotive ballet snaking toward the exits. I've watched this routine unfold every Saturday night for three years, but this time is different. Maybe the last time is always different.

I turn away from the bank of doors and grab the broom. Another ballet is about to begin. Lexi and I handle the lobby when we close. We move front to back, starting at the doors—eight sets in total—and work our way past the ticket booths and finally to the concession counters. The concessions are a big job, so we wind up doing half of that too, but tonight, there's no restocking or straightening. It's all being packed up and prepped for auction.

Closing cleanup has always sucked, but tonight has a few silver linings.

I'll never sweep this floor again.

I'll never scrape gum off the side of this trash can again either.

I'll never clean the popcorn bins or count the candy or mop the back floors.

Across from me, Lexi is rolling up the giant rugs that stretch from the lobby doors to the place where the blue carpet begins. Blue except for the occasional bursts of orange squares and yellow triangles trailing out in random directions. Maybe it's a rule that movie theater carpet has to look like a fever dream after a high school geometry test.

"Trash is done," Hudson says.

He's emerging from the theater hallway with Hannah. Both are dragging four trash bags, and they heap them next to the front doors. Hannah winds up her arm with the last, smallest bag, like she's ready to take a pitch. And since she currently pitches on an elite women's softball team, she'd know how to do it.

"Put it in the net!" Hudson says, drumming his hands on his thighs.

"You really need to learn your softball jargon." Hannah laughs. But she tosses her no-nonsense ponytail behind her back and lets the throw rip. The bag lands dead center on top of the heap, the cherry on a sundae of trash.

"Goal!" Hudson cheers, waving his long arms.

Hannah snorts. "How many sports can you jack up in one conversation?"

But Hudson just shakes his streaked hair back and forth and runs in a wild circle, whooping, until we're all laughing.

"Hey!" The shout is deep and shocking and all too familiar.

Hudson's hands drop. Hannah's smile vanishes. And my stomach clenches. The whole mood sours in an instant. Clayton always seems to have that effect.

Are we in big trouble?

It's almost ten years since that day, but my sister's words still echo back to me when I'm afraid. And Clayton is *very* good at making me afraid.

He's watching us from behind the concession counter. He'd say it's his job as a manager to keep us in line, but I think Clayton just loves proving he's in charge. I don't know what lured him out of the office where he usually festers, but something has, and now he's found his favorite thing on earth—a reason to be pissed off. He crosses his thick arms over his chest and pushes his shoulders wide. I swear he stands like this to prove he's the biggest and strongest of the bunch. Or maybe so we know he could hurt us if he wanted.

"Sorry about that," Lexi says, tapping her shiny nails against her broom handle. "They're just goofing off. Last night and all."

"Maybe they should focus up," Clayton says, his eyes locked on Hudson. "Some of us have shit to do tonight."

"Like steroids?" Hudson mumbles. Hannah stifles a laugh.

"What did you say to me?" Clayton asks. There's something different in the tone he uses.

Then he moves around the concession counter and starts toward us. That's different too.

"What did you say?" he repeats, and there's something about his face that feels… I can't put my finger on what I'm seeing, but my body knows. Adrenaline rushes through my veins, tensing my muscles and sharpening my senses.

I take a breath and remind myself this isn't a life-or-death matter. It's just a pissed-off manager that we have to put up with a little longer. Even if Clayton is even creepier than usual right now, I am almost done with this place. Done with him.

"Tell me what he said," Clayton says.

"Nothing," Hannah says. "He didn't say anything."

"No, I think he did. Didn't you, Hudson?" Clayton's voice is low and dangerous. And he is still stalking forward, his blond hair flipped casually out of his eyes.

Clayton's toothpaste-ad good looks always feel like a lie. That innocuous soccer-player hair and aw-shucks smile do not belong on someone so menacing. But usually, he stops at menacing. Tonight, he's still walking toward us. Tonight, glaring isn't enough.

My palms prickle with sweat because this isn't how this game goes. Clayton bitches, flexes, and struts around but keeps his distance. Lexi says his bark is worse than his bite, and she's always been right. Is she still right?

Are we in big trouble?

It's almost like I can feel Cara's frantic whisper against my neck again. I go very still like I did that day all those years ago, watching and waiting for whatever this is to pass.

"What should we focus on when we're done with the lobby?" Lexi asks. She's trying to distract him, but Clayton isn't budging. He's almost to the ticket booths. Hudson is watching him with his chin cocked and his foot tapping wildly. He's probably expecting Clayton to get bored, to say something snarky and move on.

But Clayton isn't moving on.

What the hell is he doing? What the hell is he *going* to do?

He passes Lexi, and in two steps he will move within arm's length of me. I need to move—I need to get out of his way, but I can't. It's like my feet are rooted to the floor beneath me, even as the air goes sour around him, the promise of violence heavier with every step.

My heart is pounding. Buzzing. Screaming. And then it stops. I jolt, realizing it wasn't my heart buzzing and screaming. It was a real sound. The awful, jarring buzz pierces the air again. It's coming from the concession area—the soda machine. It stutters once and then starts again, and just like that, the spell is broken.

Clayton turns—we all turn—to see the source of the noise. Summer is frantically grabbing at different buttons on the machine, which is still buzzing and spitting. I hear a faint splash, and Summer yelps. The buzzing stops, but there's obviously a problem. One of the dispensers is jammed.

"The machine…" Summer says quietly. She doesn't explain anything else, but Clayton pivots. My whole body sags in relief as I watch him move quickly to the concession stand. *Good. Go the hell away.*

I lean back against a ticket booth, feeling boneless. But then my eyes catch on the back of Clayton's Riverview Theaters polo. There is something underneath his shirt.

"Go before he sees you again," Lexi whispers, shooing Hannah and Hudson off.

"We'll help Naomi and Quincy with the bathrooms," Hannah says. She pushes her ponytail back with a freckled hand.

I turn to see them walking away, Hudson's forest-green Chucks slapping softly on the carpet. He flexes his fingers over and over. Because he's always jittery, or because Clayton got to him too?

Either way, he and Hannah head to the restrooms like Lexi suggested. The bathrooms and party rooms are over there, just past the doors that connect the theater to the now-defunct shopping mall. It's strange and dark on the east side of the theater now, the oversize connector doors perpetually closed, leaving a blank gray wall that reminds us this place is becoming more lifeless by the day.

"Want to do the ticket booths?" Lexi asks me.

"Sure. I'll get the floors too." My voice shakes, but I try to swallow it. Try not to look up at the soda machine where Clayton is working with Summer. Because it doesn't matter what I think I saw under his shirt. We are leaving in an hour, and I'll never see this place or that asshole again.

I force myself to power down the ticket machines and wipe down both booths quickly. I snag and stack the small trash cans and set the extra receipt tape and unprinted tickets into neat rows in a small box. Before I know it, the lobby is done.

"Concession time," Lexi singsongs.

"Joy," I say sarcastically.

I'm pretending this is any other closing shift. That I'm bored and ready for Saturday night to begin. Normally that would mean driving Naomi home to my sister, Cara. Tonight it's supposed to mean pancakes with everyone except the bulky, blond nightmare lurking at the soda machine.

I follow Lexi slowly to the concession counter. The soda machine is being triaged by Summer and Clayton on the left, but we head to the right, to the food-prep area and popcorn machine. Lexi starts dumping crusty, overcooked hot dogs, and I tear down the pretzel display on autopilot. And I keep an eye on Clayton and Summer.

No. That's not really true. I'm not looking at Summer. I'm looking at the bulge under the back of Clayton's shirt.

It must be something other than what I'm thinking. I'm imagining shapes where there aren't shapes.

A steady stream of cola starts up again with a sputter, hissing into the black spill grate with enough force to splash the walls and floor, and no doubt Summer and Clayton too. Summer hides behind the curtain of her waist-length hair, but I can still see her shoulders hunch. And I can still see the strange, squarish lump at the small of Clayton's back.

"Turn it off!" Clayton shouts.

Summer flinches but moves forward. Every part of her is

shivering, her long sweater and skirt shaking along with her hands. She pushes the button that should turn it off, but nothing happens. He shoves his way in front of her.

"What the hell did you do?" he snaps.

"I'm sorry," Summer whispers.

Lexi puts down the spray bottle. "Yeah, okay. I've about had enough."

"Me too," I whisper. But I don't move. I hold my breath and hope I blend in with the popcorn machine. Some small shameful part of me knows I can stop this. I could slip up there and quietly fix the machine and take over the cleaning so Clayton could simmer down and probably disappear. I could do it because I'm like wallpaper to him. Quiet, efficient wallpaper.

On another day, I could force myself to snap out of the ice that's trapped me, but now I can only stare at the bulge beneath his shirt while my throat squeezes until I can't breathe. I grip the counter and try to keep my heart from thumping out of my chest, but my memory is dragging me back year by year, back to the last time I saw a thing like that.

Are we in big trouble?

Clayton continues to snap at Summer, and though I burn with shame for abandoning her to this mess, I can't move an inch. The spill grate breaks loose on the soda machine and Clayton swears. Summer jumps back, and Lexi puts down her rag and starts toward them. Lexi is not wallpaper; she is patent leather pumps and red lipstick. Nothing fazes Lexi, not even Clayton.

Clayton shoves the machine so hard the legs scrape the tile beneath. Maybe he does it for better access or maybe just because he's pissed, but then Lexi is right there, sliding into the scene right between Summer and Clayton. Her voice is calm, and her hands are raised in gentle supplication.

Whatever Lexi says is lost to me, because in that moment I notice Clayton's gray polo has ridden up in the back. The thing I'd been trying to guess…the strange squared lump that I wanted to be something else. A full inch of it is visible now, above his belt. It is black and textured and curved in a way that invites a human hand.

My body goes cold, and my mind flashes back. The jangle of bells over a door. Plastic lighters on dirty linoleum. A crimson pool on the gas station floor. And Cara's voice so frightened in our small hiding space.

Are we in big trouble?

Clayton tugs his shirt back into place. He looks me dead in the eye as if to dare me to ask the question burning in the center of my throat. In the end, he skulks back to the office, and Lexi starts on the cleanup. My joints finally unlock, the spell broken. I finish the counter like it's an ordinary night. Like this was any other tantrum thrown by our temperamental manager.

But it's not any other night or any other tantrum. This time, Clayton has a gun.

CHAPTER 2

LEXI SENDS ME TO CHECK ON THE BATHROOMS TO SEE IF they need help with stocking the paper products. I cannot move fast enough. Quincy and Naomi find me wiping down the water fountain between the two restrooms. They're pushing one of the bathroom cleaning carts and dragging a box filled with paper towels and toilet paper. I still hear Hannah and Hudson in the other restroom.

Naomi comes straight up to me. My sister's girlfriend is witty and gorgeous, with enormous dark eyes and hair that is always flawlessly styled and never worn the same way twice. Last week she had an elaborate beaded updo. This week, her tight curls spring wild, spiraling in a thousand directions. Quincy, in contrast, looks exactly the same. Same tortoiseshell glasses and sideswept black hair. Same blue jeans, gray sneakers, and shy smile.

Naomi peels off her yellow rubber gloves. "Hey, Hudson came back here talking about some shit that went down?"

I stop cleaning and nod. I think about the gun strapped to his back. Should I tell them? Do they already know?

"Yeah, so fill us in already," she says.

"Hudson ticked off Clayton," I say.

Naomi crosses her arms. "It's a day that ends in *y*, so that makes sense. Let me guess, in response Clayton went and lost his damn mind."

I wince, wishing she'd speak more softly. I don't want Clayton to hear her. I don't want him to hear or see *any* of us, but I'm not likely to see that wish come true. Disappearing in plain sight is *my* specialty. Maybe Quincy or Summer could manage an approximation of the same thing. But Naomi and Lexi have two times too much personality to blend in. Then we have Hudson, a smart-ass who specializes in pissing Clayton off, and Hannah, who is six foot two and freckled. Invisible is out of the question for most of our group.

"Are you okay, Jo?" Quincy frowns, always the observant and thoughtful guy. "You seem distraught."

I nod too quickly and rapidly. "Clayton was worse than usual. He actually started coming toward us. Like he was going to...I don't even know."

Naomi cocks her head. "Do I need to give that man a lesson on boundaries?"

I wave my hands, pushing that idea away. "No, no, it's not like that. He just blew his top."

And he has a gun.

He has a gun!

Part of me is screaming the words, but what happens if I say them out loud? Does Naomi confront him? Does Quincy panic? What about Summer, who doesn't even own a TV, so has maybe never even seen a gun on screen let alone in real life? No, there is no point in making a scene. I just want us to get the hell away from him.

"He better watch himself," Naomi says. "That man does not want to play with me."

"Who better watch himself?" Hudson says, announcing his return. Hannah is beside him, holding a mop over her shoulder. The cart Hudson drags is piled with boxes of paper towels and toilet paper.

"Clayton," Quincy answers. "Apparently, he was upset earlier?"

Hudson shakes his hair out of his dark eyes. "The man's a sack of dicks."

Half a laugh breaks through my nerves, and Hudson smirks at me.

"I'm getting tired of his shit," Naomi says, her gaze drifting back toward the center of the theater.

Fear jerks at my insides like a hook. Naomi *has* to let this go. But before I can start in on that job, Hannah tightens her ponytail with a sigh.

"Forget about him," she says. "The bathrooms are done, which means we're done."

"Good, I'm starving," Hudson says.

"Are we picking up Cara on our way to IHOP?" I ask.

Naomi shakes her head. "She works early tomorrow. She said she was going to bed."

"Well, *we're* still getting pancakes," I say, forcing pep into my tone.

"Once his royal majesty unlocks the damn safe," Hudson says.

Naomi rolls her eyes. "Yeah, I will not miss that asshole one bit."

"I am not a fan either," Quincy says. His brows pull together in thought. "He's angry a lot. And it seems like he's always flexing."

Hudson laughs. "Damn, Quincy, I didn't think you were capable of being impolite."

Quincy flushes, his light-brown cheeks going splotchy. "I didn't mean to be rude. It just seems like an odd habit for work."

"You weren't rude," I say. "You were just sharing your thoughts. That's a good thing."

"Says the girl who keeps everything to herself," Hudson says.

I can't stand him for saying it, but I can't really argue with him because he's right.

"No one will miss him," Hannah says.

"Well, we still have to deal with him to get our phones and keys," Naomi says.

"He better not try to wait on opening that safe tonight," Hudson says.

My heart double thumps at the just-dare-me looks Hudson and Naomi are wearing. Hudson has already pissed off Clayton tonight, and Naomi cannot go near him now that I know about that gun. I think about my sister's arms around my neck all those years ago and clear my throat.

"I'll ask him for our phones and keys," I say quickly. Naomi looks like she wants to argue, but I hold up my hand. "He'll barely even notice me. It's probably the easiest way."

With our agreement reached, we head back to the main part of the theater. Instead of making our way toward the concession area, we take the remaining trash to the front doors.

Quincy pats his pockets. "I must have hung the manager keys back up earlier."

Slap slap slap.

The front door. It doesn't rattle or pound like another glass door might. These are reinforced monstrosities, so the sound is flat and hollow. But we can see someone out there at the door. Someone small and slender, with fair hair and a tiny frame. Probably a customer who forgot something in a theater. We get a panicked return visit at least once a week, especially since the theater doesn't have a working phone that can access a live person.

"Hang on a second," Hudson says. He's already halfway across the lobby, grabbing the keys off a hook in the ticket booth.

Shoes squeak in the back hallway, the one that leads from the concession counter to the locker rooms and Clayton's office. Clayton is poised there in the mouth of the hallway, looking stunned.

"Wait," he says.

But Hudson is already unlocking the door and pulling it open.

"Can I help you?" he asks.

"Wait!" Clayton's face has gone blotchy like he's furious again, but I have no idea why. We always check the theaters if a customer comes back for something while we're closing. It's especially important tonight since the whole place is closing forever.

But it doesn't matter because the person at the door walks inside without waiting for an invitation. She is slim and attractive in a purple sweater and a matching pair of kitten heels. Funny thing, though. I haven't seen this girl tonight. And since I've been up front all night, I would have either taken her ticket or delivered her concessions. No way would I have missed a bright purple sweater like that.

"Forget something?" Hudson asks her. "In one of the theaters?"

But the woman doesn't even look at him. She looks straight past him and past me, her eyes searching the empty lobby. She has shoulder-length blond hair and a pinched expression. She's pretty though—in that delicate-featured, forgettable way that rich white girls are often pretty.

Clayton knocks something over at the edge of the concession counter, and the woman in purple narrows her eyes. Her mouth goes hard, and I don't think Clayton is angry like I thought. I think he's afraid.

"Clay." She spits the name out like it tastes bad, and I can't disagree.

Clayton closes the distance between the concession stand and the lobby in what feels like six strides. He snags the manager keys from Hudson with a snarly look and then turns to greet his visitor. Because it's crystal clear this woman isn't a customer. She's here for Clayton, and from the looks of things, she's out for blood.

CHAPTER 3

CLAYTON AND THE WOMAN IN PURPLE STAY CLOSE TO the side of the ticket booth, and they keep their voices low. Not that it matters. None of us need to hear what they're saying to know this is a fight. What's happening isn't a mystery, but who she is? That's anyone's guess.

None of us actually voices a guess, though. We silently find things to do because humans are pack animals. We recognize the scent of danger, and we find ways to survive. In the animal kingdom, this would mean camouflage or graceful, otherworldly speed. For us it means looking busy.

Summer and Lexi are cleaning up the soda machine's mess, and I stack the leftover popcorn tubs and bags. Hannah and Naomi start wiping down the concession counters that I wiped down thirty minutes ago. Even Hudson half-heartedly pushes a broom around the splash zone, a two-foot-wide section of tile in front of the concession counter where customers who overestimate their concession-juggling skills are most likely to have a spill.

Quincy is the only one of us working like he means it. He breaks down every candy case, grouping and organizing the candy by type in a large box. I don't think he can help it. He's the kind of kid who probably keeps a spotless room and shovels the driveways of his elderly neighbors after snowstorms.

All of us pretend it is every other day.

We pretend this is normal.

We pretend Clayton is not having a whisper fight with a mystery woman. And I pretend he does not have a gun holstered under his shirt.

There's a terrible, desperate feeling rolling off their conversation, one that makes me sick to my stomach. The woman fires question after question at Clayton, but he doesn't immediately answer, and she doesn't bother to wait to see if he'll try. Mom told Cara and me that a conversation will never go well when someone asks questions even though they already know all the answers. I can't hear what Clayton is being asked, but something tells me this is definitely one of those conversations.

I line the trash cans on the customer side of the concession counters—though I doubt anyone will need them—and then hand the roll of liners back over the counter. Naomi takes them, looking up at me with irritation written all over her face.

"What is this shit?" she whispers, her eyes on Clayton and the angry woman. "We're supposed to be gone."

I shake my head because I don't want him to see us talking. We need to keep our heads down and our hands busy. We need to give Clayton *nothing* to complain about, nothing left to ask for, because the minute he's done with this weird argument, I want him to unlock our keys and phones so we can get out of here and never look back.

Unfortunately, the weird argument doesn't look like it's wrapping up anytime soon. I look up at the glass on the second ticket booth. They're standing by the first, so I can see their reflections—a silent-movie montage of their fight. Clayton reaches for her, and she cringes away. She throws up her hands, and he snaps his head to the left. She jabs her finger in the air, and he bumps his chin.

My palms and back grow damp with nervous sweat even though nothing particularly terrifying is happening. I have seen some shit go down in this theater that makes this fight look positively milquetoast in comparison. Except as far as I know, those fights never involved anyone hiding a gun.

I can't see it now. I can't even see Clayton's back. He's too far away and turned in the wrong direction, and what am I even trying to do? Do I think if I stare at it hard enough, it will disappear? That gun is probably still exactly where it was twenty minutes ago. He hasn't pulled it out or waved it around, but I still feel the dark possibilities it conjures all the way across this room.

I shake off my tension as Clayton pulls his phone out of his pocket. He's checking the time, but the woman instantly snatches for it. Clayton is too fast, locking and pocketing it with the telltale speed of a man with a secret to keep.

"What don't you want me to see?" she shouts, the sudden volume a shock in the quiet. "What are you hiding?"

Clayton's murmur is difficult to decipher, but the woman's four-letter response is impossible to miss. He hushes her, moving into her space until she has no choice but to back up. To keep moving until they are away from the ticket booth and tucked close to the farthest lobby door. The one Hudson opened to let her in. Clayton tries to push that door wide—maybe in hopes of ushering this whole scene outside. But the woman wants nothing to do with it.

Quincy leans forward, whispering, "Did I see a cell phone? Aren't phones prohibited during work hours?"

I shrug. "The 'all phones in the safe' rule never applied to him."

At the door, the girl raises her voice sharply. "Where's your ring?"

Her volume, or maybe her comment, seems to hit a nerve. Clayton shoves open the door then and grabs her arm. He doesn't quite drag her out, but it's close enough to make Naomi inhale with a sharp hiss and to make Hannah shake her head in disbelief. The second the door closes behind them with a bang, all efforts at quiet end. Clayton raises his voice instantly, throwing his shoulders wide, his chin jutting.

My stomach clenches because this is shifting. It looks dangerous. Should we do something? Say something?

Movement catches my eye by the soda machine. Lexi has

her arm around Summer's shoulders. She's moving her down the hallway toward the locker room, which is a good idea. Summer is a gentle, homeschooled kid, young for sixteen and sheltered by her protective family. When she started three months ago, she'd never even seen an R-rated movie, so I doubt she's used to testosterone-fueled assholes having screaming matches with their...well, with whatever this girl is to Clayton.

"Wonder what he did," Hudson says, sounding like he doesn't much care.

"Cheated," Hannah whispers knowingly.

They're all lined up at the counter watching now, Naomi on Hannah's left and Quincy on her right. Hudson is on my side of the counter, his hip leaned against the edge.

He frowns and the scar at the corner of his eyebrow hooks. "You think?"

"Mm-hmm. He's trash," Naomi breathes, shaking her curls.

"How does he even have a girl to cheat on?" Hudson asks. His fingers tap the glass case in an incessant rhythm.

"Isn't he..." Quincy flushes, like he doesn't want to be the one to point out the obvious.

"A little white pretty boy who spends too much time in the gym?" Naomi asks. "Yeah, he's that."

"He's also creepy as hell," Hannah says, wrinkling her freckled nose. Then she looks at me. "Did you know about this girl, Jo?"

I shake my head. "I couldn't even imagine a puppy liking him."

Hudson laughs, and one of the bleached streaks in his dark hair slides over his left eye. "Funnier than anyone gives you credit for, Jo."

I shrug and look over my shoulder. Clayton isn't watching us now, but he could. If he so much as glances back through the glass doors, he'll see all of us up here. He'll know we're watching this spectacle, and then...

The truth is I don't know what will happen if he discovers us. But I don't want to find out.

I head away from the others, down to the far end of the counter, by the condiment and paper product dispensers. Quincy follows me, and we start disassembling the paper section where customers get napkins and straws and ketchup for their hot dogs.

"Do you think Summer is okay?" Quincy asks, looking at the hallway where they disappeared.

"Yeah, Lexi will look out for her. I'm sure it was scary seeing Clayton blow a gasket earlier."

"Summer was there?" he asks, looking concerned.

"She dealt with the soda machine breaking, so he was snapping specifically at her. But it's the last time she'll ever have to deal with that. Or him at all."

"I feel bad for Ava," Quincy says quietly. He's watching the scene in the parking lot with sad eyes.

"Ava?" I ask softly.

Quincy nods. "Yes, Ava. She's Clayton's wife." Seeing my clueless expression, he frowns. "You really didn't know?"

"No idea."

Outside, things have grown suddenly quiet. I dare a quick peek and see they are much closer. Then Clayton reaches for Ava, inviting her into an embrace. My skin crawls at the idea of being so close to him. I think of the gun right there at his back. Does Ava know it's there? If she wraps her arms around him, will she feel it with her hands?

He enfolds her in an embrace. I can't tell if Ava is hugging him back, but she doesn't seem to be pushing him away. Maybe this is it. Maybe they'll wrap this up and then Clayton will come in and let us go home. Then I see Ava's arm wiggle near Clayton's side. She's struggling with something. Maybe digging around in his pocket.

My breath comes in too fast when he wrenches away from her. Ava jumps back, holding something high in the air. There is a feral quality to the way she stands, one hand stretched out to stop him, one hand gripped clawlike around her prize. But Ava is no match for Clayton's size and strength.

He lunges for the item she's holding, and they struggle. I don't know if he's hurting her. It goes back and forth, and I feel my heart clenching at the sight. My body backs up on autopilot, my feet trying to find a safe place away from him. I want to be in another room. Another city. Another universe.

Suddenly, something dark and rectangular pops out of Ava's grip. I don't hear a thing through the heavy doors, but I know what it is by Clayton's obvious alarm, the way he frantically stoops and reaches. Everyone who's ever dropped a cell phone knows the particular dance he's doing. He retrieves his phone, holding it gingerly as he stands up. Maybe it didn't break.

"Shit, she broke his phone," Hudson whispers.

Or maybe it did.

Clayton lowers the phone, the screen still dark and blank. Then he lunges, his white teeth bared, his voice a distant roar behind the glass. Ava leaps back with a yelp, and my shoulders hitch right along with hers.

"We need to get out of here." My voice is cracked and dry, and I feel my pulse in my temples. He could hurt her. If he reaches for the gun, he could do much worse than hurt her.

"I hear that," Naomi says.

I don't know when the rest of the team joined us, or when we all gravitated to the center of the room. We've unconsciously moved into a group—fish finding safety in numbers.

"Should we call someone?" Hannah asks.

"No phones," Hudson says. "This is bullshit. I'm going out there."

I grab his arm. "Don't be stupid."

"He'll pound the asphalt with your skinny ass," Naomi says.

Hudson doesn't respond to Naomi. He keeps his dark, dark eyes on me, his lips parted like he wants to argue. But I shake my head and he holds his tongue.

Hudson isn't small for nineteen. He's tall, with wide

shoulders and big hands, but he hasn't quite filled out either. He still has that hollow-cheeked hungry look of a younger man. Coupled with his father's high cheekbones and nearly black eyes, Hudson's left with a striking, but not quite finished, appearance.

"Please just don't," I say. I can feel my hand shaking on him.

To my surprise, he relents, his body relaxing.

The door flings open, and Clayton bursts back in. The lobby falls utterly silent, and my throat tightens. Clayton locks the door fast and pockets the keys. Then he whirls, fists clenched and face red.

"Show's over," he shouts. But then he seems to catch himself. He flashes that perfect smile—a bright veneer hiding the decay beneath. "I'm sure you all have plenty of important things to do when you leave tonight, and I wouldn't want your job to get in the way."

Two steps through the lobby, a noise outside stops Clayton mid-step. It stops all of us too.

Ava didn't leave. She's right there at the glass, her face twisted into an animal snarl. Her small, pale fists slam the glass twice more, the sound only marginally muffled.

"I'll figure out who she is," she screams. "I *will* find out. And when I do, I will *ruin* you."

And with that, she whirls away, leaving her dark promise to hang in the quiet.

Date: April 9, 2023

From: Delta Gamma Phi—Columbus

To: Delta Gamma Phi Sisters

Subject: Special Update

News has likely already reached you about the terrible tragedy in Sandusky and the connection to our beloved sister, Ava Drummond. We are all touched by your outpouring of support, a spirit of sisterhood and generosity that Ava has always inspired in us all. We do not have details at this time but will share them as soon as they are available. In the meantime, we encourage everyone to keep all involved in your thoughts and prayers.

CHAPTER 4

WE SCATTER AIMLESSLY, SPECKS OF PEPPER RUNNING from a drop of dish soap. Not that we need to bother. Clayton makes a beeline for his office before any of us can reach a destination.

We gather back toward the concession stand, on the far end again so we're clear of the hallway and any chance of him hearing us.

"That boy needs serious therapy," Naomi says.

"Whatever," Hannah says. "Not our problem. We're done, right?"

"Damn right. I'm never setting foot in this hellhole again," Hudson says.

"But we need to get our phones and keys," Quincy points out. "We still need him to unlock the safe."

No one answers him, but we all look toward the end of the first counter. There's a small break in the countertops for staff access to concessions and, of course, for access to the locker room and the office. The safe is in the office. Along with our very angry, very armed manager.

"I could ask him if you'd like," Quincy says, pushing up his glasses.

"No, I'll go," Hudson says.

"You kidding?" Naomi asks. "We'll never get our keys if you do that."

"No doubt," Hannah says. "He'll invent crap for us to do. He hates you."

"I'll do it," I say, though my joints feel stiff and tense, my body seizing up at the mere idea of approaching Clayton. "I said I would go, and I will. I just…I want to give him a minute."

I want to tell them the rest of it. I want to tell them he has a gun and we need to be *so* careful, but I know that situation might not be a deal for everyone else. This is Ohio, land of apple pie and Cleveland Browns and concealed carry. There could be people in this theater with guns every day. But knowing it's here is different for me.

Because I've seen exactly what a gun can do.

"Shit," Hannah says. "I left my damn sweatshirt in Six."

"Maybe Hudson can go with you to get it," I say.

Hudson looks at me like he wants to disagree with that, which doesn't make sense. I know they get along. They hang out all the time, and now is not the time for him to be difficult.

"Yeah, that's smart," Naomi says. "Clayton will be way more agreeable if you're nowhere in sight, Hudson."

There is a flicker of hesitation on his face, but then Hudson shrugs. "Fine. Let's hit it."

They lope across the lobby quickly, their long strides taking them out of the concession area in seconds. I start moving when they reach the theater hallway because we can't keep putting this off. It's going to be simple. We'll ask for our keys and phones politely. We'll offer to take all the trash out on the way. Then we'll get the hell out of here and move on with the rest of our lives.

"Hey, I forgot to ask: Did you hear back?" Naomi asks, giving me a reason to stall. Of course, this is a delay that makes me squirm.

"About that interview?" she prompts, as if I don't know exactly what she's talking about.

Of course I know. I was so stressed about it, I could barely sleep. Cara and Naomi and I went through both our closets and half of Mom's trying to find the appropriate outfit. Practicing interview questions. Coaching me on how to come out of my shell, because wallflowers don't land internships at places like OSU Medical Center.

Except this wallflower did.

I force myself to nod, and a smile slips through no matter how chill I try to be. "I did. I got a call today. I got it."

Naomi's grin is huge. "Holy shit, you got it?"

"Yeah," I say, feeling my smile widen.

"Did you tell Cara?"

"Not yet. I wanted to tell you both on the way to pancakes. I didn't know she was working tomorrow."

"You already have a new job?" Quincy asks.

I nod, my cheeks going hot.

"Not just a job," Naomi says. "This shithole is a *job*. My girl landed a full-time, tuition-reimbursing, career-launching internship."

"That's amazing," Quincy says. "Where?"

"OSU Medical Center. It's a big hospital."

"Oh, I know OSU Medical Center," Quincy says. "Like in Columbus, right?"

"Yep. Which means she'll be headed to *The* Ohio State University."

"That's so great," Quincy says, pushing his glasses up the bridge of his nose. "Congratulations. Deciding on a college is so intimidating. I'm glad you were able to choose."

"Thank you," I say, forcing a tight smile. It's not that I'm not happy. I'm more than happy. But I'd also rather gargle acid than be the center of attention. This whole line of conversation has gone on long enough.

I clap my hands and turn to the hallway. "Okay, I'm going to go get our stuff so—"

The room goes dark.

There's no buzzing or flickering, no warning at all. There is light, and then there is darkness. And dark in Riverview Theaters isn't just dark; it's like being plunged into the deep end of an unlit pool on a starless night.

"What happened?" Quincy asks, sounding alarmed.

"Electric's out again," Naomi says. "Is it a fuse thing?"

"I don't know," I admit. I lean into the counter. "Give it a second. Sometimes it comes right back."

We wait several seconds. Maybe a minute or two, but the darkness remains, bringing quiet along with it.

I turn, feeling strange and disoriented in the lack of light. Then I hear something coming up the hallway. Footsteps. Moving fast. Shoes slapping tile.

"Lexi?" I ask. And then I realize there are only three people down that hallway, one of whom I don't want to bump into in the dark. My skin goes cold. "Lexi? Summer?"

My voice trembles. And then I hear that same steady rhythm of footsteps on the carpet. I see a flutter of movement as my eyes finally adjust, someone moving across the concession stand and right onto the carpet. Before I can find my voice, the figure disappears into the darkness of the main theater hallway, the sound of the footsteps growing fainter until there is silence again.

Lexi or Summer would have answered me when I called. Which tells me there's only one other person who could have walked past me just now.

Are we in big trouble?

"Did you hear something?" Naomi asks. "I could have sworn someone was walking by."

"They were," I say, my throat thick.

"Is it Lexi? Or maybe Summer?" Naomi asks.

"No, it was Clayton." Quincy's voice is certain. And then he calls out the name I'm avoiding. "Clayton! Clayton, we're over here!"

I flinch, but there's no response. No footsteps. All is silent.

"Where is he going?" Quincy asks.

"Who knows. We need a light," Naomi says. She's patting around the counter. My eyes are adjusting now, the faint lights from the parking lot bleeding into the blanket of darkness.

In the distance, I hear the faintest whoop. A high-pitched laugh. Hudson and Hannah are probably still in Theater Six, but there would be emergency light strips along the seat aisles at least. They're probably running around like complete goofballs.

"This place is falling apart. It's the third outage this week," Naomi says.

"Are there emergency lights?" Quincy asks. "Flashlights?"

My brain sparks into gear. "Yes. In the break room. Come on, we can follow the counter."

My eyes have adjusted enough to see the outlines of the hot dog machine and the popcorn spill bucket. I search for the telltale red glow of EXIT signs, spotting them above doorways and in the center of the hallway leading to the theaters. What I don't see or hear is anyone else I work with. Where the hell is Clayton going? Is he trying to flip a breaker or fix a fuse?

And why aren't Summer and Lexi out here yet? Why can't I hear them?

"Summer? Lexi?" My voice falls flat.

"Maybe they're not back there," Naomi says.

"They should be back there," Quincy says. "We would have seen them come out."

Uneasiness washes over me, wadding my stomach into knots as I stare at that silent yawning darkness leading off the concession area. Something is wrong. I can feel it in my bones, deep down in the lizard part of my brain that keeps me alive. There is danger here.

More whooping comes from the theaters. A distant crash and a murmur of laughter. So Hudson and Hannah are clearly fine.

"Clayton?" Quincy calls again, and again, I flinch. I want to tell him to stop, to never say that name again. My nerves are jangling, and I need to calm down. It's fine. It's just a stupid power outage.

"Where the hell is everybody?" Naomi asks.

"Maybe he's getting the flashlights," Quincy says.

Maybe. But my gut says no.

"We should get the flashlights. We can check the office to see if the safe is unlocked too," I say, because I don't care about being polite or asking permission anymore. I don't care about whatever professional reference Clayton might or might not offer. Between the altercation I witnessed in the lobby and the gun I know he's carrying, I want nothing more than to never lay eyes on him again. If I find my phone and keys, I'm getting the hell out of here, manager permission be damned.

I start toward the hallway to the office, or the general direction that feels right. I immediately ram my hip into something. One of the dustpans we carry around. "Be careful. I just rammed into one of the dustpans."

The darkness is worse when we reach the hallway. Much worse. And the silence is suffocating. I hear myself breathe. My shoes squeak and hiss with every step.

The hair on the back of my neck prickles.

Where the hell are they? Why aren't they coming out here?

I open my mouth to call for Lexi and Summer again, but finally, I hear something.

Quincy jerks his head. "Did you hear—"

"Yes," I say quickly because I want him to be quiet. I need to listen. Need to make sense of this. I press my palm against the wall, and the sound comes again. It's a voice.

Someone is whimpering.

CHAPTER 5

THE WHIMPER CONTINUES, AND GOOSE BUMPS RISE ON my skin. My ears home in on the sound. It's a girl. Lexi or Summer, of course. And then the whimper shapes itself, folding into a word that answers my question.

"Lexi!"

High and thin and desperate. It's Summer. Summer is crying.

"Summer, we're here!" I call.

"What's happening?" Quincy asks. "Can you see something?"

"Be quiet," Naomi says. "Just listen."

"Lexi! Lexi!"

My heart drops down though my chest, then my stomach, sinking until I'm sure it will fall out of me. I turn, but Quincy and Naomi are barely shadows in the darkness. There is nothing but black all around us.

"What the hell is happening?" Naomi sounds terrified, and I feel exactly like she sounds, but I can't force myself to answer her.

My ears ring with the memory of bells jangling above a door.

The clatter of lighters spilling. My muscles bind up, all the liquid things in me turning to wet cement.

I have to fight this. I cannot freeze in this moment, not when he's out there. Not when I know there's a gun.

I stumble for the nearest door. The office. I keep my hand on the wall to guide me, feeling for the little plastic placard that marks the door. I find it and twist the handle, pushing it open. Inside the office the air is cool and smells faintly of paper and pencil shavings. I drag my hand along the doorframe and then along the wall to the right. I know the rack of flashlights is in here. I scan my brain to remember exactly where it is. This wall, somewhere close to the middle.

"LexiLexiLexi!"

It's Summer's voice again. She's in the locker room. Did Lexi leave her alone in the dark? Oh God, where is Clayton? I thought the footsteps I heard were his, but what if they were Lexi's? What if Clayton is in there with Summer?

And then another thought occurs. One darker and colder than the rest. What if he's in *here*, in this room? Is he watching me from the darkness?

My heart pounds until I feel it in my throat, until the surge of blood through my veins is a roar in my ears. My body begins to shake, but I force myself to continue searching the wall, my fingers reading surfaces that are strange and unfamiliar in the dark. Time clock. First aid kit.

"Summer," I say, forcing a strong and steady tone despite

the fear rolling through my stomach like a storm. "I'm getting a flashlight."

Summer's whimpers dissolve into a wordless cry. My fingers pat over the bulletin board filled with posters informing us of minimum wage and then—bingo!

I snag a flashlight and flick it on, squinting in the sudden brightness. Everything is as it should be—desk with a pile of register-access cards. A bulletin board with printouts of the schedule. The safe behind the desk, still locked tight. The room is empty though—no sign that Clayton's even been in here.

Footsteps shuffle at the door, and I swing the beam to see Quincy and Naomi blinking in the glare. Quincy grabs a flashlight too.

"Where is she?" he asks, his gaze darting around the room. "Is she in the locker room?"

"I think so."

"What's wrong with her? What's going on?" Naomi asks, looking hesitant to move any closer to the source of the crying.

"I'm going in there," Quincy asks.

"Hold on," I say. "We need to go together."

"She could be hurt!" Quincy says. He almost sounds angry, and maybe that's good. I can't keep dragging my feet. I hurry back to him, pushing into the hallway.

We find the door cracked open, and I curl my fingers around it, inching it slowly wider. "Summer?"

She lets out a low, terrible sob in lieu of answering. My

stomach is an oil slick, full of fear. None of this feels right. Maybe it's just in my head. Maybe it's the combination of a power outage and the fact that I know there is a gun in this building. Maybe the lights will go on and this will be fine, and we'll all have a good laugh at how freaked out we were.

"Summer, are you all right?" Quincy asks. His tone is low and urgent. "What's happened?"

She hiccups out another sob. Maybe that's better than an answer. I don't think I want to know what's behind Summer's wailing, but the only thing worse than finding out is standing here dreaming up what it might be. Quincy is starting along the left side of the room, where the benches would be—where it would be logical to find Summer. But I move my beam to the right...to the empty space in front of the lockers. And that's where I find her, her orange hair and slight form curved over like a C.

I take a breath, and something sharp and pungent stings my nose. The smell of urine. My skin prickles, all my hair standing on end. Something terrible is happening in this room. Something unspeakable, I'm sure of it.

"Please," Summer sobs. My flashlight beam swings past the pile of coats on the floor in front of her, landing on her pale, pale face. I shift the light out of her eyes, onto the length of tangled red hair trailing down her arms, all the way to her waist.

She takes a shuddery breath, and her voice rasps. "Please, please, please, please."

Dread sinks through my limbs like lead as I move the

flashlight to see what she's doing. What I see is that she's *not* hovering over a pile of coats. There is something else on the floor.

My vision blurs as she shakes that thing on the floor. The sight smears into blobs of black and red and pink. I blink and my vision clears. All these terrible colors coalesce into a ghastly scene.

There is a pair of legs jutting left.

There is a spray of pink hair on concrete.

There is the profile of a pale face with smeared red lipstick.

"Lexi." Her name spills out of my mouth.

"What is happening?" Quincy asks, but his flashlight has joined mine, and I think he can see enough. I think his mind is putting pieces together too. "Is she… Summer, talk to us. Please."

There is a single strange moment when I can believe this might be something else. When the truth lies buried under a thick layer of shock and disbelief. It's like seeing a thing at the bottom of a lake, the shape of it barely visible beneath the water. It could be anything or nothing.

And then, with the next breath, the water is gone, and the thing is here in front of me. Undeniable. Lexi's eyes are open, her lipstick smeared grotesquely across one pale cheek. Her body is impossibly still, her fingers curled upward but not moving.

My mouth goes dry, and I feel the heat and blood drain out of my head. Summer looks up suddenly, her face a horror, eyes ringed in shadow and cheeks wet with tears and snot. Her lips are pulled back from her teeth in a way that makes me think of a beaten dog. She grips Lexi's shirt even tighter, though her eyes stay locked on me.

"She won't wake up," she tells me. "She won't wake up!"

Summer is lucky to be wrapped up in that lie, but I am not. I know Lexi's not merely unconscious. Some people might believe that, but I know a dead body when I see one.

CHAPTER 6

THERE IS A DEAD WOMAN IN FRONT OF ME. IT IS A TRUTH
that swallows me whole. The world and all its noises are somewhere
else. Here there is only the high, electric hum behind my ears and a
slurry of memories. I think of the soles of my dad's work boots. The
spill of plastic lighters. The sound of gunshots—a flat, hard *pop*,
pop, *pop* that sounded too small to tear my world out by its roots.

Summer moves, and the spell is broken. I am back in this
room with the smell of piss and the sound of Summer's sobs. And
Lexi. Lexi is here too.

"Have you checked for a pulse?"

Quincy. I turn to see him moving slowly toward Summer.
When she scuttles back like a wounded animal, he lifts his hands.
"It's okay. I want to help. You're not hurt, are you?"

Summer sniffles, turning her whole body away, her knees up
to her chest and arms wrapped tight. Quincy stands and looks
her over, as if he has to be sure, as if Summer is the problem here
and not the body on the floor.

"Oh my God." Naomi's voice is a whisper in the doorway, her hands moving to cover her mouth.

"Does she have a pulse?" Quincy asks, his attention now on Lexi. "Is she breathing?"

"I—I don't know," I say. But I do know I haven't checked. I haven't done a thing. It's possible I could help Lexi, but I didn't even try. I didn't even think of it. I just sat here, my whole body rooted into the ground.

Is this still who I am? Is this who I will always be?

The thought is a starting pistol, and I lurch forward, breaking through my stupor to move closer to Lexi. I feel her neck for a pulse, but there's nothing. Her chest is still and flat, and when I lean close to her mouth, I hear no breathing.

"I think I remember CPR," I say. I took a class in junior high because I never wanted this. I never wanted to be frozen and helpless again.

"I can help," Quincy says.

I nod, my hands sweaty as I drop to my knees, the concrete cold beneath me. Naomi makes a terrible strangled sound as I unfasten the first button on Lexi's crisp blouse.. The collar is wrinkled and twisted, but I focus on checking her pulse again with two fingers.

Nothing.

Am I doing it right?

I don't know. I took that class when I was thirteen. When I was afraid I'd be watching Cara one night and something awful would happen again. Something else I could never undo.

My hands shake as I try it again. "I don't know for sure that I'm checking right."

Quincy checks too, his touch more perfunctory. He looks nauseated though, his forehead slicked with sweat. "I don't feel anything. Let's start."

"Lexi?" Naomi's voice is strange and high, pitched in a tone that belongs to someone else. I feel her shifting and squirming behind us, still close to the door. "Lexi? Oh my God, why isn't she moving? Why won't she move?"

I tune Naomi out, right along with Summer, who is still softly crying in the corner. Instead, I position my hands in the center of Lexi's chest, intertwining my fingers the way I remember. I lock my elbows and start compressions. It is not the same as the dummy. Lexi is a person, warm and real through her shirt. I feel the give of her skin beneath my hands, and it makes my stomach roll. The nausea grows stronger with each compression because this is not a class. This is not a video. This is real.

Naomi is so loud behind me, her panicky cries hitching as she shuffles back and forth, her flashlight beam making light strobe across the floor.

"Is she breathing? Tell me she's breathing," she says. I don't think she wants the real answer, so I stay quiet.

"Two minutes," Quincy says. "Are you tired? I can take over for a bit."

I nod quickly, because my wrists are aching, and my own breath is coming heavier. It's hard to believe it was only two minutes. It felt like ten minutes. Maybe more. I pull back, and Quincy steps in, assuming the position with the interlaced fingers and locked elbows. He's obviously taken the class more recently because he doesn't hesitate before starting compressions.

I roll my shoulders, surprised at the fatigue. It's harder work than I remember. Or maybe it's the panic surrounding me, wearing me down. Summer is rocking in the corner. Naomi is pacing and pacing.

"Is she breathing?" Naomi asks. "Is it working now?"

I close my eyes to the strobing beam of her flashlight swinging back and forth across us, and put my hand up in supplication. "Naomi?"

She stops, and I try to find my voice. Try to remember her beside Cara on my bed when I tried on four hundred outfits and practiced interview questions. *You've got to speak up*, Naomi said. *If you're going to be a doctor, you have to show them you're a person who can speak up and take action.*

This is not the action she was talking about. Not right now. I'm not ready for any of these choices. But I've known for a long time that you only get to play the hand you're dealt, and these are my cards today.

I open my eyes to find Naomi looking at me. She's waiting on me to finish.

"Can you…" I try to think of a job. She'll want to help, even if she's afraid. And then my mind supplies the answer. "Keys. We need manager keys to get outside so we can get help."

"Yeah, Clayton has them," she says, and she doesn't add that we don't know where he is. Or how strange it is that he isn't here. Or that he walked right past us into the darkened theater hallway. But she bites her lip in a way that tells me she's aware of all of those things. "Maybe there's a spare set somewhere. I'll look."

She swipes at her eyes and nods, and then she sets out for the hallway. I look down at Quincy, who's still going strong. I can tell his breath is coming faster though, his face strained with the effort of the compressions. I move closer again and gesture for him to let me take over.

I lock my hands into place on her sternum and start again. I try not to look at the red lipstick smeared across Lexi's cheek or the thin gold chain on her wrist.

"Should we breathe for her?" I ask, because I've been taught both ways, and honest to God, I can't remember.

He shakes his head. "My instructor said it's not needed for adults. It's best to just keep up with the compressions and call for help."

I continue the firm, fast rhythm. My arms are growing heavy, a dull ache blooming in my shoulder joints. It is so much harder than I realized. After what feels like hours, Quincy shifts.

"We should switch."

"How long has it been?" I ask, panting as he takes over.

"Eight minutes total," he says. "We should check for a pulse again."

He pauses, and I feel her neck for a pulse. Her wrists. Lean down until my ear is close to her mouth so I can hear if she's breathing. But there's nothing except silence and stillness.

"Let's start again," I say.

He goes for another two minutes, and then I start, counting one push after another even though I know there's no reason to count. Both of the classes I took drilled one thing into my head— keep going. No matter what, keep going until help comes.

But what if help doesn't come? How would anyone know we need help?

Panic bubbles up through my middle, but I push it down, put all my focus into the rhythm of my compressions. Lexi's ribs feel small and fragile beneath my palms, but I ignore it.

I try not to notice her mangled collar.

I try not to look at her snarled hair.

I try not to see the two broken nails on her curled-up fingers.

Wait a minute. I sit back, and Quincy moves to start again, but I open my mouth, feeling breathless.

"Wait."

"Is she—"

"No," I say. "Something's not right."

It's a stupid thing to say. Nothing about this is right. Lexi is utterly still. All those tiny, infinitesimal shifts and movements that make us human are absent. I've seen this before. I know what death looks like, the way it takes a person and turns them into a body. But I also know it doesn't happen to people who are young and healthy like Lexi. Not unless something happened.

Out of the corner of my eye, I see Summer rocking near the wall. She is silent, her face pressed into her knees, her arms wrapped around her legs.

She is more than upset; she is traumatized. Whatever Summer saw here, it was the sort of thing that rips your life into two pieces: the part before and the part after.

I don't know how to voice any of this though, so I tilt my head and look at Lexi's twisted collar again. There's a dark smear under her jaw. A chill zips through me. What happened here? What happened to Lexi?

"Should we start compressions again?" Quincy asks.

I swallow hard. "I don't think..."

"We need to get help," he says. He sounds like a kid who has always been able to get help when it was needed. He probably *is* that kid. "We need paramedics. Or the police."

"We don't have phones," I say quietly, racking my brain for how to solve this problem. Because he's right. Or partly right at least. I think it's too late for paramedics, but I do think we need the police.

"Clayton has the keys, and he can get in the safe," Quincy says, standing. "We need to find Clayton right now."

"No!"

Summer's voice makes us both jump. I'd almost forgotten she was here. She scuttles backward until she bangs into the lockers. Her eyes are wide, darting back and forth between us.

"No, no, no, no, no, no," she says, her voice a hiss of dry air with almost no sound at all.

My body goes cold, and everything seems to slow. My vision sharpens, and I scan the room warily, my eyes landing on Lexi's tangled hair. Her broken nails. This is not natural. Someone did this. Did Clayton have something to do with this?

Did he...*hurt* Lexi?

I remember the bells jangling above the door and the *pop, pop, pop*. I remember the pool of blood slowly spreading. This is not that night, but the shadow it casts in my mind holds the same shape. Evil has been here too, just like it was then.

Are we in big trouble?

I shiver, wishing there were no trouble. But right now, trouble seems to be everywhere I look.

"We need to do something," Quincy says.

"We shouldn't touch her anymore," I say gently. There are other things to consider now. Evidence-shaped things. Because this isn't just a medical emergency anymore—it's a crime.

A murder.

Crime and Safety

PINKERTON GRADUATE STRANGLED
IN SANDUSKY KILLING SPREE

Tracie Gavin, Pinkerton Gazette *Staff*

Alexis J. Patterson, 19, was found fatally strangled in Riverview Theaters, where she had been employed for more than two years. Patterson, who was a 2021 graduate of Pinkerton High School, was one of four who died on the evening of the theater's permanent closure. Ms. Carol Christie, Patterson's high school theater director, expressed shock and grief upon hearing the news. "Lexi was the head of our costume department from her sophomore through senior year," Christie said. "She was smart and talented, and this is just a tremendous loss." The investigation of this situation is ongoing.

CHAPTER 7

"MAY I HAVE THE FLASHLIGHT?" I ASK. QUINCY PICKS IT up from the shelf he'd set it on, and I move it so I can see Lexi's neck better. I am careful not to touch her again, but I shift the light beam until I'm sure of what I'm seeing. There are two oblong bruises on the right side of her throat and another, thicker bruise on the left.

Goose bumps rise on my arms, and I sit back on my knees.

An accident did not cause those bruises. An accident didn't tangle her hair or twist her collar either. I look up at Summer, thinking of the last word she reacted to, the word that was the beginning and end of all this in her mind: *Clayton.*

The fragmented facts fall into place, reinforcing the singular terrible truth. Clayton is the reason Lexi is dead. She didn't fall; he *put* her on this ground. Clayton grabbed her by the neck and squeezed until she stopped breathing. He killed her.

This is a murder.

The word rolls around in my head with the sound of bells

over a door. The smell of salt and copper. The memory of the last murder I witnessed. Because this is not my first rodeo.

I step back, feeling my head swim. "Summer, did Clayton do this?" I ask. "You saw Clayton…"

Summer cries, her body still rocking back and forth. Back and forth. "It was dark. The lights—it was *so* dark."

Quincy shakes his head and adjusts his glasses. "Wait, what are you saying?" he asks. "Are you saying Lexi was…killed?"

He struggles to pronounce the word, like the shape of it doesn't quite fit in his mouth. Quincy doesn't live in a world where people are murdered. Hell, I'm not even sure he lives in a world where people die.

But he does now, doesn't he?

"What happened?" Quincy asks. "Can you tell us what happened?" His voice and expression are gentle with her, but there's an urgency in him too. As if knowing the ins and outs of it will fix this. As if lining up the facts will make them less true.

"He was angry," she whispers. "He heard us."

"He heard you in here?" I ask. "You and Lexi?"

"Was there some kind of accident?" Quincy asks. "Did something fall or—or—" He looks around, clearly trying to force some story to emerge, some explanation less ugly than the one we have. Of course, he doesn't find anything to fill in the blanks. Unless one of the lockers came to life and flew into a homicidal rage, there's no way to explain this off as an accident.

Quincy's shoulders slump, and he leans against one of those lockers in defeat. I feel a wave of pity for him because he isn't going to find what he wants. And he can't go back from this moment. None of us can. But the rest of us have the option to move forward.

I look at Lexi sprawled on the ground, and my throat goes thick.

"Tell us what happened," I say. And then I look at Summer in case she wasn't sure who I was talking to. "Please, Summer."

"He heard us talking."

"About?"

She bites her lip, looking ashamed. "About him. We were…"

"Complaining?" I try. She nods and I nod back, trying to keep her going.

"You were complaining, and he overheard you, and then what happened?" Quincy asks.

"He flew at her," Summer says. There's nothing left in her voice but air. She takes a shuddering breath and closes her eyes. "They were fighting. And then the lights went out. And I heard them on the ground."

Summer begins to cry, and Quincy moves to her side. He reaches out like he wants to touch her, to offer some sort of comfort. But in the end, he just stands there, tortured and still.

"Why would he do this?" Quincy asks.

I shake my head, but my mind drifts back to Ava, to her small fists slamming into the glass door. When she screamed through the glass, she looked like a feral animal.

I will find out! And when I do, I will ruin you!

Ava thought Clayton was cheating. She was sure of it. Is it possible Lexi was the one he was cheating with? My head whirls at the idea. It doesn't seem possible. But thirty minutes ago, Lexi had been mopping the tile in front of the soda machine, so what the hell do I know?

"I have no idea," I admit to Quincy. "But it doesn't matter right now. We need to get the others and get help."

"But he's out there," Summer says. "I heard him leave."

"He left after doing this?" Quincy clarifies. "He just walked out of here?"

My breath catches. Summer isn't the only one who heard him. I heard Clayton too. The footsteps when the lights went out, that was him. I remember the slap of shoes against tile and then the softer steps on the carpet. That was Clayton. He murdered Lexi and strolled right past me without a word.

"I heard him too," I admit. A shudder runs through me. "We have to go. We need to get the police. Right now."

"Where did you hear him?" Quincy asks, his eyes darting nervously. "Could he be back here somewhere?"

I shake my head. "We both heard him near the concession area. I think you saw him, remember?"

"Where was he going?" Summer asks.

"The front doors, most likely." Quincy nods at me for

confirmation. "That's where he must have been going, right? He'd want to run. He has the keys so he could get right out."

I open my mouth to say yes, but the word stalls out in my throat. Because I remember—he *wasn't* headed toward the front doors. When Clayton reached the carpet, he turned *right*. He was headed for the theaters. Toward Hannah and Hudson. And now, Naomi.

"Jo," Quincy says. "Where is everyone else?"

My stomach tumbles into free fall. Oh God. They're all out there in the dark, and there is a *murderer* out there with them. A murderer who happens to have a gun.

Fear runs through me. I lock eyes with Quincy, and Summer steps away from the wall, shuffling closer.

"We have to find them," I say.

At the door, I hesitate. There should be four of us leaving this room. I turn to see Lexi's legs, her knees bent. One patent leather pump has come off her heel. I stare at the graying flesh of her foot and feel my heart crack.

In another world, I would have gotten here earlier. Maybe if I had, I'd have saved her. But that's not where we are tonight. In this world, Lexi is gone.

I slip back inside the locker room long enough to drape my sweatshirt gently over Lexi's face. I am not brave enough to look at her when I do it. And I'm not tender enough to linger or say a kind word. I go back to the doorway, my mind flat and numb.

Summer, Quincy, and I make our way into the dark hallway. It should feel stranger than it does. Maybe it's different for me because it isn't entirely unfamiliar. After all, this isn't the first time I've walked out of a room and left a dead body inside.

I wonder every day if we should have known he was capable of this. If I had paid closer attention or taken all his outbursts more seriously, could I have changed what happened? Could I have stopped the killing before it started?

CHAPTER 8

AT THE MOUTH OF THE HALLWAY, WE'RE FORCED TO abandon the safety of darkness. The power is still out, but now that our eyes have adjusted, the parking lot lights cast everything in a faint yellow glow. We hesitate at the very edge, staring at the empty concession counters. Beyond that, the ticket booths loom like sentries with the lobby doors flanking the back half of the room behind them. The hot-drinks machine finishes its cleaning cycle with a *click*, leaving an eerie, hollow silence in its wake.

When the lights went out, the darkness itself was the monster I feared. But now I know there is a real monster in this theater. Once we step out of the hallway, we'll be exposed to him.

"Do you hear anything?" Quincy asks softly.

"Nothing," I whisper.

Summer shakes her head too. There is a faint, rapid tapping beside me. It's confusing until I see her chin trembling. Summer's teeth are chattering in the quiet.

Quincy looks left toward the condiments station and right toward the hallway that leads to the theaters. "Should we call for them?"

Summer looks like we've suggested lighting her hair on fire. I don't actually blame her. Being exposed is bad enough, but literally calling attention to our location? No, thank you.

"Clayton will hear us," Summer says.

"Clayton might be long gone," Quincy explains. "We need to check those front doors. If they're open, we can get out."

"Wait a minute," I say. "We need to be sure he isn't lurking out here waiting on us."

Quincy hesitates before nodding, but I know I'm right. We can't just waltz out into this lobby. We've got to be smart if we're going to keep Clayton away from us. And away from Hudson, Hannah, and Naomi. A sharp pang of warning zips through me.

Naomi. Naomi should have come back to us by now. Come to think of it, Naomi should have been back fifteen minutes ago. How could I forget about something like that? I'm the one who sent her out here, and now she's missing, and Clayton's out here somewhere. I try to imagine my sister's dark eyes and heart-shaped face if I had to tell her something happened to Naomi because of me.

No. I can't go there yet.

"It's so quiet," Summer says. Her whole body is shaking.

"Maybe everyone got out," Quincy says. "Maybe everyone ran to get help and they'll be back any minute."

It doesn't make sense. If they went to get help, they'd have propped open a door. Or maybe shouted to try to get us too. But I don't say that. Instead, I turn off my flashlight and gesture to Quincy. "Turn your flashlight off. We can try to stick to the shadows."

"Should we try the doors first?" Quincy asks, voice low.

I nod, and we move into the concession area. We pad quickly past the tile and onto the strangely patterned carpet. Quincy's steps are heavier than I expect from his slight frame. I wince with every fall of his feet, wishing I'd had him take his shoes off. Wishing boys were quieter. Wishing I were eating a damn waffle instead of worrying about escaping a killer.

We keep moving until our bodies are pressed against the side of one of the ticket booths. Adrenaline is popping through my veins like a second pulse, and I swear I see flashes of movement out of the corner of my eyes. I hold my hands up to Quincy and Summer, forcing them to wait while I listen for long, long seconds.

I do not know what I'm waiting to hear, but it doesn't happen. There is no one slipping through the shadows. Everything is still and silent. Eventually, I lower my hands and take a breath.

"I'll check the door," Quincy says, but I shake my head.

"Your shoes," I say. "They're…"

"Loud," Summer says softly. I grin, and her cheeks go dark. She ducks her head, and her hair slides to cover her like stage curtains drawing closed. Quincy looks at her with a bashful smile.

"She's right," I say. "I'll go."

Every ounce of my body and soul screams at me to stay right where I am, to glue my back to the side of this ticket booth and stay in the safety of its shadow until help comes. But Mom is out of town again, and Cara is asleep. They don't know to look for us. I don't know if anyone knows, so it's up to us to get out of here.

I push myself off the booth and take long strides to the first door. My heart is thudding in my ears when I try the handle. It doesn't give under my tug. I move from left to right, finding the second door locked. And the third. And the fourth. And the fifth. And the—

A hand lands across my mouth with a hard *clap*.

Panic erupts in the center of my chest. I inhale to scream, but a long arm hooks around my waist, hauling me backward so quickly, it kicks all the breath out of me. I flail desperately as whoever it is drags me across the lobby, to a side door—the emergency egress hallway door.

I squirm wildly, thrashing until I wrench my mouth free. I take a sharp breath, smelling soap and cardamom. Then I toss back my head hard, my skull cracking into something sharp and bony. There's a muffled grunt, and the egress hallway door clicks shut, trapping me with my attacker. With Clayton. I crack my head back again.

"Ow!"

That's not Clayton's voice.

And come to think of it, Clayton doesn't smell like cardamom.

I whirl around with my hands up defensively. I drop them the second I see brown skin and streaked hair.

"Hudson?"

"Wish you'd figured that out before you bashed your head into me," he says, rubbing his chin and testing his jaw.

I blink, taking in my surroundings. It's brighter here, the hallway lit by a sickly, flickering row of emergency lights in the ceiling. Hudson is still rubbing his chin and watching me with dark eyes.

"The hell are you doing walking around in the open like that?" he asks.

"What am *I* doing?" I snap. "You grabbed me from behind and *dragged* me into this hallway."

"I couldn't take the chance of scaring you and having you scream."

"So you did the scariest thing imaginable?" I wave my hands around. "How did this seem like a good idea?"

"Look, I didn't want Clayton spotting you. He's acting hinky as shit!"

I open my mouth, and the hallway door opens. My body tenses, but then I recognize the silhouette of Naomi's curls. Summer and Quincy trail after her, and Hannah is at the back. They're careful to close the door quietly, and then we all shift around each other. Before anyone can say anything, Hannah points down the hallway.

"Not here," she whispers. Then she moves between us to take

the lead. We follow her in silence, a dutiful class in an elementary school hallway. She passes by plain gray doors marked with stenciled numbers. ONE. TWO. THREE. They're the emergency exit doors from the theaters. One end of the hallway exits in the lobby, and the other end leads to a set of back doors.

Theater Three is our largest theater, so it has two exit doors in this hallway. Hannah stops nearly dead center between them. We arrange ourselves into an awkward circle. Naomi stands between Hudson and Hannah, and Summer and Quincy flank my right and left.

Hannah straightens her broad shoulders and tightens her ponytail. Naomi's arms are crossed tightly over her chest, and her eyes are swollen like she's been crying. Hudson looks how Hudson always looks. Tall. Striking. Twitchy.

"You okay?" I mean the question for Naomi, mostly, but they all nod.

Naomi bites her lip, like she's afraid to say what comes next. "Is Lexi…"

I open my mouth, but there aren't any good words to fill the space. My expression must say plenty, though, because I watch shock and then pain shimmer across her expressive eyes.

"I'm sorry," I say.

"We tried CPR for a long time," Quincy adds.

"Was it some kind of medical thing?" Hannah asks, her freckled nose wrinkling.

I shake my head slowly.

"Did Clayton do something to her?" Hudson asks.

There's a pause where no one speaks, and the answer takes shape in the silence.

"He hurt her," Summer says softly. "I saw it."

"Why?" Hannah asks. "Why would he hurt Lexi?"

I shrug, but Quincy answers, "We don't know why. We just know there were bruises on Lexi's neck. And Summer saw him attack her just before the lights went out."

"Is that true?" Hannah asks. It's a ridiculous question. But what's happened here tonight is ridiculous. Lexi went to work. She swept a floor and fixed a soda machine, and then she got murdered. How are we supposed to make sense of that?

Summer nods slowly. I hear that same rapid-fire tapping of her chattering teeth.

"He killed her," Hudson says. His eyes are darker than usual, and maybe this is what anger does to his features. "Son of a bitch killed Lexi."

I tilt my head, trying to find something to say, but what words could possibly feel right in this moment? Hudson's face twists before I speak. He lunges off the wall. "I'm going."

"Going where?" Naomi asks. "What kind of fool idea is in your head?"

"The idea that there are six of us and one of him. I think it's time we make sure he doesn't get out of here. He needs to pay for what he did."

"We can't go after him," I say.

"Watch me."

"He's right," Hannah says. "Screw this dick."

"You *can't* go after him," I say, my chest feeling fluttery and strange.

"We can't get out until he unlocks the doors. And the safe for that matter," Quincy says. "I'm not a fan of fighting, but we need to get his keys, so we have to confront him. And Hudson's right. He is severely outnumbered."

"It doesn't matter!" I snap. "It doesn't matter if there are a dozen of us. We have to stay away from him."

"Why?" Naomi asks.

"Because he has a gun!"

Questions fill their eyes, and I shake my head before anyone can ask. "I saw it tonight, under his shirt. I know you might not believe me—"

"I believe you," Hudson says. "He's got NRA stickers on his car."

"He's worn it to work before," Quincy says. "I've seen it too. I just didn't think of it."

Naomi offers a laugh that is hollow and humorless. She shakes her bouncy hair and holds up her hands. "So you're telling me we have a murderer stuck in this building with us. And he happens to have a gun."

"To be fair, a lot of people have guns," Quincy says.

"Yeah, well, it's a little unnerving when the person carrying it just murdered somebody."

None of us has anything to refute her. We stare at the walls and clench our fists and face a terrible truth. We are trapped in this building with an armed killer. Sooner or later, he's going to find us, and when he does, someone else might die.

CHAPTER 9

"LET'S BREAK THE GLASS IN THE DOORS," HUDSON says.

Hannah turns so quickly, it sends her ponytail swinging. "What?"

I don't have a ponytail, but I feel the same whiplash of surprise. Hudson's solution is shattering giant glass doors? Is he serious? Does he even remember why that's not possible?

"Yeah, I'm not sure it's that easy," Naomi says.

Quincy frowns. "Do we even have anything we could use to break glass?"

"Chairs?" Hudson tries. "One of the stools from the projector rooms?"

"Those flimsy-ass plastic chairs?" Naomi asks.

"Isn't the projector room locked?" Hannah asks.

"Yes, it's locked," I say. Everyone looks at me, and I hate it. I savor being a person who's easy to overlook. People don't notice if I trip on the carpet or flinch at a jump scare, but as Cara and

Naomi love to remind me, if I want to be a doctor, I need to get over it. Besides, staying hidden might have saved my ass now and then, but it's cost me plenty too.

"Hell, I can pull out one of the printers and throw that shit if I have to," Hudson says.

"It won't work," I say, forcing more volume into my words this time.

Hudson cocks his head. "Why the hell not?"

"Because they replaced those doors the year I started. Kids were breaking them by throwing rocks from their cars," I say. "You were here when they did it, Hudson."

"Like a drive-by stoning?" Naomi asks.

"Shit, you're right," Hudson says with a frown. "They installed some kind of impact-resistant glass doors."

"Because of course they did," Hannah says with a sigh. "So our only choice is trying to get out through the mall?"

Quincy adjusts his glasses on his ears. "What about the emergency exits?"

"Tried that," Hudson says. "Every last one is locked. All the front doors too."

Hannah rolls her shoulders. "The back door isn't locked, but it's actually boarded over from the outside."

"Why?" Summer asks softly.

"They're redoing the whole place," Hudson says. "They've already prepped the entire mall. They were just waiting on some of the demolition pieces until we're out."

"But we're *not* out," Hannah says. Her freckled brow furrows. "Isn't boarding over a door premature?"

Hudson shrugs. "Dad says they're behind schedule. They're probably trying to get ahead."

"But I thought emergency exits had to stay unblocked," Quincy says with a frown. "It's the entire purpose of them, isn't it? To function in emergencies?"

Hudson waves that off. "After tonight, the whole place is shut down for total overhaul and reconstruction. That's a whole different bag. They're probably worried about someone sneaking in and getting themselves killed during demo."

"So they literally nailed us into this damn hellhole?" Naomi asks. "I can't with you men."

Quincy frowns. "Couldn't there be women on the crew?"

"No woman is nailing an emergency exit closed, I promise you that," Naomi says.

"Look, we've got to get out of here," I say, trying to think. "Let's talk about the mall. The connector doors—are those keys still above the frame?"

"If it's even locked," Hannah says.

"But I thought everything in the mall was closed," Summer says softly, her thin arms crossed over her chest.

"You're right," Quincy says, nodding at Summer. "The mall has been closed for weeks."

I nod. "But there are still lots of emergency exits in that building."

"The contractor will have most of it buttoned down tight," Hudson says. "Emergency rules sort of go out the window when a building's shut down like this. But there could be something, I guess."

"Do we have any other options?" Quincy asks. "Anything else we should consider? Should we try throwing something at the doors?"

"He'd hear us," Summer whispers. She is shaking; even her words vibrate when she speaks. "If he hears us, I don't know what he'd do."

"Yeah, I'm not a fan of whistling him over," Naomi says. "I didn't see the keys anywhere, and I hit a couple of the fire alarms, but they aren't working. Maybe because of the power?"

Hudson nods. "We tried one of the fire alarms too."

"And the panic button under the ticket booth," Hannah says. "That's when we heard her."

"What do you mean you heard her?" I ask.

"We were in the theater when the power went out," Hannah says. "Just killing time."

Hudson nods, his gaze losing focus. "Sometimes the power comes back, you know? After a while, we gave up. Made our way to the door, and the second we stepped outside—"

"He was right there," Hannah says. Her face goes pale, the smattering of freckles on her nose and cheeks turning dark against her skin. "He practically *ran* past us. He looked like he'd seen a ghost."

"And he was talking to himself," Hudson says. "Freaking the hell out, especially when he figured out that back door is blockaded."

"What did he say?" I ask, chills rolling up my arms.

"He was looking for something," Hudson says. "He was upset and muttering, '*Where are they? Where the hell did I leave them?*' Shit like that."

"I think it was his keys," Hannah says. "Bastard's probably looking for a way to run."

"Anyway, that's when Naomi called out." Hudson rakes a hand through his hair. "As soon as she started hollering for us, he ran like hell."

"Where did he go?" Quincy asks, but his eyes keep drifting to Summer whose shaking is growing worse.

Hudson bounces on the balls of his feet. "No idea."

"We knew it was weird, but we didn't know he was dangerous or whatever. We didn't have any clue about…" Hannah trails off with a shaky sigh.

Hudson shakes his head, and Naomi closes her eyes. Summer sniffles, curling inward into her shroud of red hair. The reality of Lexi's death rolls through our bodies again, and we all crack in different places under the weight. But I have felt this weight before. Does that mean there's something too broken in me? Something that doesn't feel this the way I should? Or does it just mean I'm braced for what comes next?

Because I know this won't be the last time it hits us. Death is like the tide; it rolls in and out in an endless cycle. Waiting in this hallway won't change it. If anything, it might give us another death to worry about. And I'm not about to take that chance. We need to move.

I look around, but everyone seems trapped in a haze of shock and horror. I clear my throat and think of Naomi and Cara again.

This isn't how I wanted to find my voice. I was supposed to save trauma victims, not shepherd my coworkers away from a killer. But right now, I seem to be the only person who isn't lost in a shock-induced haze.

"Maybe we should vote on what to do," I say.

Hannah nods. "I think we should go to the mall."

Quincy steeples his fingers under his chin. "It seems like the only choice."

Hudson shrugs. "We get a hold of Clayton's gun; a bullet might take care of the glass."

"Or it might end up in one of us!" The sharpness of my tone surprises me, but the words are already out, and even with everyone looking, I still can't hold the next words in, though my voice peters to a whisper. "*Nothing* good is coming from that, Hudson."

He looks at me, and I can see a million questions in his gaze. I feel like a locked door that's been cracked open. If I don't stop this now, he'll curl his fingers into that opening and pry my secrets out. I turn to Naomi to shut him down.

"So what's your vote?" I ask.

"I want to be as far away from Clayton as I can," she says. "I vote for the mall."

We go around the room again, but in the end, everyone votes to go to the mall, even Hudson. We make our way back to the door that opens to the lobby. Hannah is in the lead, but she pauses at the push bar on the door, her brow furrowed.

"What is it?" Quincy asks.

"I hear something," she says.

I'm opening my mouth to ask when I hear it too, a distant murmur. A voice.

My heart shoots into my throat, and Summer meets my eyes. I see my fear mirrored in her face and know instantly that I'm not jumping to conclusions. That isn't the voice of someone here to rescue us. It's Clayton.

Hudson moves forward and presses the door open the tiniest sliver. Clayton's voice is instantly clearer.

"I'm not mad. I get it. It's been a tough night for all of us. We're all scared. But we're *all* stuck here without those keys. So stop hiding."

He's by the concessions, maybe by the soda machine from the sound of it. The angle of the egress door will make it impossible for Clayton to see, but it makes me nervous all the same.

"Just bring me the keys, and we can go outside," Clayton says. His voice is rising. It's obvious he's getting antsy. It's just as obvious he's been at this a while. We must not have been able to hear him while we were in the emergency hallway.

"Hello?" he shouts. And then, more softly: "Damn it."

For long, long seconds, he does not speak again. We stand in the cramped space of the dim emergency corridor staring at one another. I can feel my heartbeat under my skin. Summer's breath comes faster and faster until I'm worried she might start screaming—might launch into a full-blown panic attack. Hannah takes her hand, and Summer steadies.

I'm steady too. Steady because I'm not moving at all. My eyes stay locked on the sliver of a gap between the door and the frame. Hudson is positioned between me and that gap. My eyes graze over his angular jaw and prominent Adam's apple. I notice a utilitarian silver chain peeking out from his T-shirt and a blue stain near his collar.

"None of us are getting out of here until you bring those keys back!" Clayton shouts. And then he mutters something under his breath. A minute later we hear a door creak open. His voice comes again, much more muffled than before.

"He's in one of the theaters," Quincy whispers.

Hannah nods. "He must be checking them. He's looking for us."

"He'll eventually check this hallway, then, right?" Summer asks. Her voice is a squeak, and her theory is difficult to argue.

My pulse races even faster. Hudson has pushed the door open another inch, and I can see the connector door all the way across the lobby, the one that will lead us to the mall. Hudson pushes the door a little wider, sticking his head out. He listens hard and then, without warning, pushes the door wide.

"He's in Theater Three. This is our chance."

My stomach folds in on itself. I know exactly why I don't like the idea of being out there again, exposed in that cavernous lobby. Clayton won't stay in that theater. He could come out at any second. He could see us.

But Hudson doesn't see it as a risk. He sees it as an opportunity. He pushes the door wide and waves quickly. "Go! Go right now!"

I open my mouth to argue, but everyone flies into motion. Quincy and Hannah and Naomi and even Summer are rushing into the lobby. Hudson whispers my name, but I hear other things as well.

Bells jangling over a door.

Lighters spilling on the floor.

A final gurgling breath.

And then Hudson takes my hand, and I do the only thing I can. I run.

10:04 AM / April 13, 2023

CITY REVOKES CONSTRUCTION
PERMITS AT SITE OF TRAGEDY

Darrin Roberts—*Northeast Ohio News*

City Council revoked all active construction for the site of former shopping mall Riverview Fashionplace following the April 8 tragic deaths of four Riverview Theater employees. City Council President Troy Feibel cites egregious safety issues among other factors in a lengthy council statement on this topic. "Four of our neighbors are dead, and that building played a significant role in their deaths," Feibel said in an emotional statement before the council and many community members. "Four people are gone, and I'll wonder for the rest of my life how many of them might have lived if these so-called oversights had been resolved." Construction, which included a partial demolition of the former mall, has been halted since the time of the tragedy. Neither Coplex Construction nor PDG Development, who held the majority of the permits, provided comment on this matter.

CHAPTER 10

WE FLY ACROSS THE LOBBY, PAST THE TICKET BOOTHS and geometric carpet and the condiment stand Quincy and I straightened. We bunch into a tight pack at the door and fumble with the handle. I am nudged by shoulders and jabbed by elbows, but I stay right in the middle of it.

"It's locked," Quincy whispers.

"Get the key," Naomi says; she's too short to reach.

Hannah grabs it for them, and I hear her fiddling with the doorknob. The key scrapes at the metal lock, and it is so loud. I know he'll hear us. He *must* hear us. A whine rises behind my ears as Hannah lets Hudson take a turn at the key. It isn't working. They can't get it open, which means we're trapped here. We'll never make it back to the hallway before he sees us.

My throat squeezes tighter with every breath. I know what's coming for us—I know what we will look like on the ground, how we will sound when we are bleeding out on this ugly carpet.

And then—finally—there's the *click-click* of the lock

disengaging. The door swings wide, and we snake through into the connector hallway, a desperate centipede rushing for the safety of the darkness. I wedge my foot into the doorframe before it can fully close.

"Should we leave this propped open?"

"It's a good question," Quincy says. "There isn't a doorknob on the mall side. Maybe we should."

He's still hanging close to me in the darkness, but the others are already down the hall—out of sight and maybe inside the main atrium of the mall.

"*Stop playing games!*"

Clayton's voice sends goose bumps up my arms. He is losing patience now. The anger is clear in every word. My heart trips over itself, like it, too, is trying to escape him.

"*How the hell do you think this will work? You think you're walking out of here without me knowing?*"

I close my eyes, trying to place him, trying to calculate angles and add distances in my head like I'll be able to suddenly figure out how sound travels. As if I have any chance of pinpointing his location. Of course, I have no damn idea where he is.

What I know is this: Clayton is out there. And he's looking for us.

A rush of shadow and footsteps moves back up the hallway from the mall. I inhale sharply, but it's just Hudson, his angular face cast in strange shadows by the flashlight he's holding.

He reaches and pulls my fingers from the gap before I can

think. The door slowly, quietly clicks shut, leaving us in the connector hallway. The theater—the one piece of this building that's familiar and habitable—is now sealed behind a steel door, one with no knob on this side.

Panic bubbles up through my middle. I drag my fingers over the door, feeling for a knob I know isn't there. This is a one-way door, but Hudson wouldn't close it if there weren't a way back in, would he? There must be a gap. Something. I keep feeling and patting, and over and over I come up dry.

There's nothing. We're trapped here. Hudson has pulled us out of one prison and locked us right into another.

"What did you do?" Quincy asks.

"Only chance we have of him not finding us is if he doesn't know we're in here." Hudson shifts his flashlight to point down the hallway, toward the mall. "Come on."

He urges us both down the hallway, and I stumble after on legs that feel wooden and strange. The darkness of the hallway gives way when we meet the mouth of the now-defunct Riverview Fashionplace, a three-story shopping mall with a river running through the full length of the main atrium. Once, there were walls coated in faux rock, and sheets of Spanish moss dangled from the bridges that spanned the river. Back then, this place featured everything a cheesy mall designer could muster up, from fountains to waterfalls to misters.

When I was little, Mom used to bring Cara and me. We would run over the bridges that connected the east and west halves of the mall. We would sit, enraptured by performers on the kitschy clamshell stage, and sometimes we'd try to find more of the carved frogs and fireflies hidden throughout the waterscape. When we were little, I always counted the most. But after the gas station, after that awful day, I always let Cara win.

Now, even in the dim light, the mall is barely recognizable. A bone-white channel stretches out behind Naomi and Hannah, the remnants of the river that once bisected the entire mall. I can see the first bridge maybe ten yards behind them, some of the boards busted loose, the handrail completely missing on the left side. Even when I started at the theater, a lot of the mall stores were permanently closed. Wallboards stretched across long expanses of the mall, turning a former Bath & Body Works or American Eagle into a mural advertising YOUR NEXT FAVORITE SHOP—COMING SOON.

Now those murals are interspersed with giant yellow-brown plywood sheets and enormous plastic drapes. Some of the stores are empty, yawning dark cavities behind pull-down security gates or taped-over glass doors.

"Hudson closed the door," Quincy says.

Hannah's shoulders pull back. "What the hell were you thinking?"

"We heard Clayton. He's looking for us, so I closed the door," Hudson says.

"There's no *handle* on those doors on this side," Hannah says.

"We don't need a handle. We're getting out," Hudson says, and he's already looking to the left, where plywood entirely covers the hallway that once led to the emergency doors. Plastic cover drapes the area to the right, but I'm not feeling much better about that.

"You aren't going to say anything?" Hannah asks. She's looking at Naomi, but Naomi shakes her hair with a hard laugh.

"Hell no. It doesn't matter if it's open or locked to me. I'm never going back in there."

"Please hurry," Summer says.

The softness of her voice confuses me. We all stop and look at her, and her eyes are wide and terrified, her red hair hanging in tangled lines around her shoulders and waist, her long skirt and cardigan trembling. Her eyes are locked on the dark hallway we exited, on the locked door we left behind. "Please. Before he comes for us."

There's a thinness to her voice, a desperation that reminds me this is not just a power outage and an inconvenient misplacement of the keys to unlock the main doors. Clayton *killed* Lexi, and Summer was there when it happened. She is pale and trembling— the way she's been since I found her in that locker room.

Summer saw exactly what Clayton did, and she is terrified. Maybe we should all be terrified. And maybe we should all do exactly what Summer said. We need to hurry.

"She's right," I say. Everyone's eyes turn to me, and I squeeze my hands into fists. They look like I need to say something else, but I need to think. I can't just blurt out the right thing without thinking.

Is that even something a person can learn? How can I be a doctor if I can't make quick decisions?

Hudson goes over to the plywood section first, jogging the length of the diagonal slab, checking all the places where the sheets overlap. Soon enough, he comes back shaking his head. "No dice. Let's try through all that plastic shit."

Irritation flares in my middle. Hudson lives like every single second of his life is a call to action. Like the only wrong choice he could make is sitting still.

He disappears through the curtains of plastic. A few seconds later, he swears, and I know the other exit is blocked too.

"What the hell are we going to do?" Naomi asks.

"There are other doors, right?" Quincy nods toward the dry riverbed and the mall atrium beyond it. "There'll be doors in the middle, won't there?"

As familiar as I am with this building, I'm having a hard time reconciling the scene before me with my memories of the tacky, water-themed mall scape. I remember walls molded to look like streamside vistas and lights that shimmered blue, green, and purple. It was like slipping into a fairy tale when I was little. Now there are heaps of two-by-fours and piles of busted drywall and plastic sheets hanging as far as the eye can see. The place was in slow decay for years, but now it's a foreign land. The backdrop of a sad documentary.

I scan the area and spot a large door between two boarded-over shops labeled STAIRWELL and another alcove labeled RESTROOMS.

I can also see the signpost that once held a map of the mall. There are bits and pieces of the place I remember, but it's like looking at the carcass of a once beautiful bird, its bones and innards splayed across oil-stained pavement.

Hudson returns, and we move together toward the atrium, following the white channel of the riverbed. Quincy, Naomi, and I stay to the right, but Hannah, Summer, and Hudson veer left. Hudson kicks at one of the plastic vines still clinging to the side of the riverbed.

I hate that our party has been split. It's a five-foot-wide river, maybe two feet deep at the worst. We're a few steps away from them, and logically I know that's not a big deal. This isn't dangerous. But I can't help the uneasy feeling rolling through me.

"The next set of doors will be up here across from the stage," I say.

"I don't remember the mall very well," Quincy says.

"Not much to remember," Hudson says, kicking a scrap of wood out of his path. "Shops on this floor and the one above. Third floor is all private offices. Creepy, identical offices."

"They had offices up there?" Hannah asks.

Hudson nods. "That's how the failing started. Sandusky was never going to be big enough to handle a mall this size, so when they couldn't find vendors for the third floor, they rented it out as office space to attorneys and psychiatrists and whoever else."

"Did that work?" Naomi asks.

"Well, we are standing in the middle of a dead shopping ma—"

"Shh."

It's Quincy who cuts Hudson off. He has his finger up, like maybe he was going to physically hush us, but he isn't looking at any of us. He's looking back down the mall the way we came, his eyes trained on the connector hallway to the theater.

"Did you hear that?" he asks, pushing his glasses up the bridge of his nose.

"Hear what?" Hudson says.

"I thought I heard something creak," Quincy says.

And then there's a sound that turns my blood cold. It is a simple *click-thunk*. As familiar as my own voice, but this time it's enough to steal my breath and leave my knees wobbly.

It is the sound of a heavy door closing. And I know in an instant what door just closed and why. It's the door to the theater. Clayton followed us in, and let the door swing shut behind him.

We are trapped with a killer. Again.

CHAPTER 11

I LOCK EYES WITH HUDSON ACROSS THE RIVER CHANNEL for the span of a breath. Maybe Clayton didn't come inside the mall. Maybe he opened the door and peeked in, but decided to let it close when he didn't hear anything. It's possible he's still in the theater. And then I hear footsteps.

Hudson breaks our gaze, and both groups spring into action, rabbits running for the darkness of our burrows. Quincy and Naomi choose a tall, plastic-draped fountain for cover. I crouch with them but immediately scan for a better option. Tucked behind the north side of the fountain, we can't see anything to the south, which is exactly where we heard Clayton.

I feel like the years are rushing in reverse, sending me back to that day in the gas station. My world is about to shatter into a million pieces again, and I am powerless to stop it. I press my hand to my chest, trying to force myself to calm down.

"Is he even hidden there?" Quincy asks.

I'm not sure what he's talking about until I follow his gaze across the mall. Hannah and Summer are huddled behind a kiosk that sold Christmas ornaments during the holidays and weird face cream the rest of the year. They're tucked into the shadows like us, and vulnerable too, utterly cut off from any view of the entrance to the theater.

But Hudson is behind a tiny information booth, and he's not crouched low like the rest of us—he is bent over at the waist with his chin resting on the counter, his fingers drumming like hummingbird wings. I'm not sure if he's fully hidden, but relief washes over me all the same. Because unlike the rest of us, Hudson is facing the south side of the mall. He's looking straight down the river channel to the place where Clayton will be.

"Do you think it's the police?" Naomi whispers.

"What?" Confused, I glance at her to see the uncharacteristic worry in her eyes.

"Shouldn't someone be looking for us?" she asks. "It could be the police, couldn't it?"

I can list half a dozen reasons why I'm sure it's not, starting with the fact we're supposed to be eating waffles right now and I can't imagine anyone looking for us, and ending with the fact that police officers generally announce themselves when entering a building for a rescue.

But I don't say that. I don't want to talk at all, because I don't know where Clayton is or how much our voices will travel. I don't even know if he's come out of the connector hallway until

Hudson's fingers stop tapping. He goes entirely still, his dark eyes fixed on something I can't see—something to the south.

"Hudson sees Clayton," I breathe.

We are all beyond quiet. A whine rises behind my ears, and I feel like I can't get enough air. Hudson is motionless. Every part of me tenses like I'm waiting for an explosion, like the seconds are counting down closer and closer and—

Hudson bolts away from the kiosk without warning.

"What is that fool doing?" Naomi whispers.

"Is he coming over here?" Quincy asks, voice alarmed.

I do not answer, because Hudson is sprinting over the first bridge that spans the empty river. My heart rate doubles as he rushes toward our fountain, his hair flying up in tufts.

He crouches in front of us, breathing hard.

"What are you doing? Where's Clayton?" Naomi asks.

"He's in the hallway with the plastic right now," he says. "I don't think he knows we're in here. Not yet, anyway."

"He has to know. I don't think we took the key out of the door. Obviously we used it to get in here," Quincy says.

Hudson shrugs. "Maybe. But we've forgotten that key in the lock a hundred times. It doesn't prove anything."

"But he didn't find us in the theater," I say. "He *has* to know we're in here."

"Even if he knows, he hasn't found us yet," Naomi says.

Hudson clings to that, whirling. "Exactly. Which is why I think we've got to take advantage of the element of surprise."

"How?" Quincy asks.

Hudson's eyes are wild. "We rush him. Tackle him to the ground and get his gun away from him."

I feel heat and then cold race over my whole body in successive waves. "You can't be serious."

"Dead serious," he says. Then he puts his fingers to his lips and peeks his head around the fountain, slowly stretching, presumably until he can see Clayton. He holds his hand up behind him, urging us to be quiet.

Then he turns back to us, whispering very softly, "He's checking out the connector door again. I'm telling you, he just wants to get out of here."

"Then let him!" I whisper. "Why would we go after him when we know he has a gun?"

"Because he killed Lexi, Jo." Hudson shakes his head. "No way I can live with letting him get away with that."

I swallow down the snide comment in my mouth. Because the truth is he could live with it. You can learn to live with all kinds of terrible things, and I would know. The important part is that you live to begin with.

"He's right."

To my shock, it's Quincy who says it. And when I gape at him, he pushes up his glasses, his cheeks going a little dark. "Even without the Lexi situation, we aren't going to be safe in here until we get that gun away from Clayton."

My breath is coming faster and faster. I can think of dozens of ways this can all go wrong. Clayton could shoot someone before he's disarmed. Hudson could shoot himself trying to get the gun away from Clayton. My mind is conjuring one bloody scene after the next, and before I can bring up a single one of them, I hear something roll and drop with a clatter.

My heart leaps into my throat. It's coming from the other side of the riverbed, near the kiosk where Hannah and Summer are hiding. Did something fall off it? Did one of them throw something?

"Shit," Hudson says.

"What happened?" Naomi asks. "Is it him?"

"Shit," Hudson repeats, moving to a crouch. "Clayton's looking around. He heard them."

"Heard who?" Naomi asks.

"Hannah and Summer. They dropped something," I say, my heart beating faster. Harder.

They're more active by the kiosk now, clearly alarmed by the noise they've made.

"Something fell off the top of the kiosk. A pipe or something," Hudson says.

Hannah and Summer are still close together. They're twisting this way and that, and I am terrified they'll run. Terrified that I will stand here, hiding again. Watching again. That I will hear that terrible *pop, pop, pop*, the one that's echoed in my memory for nine years.

Hudson turns back toward us, looking at the ground. The

plastic sheeting. He's hunting for something, and then he finds it, lifting the plastic quickly to pull up a couple of small board ends, the pieces left after a cut.

He hands them to Naomi and me. "Take these. Quincy, you and I will run around back here."

He points at the boarded-over shops behind us. "Count to twenty, and then throw those as hard as you can at the bridge."

"Hudson, stop," I say, but my voice is weak. I feel so breathless I can barely get the words out. My body is freezing up, my voice trapped. "Don't."

But he slips away, Quincy right on his heels. They melt into the darkness by the stores, and I am left holding a hunk of wood. Beside me, Naomi is softly breathing out the count, just like Hudson asked. She is crouched and focused and ready, but I am frozen while the world moves past—smears of chaos as far as I can see.

"Three. Four. Five."

I adjust my grip on the wood and look at the bridge. I can hit it, sure, but why? What good is that going to do? Clayton could shoot the bridge and miss and hit one of us. He could see exactly where the wood came from.

"Nine. Ten. Eleven."

I can't hear anything. I want to warn Summer and Hannah, but how? Across the channel, they're still crouched together, but Summer is pulling hard where Hannah is holding her hand. She looks like she wants to run. Oh God, if she runs, we're all screwed.

"Fourteen. Fifteen. Sixteen."

Summer breaks free of Hannah's grip and bolts, and that's when I know. Everything is about to fall to pieces.

Maybe it wouldn't have mattered, but the wondering messes with me. The whole world is a set of dominoes—everything we say and do touches another domino, and they all tumble this way or that. Your choices might ripple out to someone who cures cancer. Maybe my recent choices opened a window of opportunity for a killer.

CHAPTER 12

NAOMI SHOUTS, "THROW THE WOOD. THROW IT NOW!"

I do. We both do. The boards fly at the bridge, and I hear them both hit. But it won't matter. Summer is racing down the middle of the mall. She is next to the stream, and she is rushing toward the theater. Directly toward Clayton.

"Leave them alone!" she cries.

Hannah is bolting after her. "Summer, wait!"

Footsteps thunder everywhere, and the world snarls into a tangle of noise and fear and darkness. It pulls me back—drags me under like the riptide until my mind is back in the gas station. But I am not there. I am *here*. This is real and it is happening.

I stumble for the edge of the fountain, trying to see where everyone is. Trying to make sense of the movements and noise around me.

"He's got his gun!" Quincy yells. "Get down, get down!"

I whirl and there he is: Clayton. Blond and perfect, he holds his black handgun like a man trained to do it. And maybe like a man who's dreamed of this all his life. He is staring straight at Summer.

And then a shadow moves across the streambed where Clayton is standing—a streak moving before I can see it. Before Clayton can see it either. Hudson is cutting across the mall, sprinting toward Clayton. But our manager's gaze and gun stay locked on Summer. What is she doing? What is she thinking?

I open my mouth to scream at her to duck. To run. But Hannah tackles her before my voice emerges. And one breath later, Hudson slams into the side of Clayton's legs.

Clayton topples, and the gun flies out of his hands, hitting the ground with an awful clatter. The gun skids across the tile floor away from Clayton and closer to Hannah and Summer.

Clayton roars from the ground, and I don't know what's happening. I can't see anything but a flurry of arms and legs and punches and kicks. Hudson cries out, and Clayton pops to his feet.

"Get the gun!" Hudson cries. His voice is rough and pained. "The gun!"

His voice kicks me into action. I bolt as fast as my feet will carry me, around the kiosk and along the stream. Clayton shifts into a run—barreling toward Hannah, but Hannah's stooped over. She's scrabbling for something on the ground.

And then she raises it in two shaky hands, and everyone freezes.

I don't know enough about guns to know what they're

called—I don't want to know—but this one is black and squared at the edges. And it is pointed right at Clayton.

For one second, Clayton is as frozen as the rest of us, and then he bolts off to the right, to the large door I saw earlier. *Why would he want to—* Then I see the word above the door. He's going for the stairs. Clayton pushes the door open, and it closes with a hard bang behind him. I hear the soft thumping of his steps. He's going up. He's leaving.

My shoulders sag in relief, and Hudson leans back against a rail with a heavy sigh.

"Good job, Hannah," Naomi says.

Hannah doesn't say a word. And she doesn't put down the gun.

"Hannah?" I ask. Her name sounds like fear on my lips.

Hannah still doesn't speak. She looks at the gun in her hands for the span of one breath.

Then she turns like she's in a trance and sprints for the same door Clayton used. It's only when it bangs shut behind her that I realize what's happening. That's when I know she's going after him.

"Hannah?" Summer's voice is small and shrill. I expect her to burst into tears, but she runs for that same door too, pushing it open. And then Hudson is moving, running across the mall.

The door bangs shut once behind Summer.

Again, behind Hudson.

I hear another door open above us. The second floor? The

third? I can't tell, but there are footsteps. Who is it? Clayton? Hannah? Why in God's name is she going after him?

Quincy and Naomi approach me from behind, and we look up at the balcony.

"I can't see them. Can you see them?" Naomi asks.

Quincy scans the balcony above on the west side. "It's too dark. Did you hear them come out on the second floor or the third?"

"They're up there. If they come closer to the railing, we'll see them," I say. In the next seconds doors open and footsteps thunder. I can't tell what's happening. I only know they're above us, somewhere up there in the darkness.

"What is Hannah doing?" Naomi asks. "What the hell does she have in her head?"

"I have no idea," Quincy says, and then he points at the balcony on the west side, nearly a third of the way down the mall. "There! Do you see?"

As he says it, I do. Flashes of shadows streak along the second-floor balcony. They're moving fast. If we don't head deeper into the mall, we'll lose sight of them.

I am shaking to the marrow of my bones, but I know I can't stay here. Even though my heart is pounding at a gallop in my chest and my legs are turning to lead, I have to move. Quincy and Naomi rush forward, walking along the dry streambed.

I follow with dread weighing each of my steps. My body tries desperately to overrule my willpower. No matter what I *should* do, I don't want to rush ahead to see how this turns out. Given the fact there's a gun up there, I don't even want to be inside this building. But I am inside, and I have to do something. I can't keep freezing up—I have to try.

I follow Quincy and Naomi, moving past another kiosk and several stores with glass fronts instead of plywood or metal grates. We pass the giant clamshell stage surrounded by sunken stair seating. The exit doors here are blocked, but the wide elaborate staircase leading from the ground floor to the second is clear and open. There used to be a waterfall that ran down the middle of those stairs, into the river bisecting the mall. Now it's a streak of brown-gray rock in the center of the white stone steps.

Above us, voices murmur and footsteps thunder, and I turn around, trying to make sense of the noise. It feels like it's coming from everywhere.

"They're on two floors. Someone is on the third floor. Perhaps two of them," Quincy says, and I don't understand until I see a hint of movement higher—on the third floor. But who is who? It doesn't make sense! From the sound of it, they're on opposite sides of the mall on two different floors. It's hard to pick anyone out in the darkness, the moonlight from the skylights doing little to illuminate the balconies beyond the railing.

"Clayton!"

It's Hannah's voice, and it is sharp and high. The third floor. It's easy to find her now, tall and moving fast high above. She's close to the railing now, and she's not quite jogging, but she's a high-performing softball player who runs four miles a day, and it shows. She has caught up with Clayton. In contrast I can hear Clayton rasping, the heavy breaths of a man who isn't as accustomed to running.

"Summer and Hudson must be on the second floor. Hannah's alone with him up there," Quincy says.

"Oh shit, Hannah," Naomi says, her voice low.

I look up in time to see Hannah right at the balcony railing on the third floor. Her ponytail swings as she lifts the gun, aiming down the balcony. "Stop or I'll shoot."

Clayton freezes. Quincy quietly crosses himself and turns away. On the second floor, Hudson appears at the railing. His dark head moves right and left. He is searching for something. For Hannah, I think. Then he disappears from the railing, and I can hear him running. Maybe for the stairs?

"I know what you did!" The fury in Hannah's voice is too big and deep to belong to the Hannah I know. A door opens on the second floor, and I can't see, but I think it's Hudson entering a stairwell. He must have realized Hannah's up higher, and he's going after her, but he's on the wrong side of the mall. I don't know if he can get to the other side in time, even if he makes it up those stairs like an Olympian. My heart is in my throat again.

"I *know*," Hannah repeats.

Clayton's laugh is a shock in the quiet. When he turns, I feel every inch of my skin turn cold. He has his hands up, but he cocks his head in a way that scares me.

"You're not going to shoot me, Hannah," he says.

Hannah's arms tremble. The gun shakes, but she still has it up.

"Oh God," Naomi says. "I can't watch this. I can't look at this. I can't—"

But I can't look away. Just like before, my eyes are glued to this awful scene and I am frozen. My body is paralyzed by this moment.

I am waiting for lighters to spill.

I am waiting for a *pop, pop, pop.*

I am waiting for someone to die.

Clayton is inching closer now.

"Don't!" Hannah screams, the gun shaking in her grip.

I hear the bang of a door being thrown open. Half a breath later, Hudson appears at the railing on the third floor. He's on the opposite side of the mall like I feared, a million miles too far to do any good, a million miles too close to avoid seeing what awful thing comes next. And it will be awful. That is the only way this ends.

"You son of a bitch," Hannah says, and her voice is halfway to a sob.

Clayton laughs again. "Stop playing, Hannah. You know you're not going to shoot. You're going to be a good girl and give me that gun."

Hannah stiffens her arms, but she hesitates, and my soul aches because deep in the marrow of my bones, I am sure she won't do this. I've seen her carry spiders outside on the rim of a dustpan. She made us call a wildlife rescue center when a blue jay hit the front doors of the theater. Hannah is not a person who can take a life.

But Clayton is.

"Hannah, run!" Hudson screams.

Hannah turns to look across the mall at him, and Clayton does not miss his chance. He lunges into a sprint, and by the time Hannah turns back, he has almost closed the distance. She tries to adjust the aim of the gun, but he crouches mid-stride, and my stomach drops.

I know what will happen now; I can see it.

Hannah tries to bring the gun down on his head, but Clayton shifts low as his body plows into her. And he doesn't just hit her—he pushes his shoulder upward. The momentum of his run amplifies the force and she goes airborne.

Something sour blooms in the back of my mouth when I see Clayton's thick palm shoot toward the center of Hannah's chest. She lands halfway on top of the railing, and he reaches for the gun, but she holds it high in the air, just out of his reach.

"Give me my gun, bitch!"

Hannah arches to keep it from him, and she wobbles on the railing. Naomi gasps and Quincy is speaking, praying maybe, but I'm silent even though every cell inside my body is screaming for Hannah to give him the gun. To run. But Hannah doesn't give him the gun—she throws it over the balcony.

Clayton's thick palm shoots out like a cobra, striking her dead in the center of her chest.

It's over before it even happens. Hannah flails for her balance—for her *life*—and a terrible, desperate noise comes out of her. But it is too late. Her precarious balance is gone, and her body pitches backward. I see her feet fly up over her head. And gravity does the rest.

FIRE MARSHAL TAKES HEAT OVER
SHOPPING MALL DISASTER

TV8 INVESTIGATES

The tragic killing of four locals shocked and dismayed the sleepy town of Sandusky, Ohio, in early April. In the weeks that followed, chatter on neighborhood groups and at city council meetings has focused on a point that has little to do with the crime itself. Namely, how did the Riverview Fashionplace building ever pass fire inspection? According to a public records request, the fire marshal has received thirty-four requests involving the inspection of this property, more than three times the number of requests than any received this year on an individual property. While most of the building was closed for active construction, one portion—Riverview Theaters—was still open with employees and customers both having access to unsafe conditions in the connected mall. *TV8 Investigates* is asking viewers with personal information or tips to reach out about this ongoing investigation.

CHAPTER 13

THE END COMES WITH A TERRIBLE, DULL *CRACK* THAT I know will echo in my ears forever. There are some sounds you never forget.

"Oh my God," Naomi says, and her voice sounds flat and distant.

Everything sounds wrong, like a badly dubbed foreign movie. My feet carry me with strange slaps on the tile. A door slams somewhere above us. Distant footsteps tap across the balcony. Clayton? Summer? Someone is running.

And there is sobbing—soft and low and quiet. I recognize the anguished voice. It's Hudson, and it's the only thing that makes sense in my brain.

I stop a few feet from where Hannah landed, and my eyes try to comprehend what I'm seeing. Because Hannah is like a child's drawing, and my brain can't put the pieces together. Her limbs are generally in the right location on her body, but the angles are impossible. Everything is broken, but her neck is the worst part, twisted on the edge of the bottom step. She is a Picasso in real life, her face mashed into her shoulder, her right hand folded entirely under her arm.

Hannah is not moving, and she is not breathing, and I know there is no CPR or phone call or medical miracle that will change anything here. She is dead.

My knees give, right there, dropping me in a heap on the tile floor. Some part of me knows there is wailing. Footsteps. Someone is retching. But all of it is a thousand miles away from me. I am floating in a soap bubble at her feet, and I let myself have it. Maybe I don't even have a choice.

I close my eyes and touch the buttery suede of Hannah's worn Adidas sneaker. Her foot is still warm through the thin canvas. I am desperate to shake her foot. To roll her over or turn back time. To make this something other than what it is.

I press my lips together tightly to hold in the scream climbing inside me. If I let one peep of that out, I don't think it will ever end. So, instead, I keep my fingers pressed to her foot while my ears ring and my head whirls. Maybe if I hold on tight enough, I'll remember how to do this, how to keep living when death is all you can see.

Murder doesn't have space for how the survivors will manage, for what you can or cannot do. Death is absolute. It's always accepted in the end, because there aren't any other options on the table.

"Jo?"

Quincy's voice pulls me back into the world. Everything spins into focus. Hudson sobs somewhere high above us. He is still up there, somewhere on the third floor. Naomi is crying softly. Quincy is waiting to my left, his dark eyes searching my face. And Summer is back. I see her now, halfway down the stone steps. She is whiter than paper, her arms crossed over her middle and her breath coming in awful hiccupping gasps.

I look at Quincy, and he wipes his mouth. I think I smell vomit and realize it's him. He's been sick. His eyes are still watery from the effort of it.

"I'm sorry," he says, his cheeks going pink. "I don't know why I got sick. After Lexi…"

"Lexi was…different." The right word is *cleaner*. It was hard to look at Lexi. It's a whole different animal to look at someone whose limbs and neck are bent in the wrong direction. Or when someone is bleeding out in a pile of cigarette lighters.

And it's always harder when you see the person die.

Summer slumps at the edge of a stairstep, her forehead pressed to the railing. Her hair seems endless, a tangled orange river blocking her from me entirely. I look up, trying to spot Hudson above, but I can't see him.

Or Clayton for that matter. A chill runs through me. Where is he? I remember the sound of the door closing, right after Hannah fell. Was that Clayton?

I keep my voice low—just for Quincy. "Did you see what happened to Clayton?"

"He's on the second floor. Or he was at one point. I saw him duck out of the stairwell, but he's staying back from the railing now."

Hiding. He's hiding from us so we won't see what's coming next.

"What about the gun?" This is Naomi, her voice rough from crying, her eyes swollen and raw.

Quincy winces. "It's somewhere down here. I couldn't... I didn't look."

"It's okay," I say, glancing around.

"Like hell it's okay. He's still up there somewhere, right?" Naomi asks.

Quincy gestures above us. "He's up there somewhere, possibly watching us."

"But he doesn't have his gun now," I say softly. "Five against one is very different when there isn't a gun involved."

Quincy pushes his glasses up, thinking this over. He nods. "Yes. There are too many of us. If he isn't armed, he won't stand much chance against five people."

"Right," I say, twisting to look up. I still don't hear Hudson, and I don't like it. He should be down here by now. He should be with us.

"Yeah," Naomi says. And then she looks up. "You hear that, asshole? We've got your gun!"

Alarm flares through my middle, and I reach for her, but she's raging at the darkness of the balcony, her fists clenched at her sides. "And don't you get it in your head that I'll hesitate, because I won't. You come near us, and I'll shoot you cold."

I grab Naomi's arms and pull her close to me, whispering, "What are you doing? We don't have the gun."

"He doesn't know that," she says. "If he thinks we have it, he won't bother looking for it, right?"

I release her because it suddenly feels like holding a stranger. Naomi has dated Cara for six months, so I know her. She loves flowers, hates anything grape-flavored, and makes everyone laugh. Naomi is strong and witty and rattled by nothing.

I've never seen Naomi afraid like this. And I've definitely never seen her lie. Then again, I've never seen Quincy so calculating. Or Summer so silent. When you brush this close to death, the trauma messes with you: it strips you to the bone until all the hard, brittle parts are right out in the open.

Maybe that's my power right now. None of this is new to me. I've already had my world implode on an ordinary Sunday afternoon. I've spent years pretending I'm not afraid of the sound of bells. That I don't flinch at the sight of guns or shake every time I approach a gas station counter. If you don't give anyone reason to pay attention, secrets like that are easy to hide.

For me, going through the motions is practically second nature. I learned how to smile and move along when it feels like your insides are coming unraveled. I know how to fake it. Maybe I can give that to everyone else. Cara and Naomi told me I should be able to take charge. This sure as hell isn't the opportunity I'd pick, but I guess it's the one I have.

"We have to find a new way out of here," I say.

"What way?" Quincy asks. "Everything is locked up or boarded over."

"There must be a way we haven't found," I say. "Or people who'll be coming to look for us soon."

I force myself to my feet, faking a steadiness I don't possess.

"Naomi," I say. "I'm going to go get Hudson."

They look up at me, even Summer lifting her gaze.

"Where is your head?" Naomi asks. "No one should go up there."

"We could call for him," Quincy says.

I think about it but shake my head. "We don't know where Clayton is exactly. I don't want to announce that Hudson isn't with us. That's why I want to sneak up alone. I can be quieter on my own."

"Are you hearing yourself right now?" Naomi asks. "Because you just said we don't know where Clayton is. And now you want to go flitting up those stairs alone?"

I point at the open staircase behind us. "Hudson is right up there. I heard him earlier. If Clayton comes back, you will see him and you will yell. And if we get lucky, I'll get back down here with Hudson before he even sees one of us is missing."

Naomi and Quincy don't like it, but they're probably in that blurry shock-induced place where it's hard to find the words to argue. I pause at the bottom of the stairs, looking at Summer, who's rocking on the step.

"Summer? Are you okay?"

"He's coming for us," she whispers.

A chill rolls through me at her words. At the motion of her rocking, back and forth. Back and forth.

"We're going to find a way out of here," I say, trying to be reassuring.

But Summer keeps rocking, that tangled red hair framing her pale face when she looks up at me.

"He won't stop now," she says, her eyes feverish. "He won't stop until he kills us all."

Date: April 9, 2023
From: Coach Schneider
To: Lakesider Girls Team
Subject: Hannah

Team,

I'm devastated to share that your friend and teammate, Hannah Price, was killed last night in a horrible tragedy at the theater where she worked. We don't have many details, as the police are still working to solve the crime, but our hearts are broken at this news.

Hannah has pitched for the Wildcats for three years, leading us to regionals every year and helping us snag the state championship in 2022. I think most of you know she'd received several offers from colleges with fantastic softball programs, and in typical Hannah fashion, she had a detailed spreadsheet outlining the pros and cons of each one. Hannah had a bright future, not only in softball but in chemistry, which she planned to study in college. We are heartbroken to know her future has been cut short.

Mr. and Mrs. Price asked me to convey their gratitude for those of you who have reached out. This is an understandably painful time for them, so they asked that we bear with them on the details for Hannah's arrangements.

Team, it's hard to know how to close an email like this. We lost a champion. We lost a teammate. We lost our dear friend, and we are all terribly saddened by her passing. We know Hannah was tough as nails, so we're going to have to follow her example as we get through this tough time. Be good to each other. I know we can get through this together.

—Coach

CHAPTER 14

I CAN'T MUSTER ANY WORDS TO COMFORT SUMMER. I can only nod and face the stairs because I cannot think about Clayton. What he's planning or where he's hiding can't be in my head right now. I have to focus on the thing in front of me: getting Hudson back to the group.

I climb the first flight of stairs braced for Clayton to leap from the darkness, tensed for the crack of a bullet, even though I know he doesn't have the gun. But I reach the second floor unscathed and keep climbing to the third. I'm grateful for the thick blue carpet that replaces the white stone from the staircase. It swallows the sound of my footsteps. If I can't stick to the darkest shadows, I'll at least embrace the silence.

"Hudson?" I whisper at the top of the stairs.

There is no answer—no sound at all.

I take a few tentative steps south on the balcony, scanning the shadowy hallway. There's a row of emergency lighting along the floor by the railing that casts a pale purple glow, one that reflects on some of the offices beside me. Each space is a clone of the one before. They boast the same door and window, with a changeable sign placard on the wall. Now the signs are mostly empty. Some of the windows are barren and dark, but in most offices, there are curtains. Some are drawn tight, but as I walk, some are parted a few inches. Not that it matters. I can see nothing but blackness beyond the glass. But goose bumps rise on my arms all the same.

Anyone could be inside those rooms. Anyone could be watching. Waiting for me. My heart pounds hard at my ribs. For a moment, my mind imagines Clayton in one of those rooms. He could be standing behind that murky glass, watching me from the darkness.

I shiver and speed up, catching a glimpse of movement below. I sneak a look, spotting Quincy ushering Naomi and Summer to the other side of the staircase below. He's moving to a place where there's no chance of seeing Hannah's sprawled and motionless body, her long legs broken into strange angles.

A sniffle catches my attention, and I pause mid-step. Another sniff and I'm sure it's Hudson. I guess it's hard to work with someone for two years without all their sounds becoming familiar.

I keep moving across the carpeted balcony until I find him. Hudson has his back to the railing, his oversize knees drawn up and bony elbows popped on top. He has a scar above his left ear, one that curves and disappears into his hairline. I've never asked, but I've heard him explain how he got it to half a dozen people. Each reason he offers is less feasible than the last. An ice-dancing accident. A walrus attack. A tattoo attempt gone terribly wrong. It's hard to reconcile the smart-ass I know so well with the guy who looks up at me now.

His dark eyes are swollen, and his face is streaked with drying tears. I'm surprised by how soft he looks in this broken moment, his bleached hair a mess that seems to soften the sharp angles of his face.

"She's dead, isn't she?"

His voice is gravel in a desert, and his look dares me to lie to him.

"She is," I say. "I'm sorry."

I don't know what Hannah and Hudson were exactly. Friends, certainly. More? It never seemed like that, but I guess I don't know. The grief all over his face tells me he lost more than a work buddy tonight. How much more?

"We grew up together," he says. "Did you know that?"

"No."

"Played baseball together when we were little," he says. And then he laughs, strange and bitter. "I couldn't throw for shit, and believe me, she tried hard to teach me. It wasn't a long season, but we became friends. Not that she stuck around the little leagues. Pretty obvious she wasn't destined for life in the amateur lane."

He's right. Last time I checked, she had five different offers for a full ride. Sometimes she sent messages or videos she filmed in her bedroom, and you could see nothing but trophies and ribbons along the back wall. She got calls and texts every day from college scouts. Hannah's not just an athlete—she's a star.

Except now she's gone.

Hudson is quiet again, his gaze a thousand yards away.

"So no dreams of sports glory for you," I say, trying to bring him back.

"No dreams for her either now." His expression turns darker. It's like watching a heavy curtain pulled across a window, the light vanishing in one fell swoop.

"This is on me," he says.

"What? Hudson, you can't think like that."

He shrugs one shoulder. "The hell I can't. I yelled her name. She looked at me, and that's when he ran at her. That was it. I'm the reason she's dead."

His voice breaks, and he drops his head, tears starting again.

It wouldn't have mattered if he hadn't yelled. Clayton called her bluff with the gun. He was bigger and stronger, and he was going to win that one way or another. Hannah sealed her fate when she chased after him, but Hudson's not ready to hear logic right now. He only has space for anger.

"You knew better," he says. "You told me nothing good would come from going at him, and you were right."

I sigh. "I didn't say that because I knew better."

He gestures. "But you did. You *knew* something bad would happen."

"I'm not psychic, Hudson. I'm afraid."

"Afraid of Clayton?"

"Sure, afraid of Clayton. But even without Clayton, I would have been afraid."

"Why?"

"Because there was a gun."

"You're afraid of guns?" he asks.

Afraid doesn't feel like a big enough word. I'm not sure there's a big enough language for the feelings I have about guns.

"Aren't you afraid of anything?" I ask.

"The dark," he says. "My nani dying."

"Your nani?"

"My grandmother," he says.

How is he like this? He just offers up every truth about himself without a second thought. It mystifies me.

"Why are you afraid of guns?" he asks, still straight to the point.

Maybe he thinks I'll spit out my answer as easy as he spit out his. I hate that about him—how easy he makes it look to be an open book. But I don't want to be open. I don't want people to see the blood-spattered pages in the gas station, the parts of my life that make people look at me differently.

And yet, despite all those feelings, it blurts out of me.

"When I was nine, I was in a gas station during a robbery. Someone got shot."

"They didn't make it," he says gently. I'm surprised he doesn't phrase it as a question. Something in my tone must have given it away.

I nod, and the memory echoes through me—the bells over the door and the *pop, pop, pop*. The gurgle of my father's last breath. I close my eyes against the tears threatening to build, and then I clear my throat. "So, yeah. I don't like guns. And I don't want to keep our group split up like this, because I think you were right too."

"Right about what?"

"Clayton isn't going to stand much of a chance against five of us. But if we're going to stay alive, we need to stay together."

CHAPTER 15

WE WALK ALONG, AND HUDSON'S GAZE DRIFTS SLOWLY to the railing, to the floor below. I know he can't see Hannah from here, but his expression darkens.

"You need to keep an eye on Summer," he says. "I don't trust her."

It is the last thing on earth I expected him to say. I wrinkle my nose. "Summer? Why?"

"Because she might have something to do with this."

"We're not doing this, Hudson," I say, and I keep walking, making sure he knows how little credence I'm giving this new theory. "You're angry about Hannah. I get that. But we know exactly who did this. We don't need to invent a monster here."

"Summer said something to Hannah." He says it like he didn't hear me at all. "When they were by the kiosk, I saw them talking, and Hannah looked upset. They both looked upset."

"And? This is an upsetting day, and Hannah was a good person—the kind of person who'd be upset about Lexi."

Hudson shakes his head. "This was more than that. I'm telling you, Summer told her something—and whatever it was, I think it's what made Hannah go after Clayton."

We're near the top of the stairs now, and I stop, wanting to end this conversation before we go one step farther. "We don't know why she went up there. People do all kinds of things when they're traumatized."

"Really? You saw someone get shot, Jo. Did you pick up a gun and run after them?"

No, I didn't. But I wish to hell I had.

"Let's just get down there," I say, and I shake my head, making sure it's clear that what he's saying feels ridiculous to me.

And it is ridiculous. But for all my protests, there's a voice whispering in the back of my mind. Summer was with Hannah before she died, and she was with Lexi when she died too. Is there anything to that? Anything more than a terrible coincidence?

Who the hell am I to question it? This is the second time in my life I've been present for a murder. Nobody lists shit like that in the life-goals section of their bullet journal.

At the top of the stairs, I catch a glimpse of Hannah's body below. I steer my gaze away, but my mind conjures horrifying visions as sharp and clear as if I had seen it close up and not three floors below.

Hannah's body wobbling over the edge.

Hannah's eyes gone wide, her fingers splayed.

Hannah's arms and legs flailing. Desperate.

I didn't see these details clearly when it happened, but I dream them up in high definition.

Halfway down the stairs, my heart gives a little jolt when I don't see Quincy, Naomi, or Summer. But then I remember they moved behind the stairwell, to an alcove with a cluster of long empty planters.

They're talking softly when they notice us. Naomi stops and looks up. Relief softens the tightness in her jaw.

At the bottom of the stairs, I start toward them but realize Hudson hasn't joined me. He's looking at Hannah's body. My stomach drops as my own gaze drifts, catching on the sole of her left shoe and a strangely bent arm. I scale the stairs quickly back to Hudson.

His normally bronze skin has gone ashy and gray, and his whole body is tense. I touch his hand, fingers twitching at the sides of his legs.

"Hudson?"

His eyes blister me with their intensity. All the anguish and fear and revulsion that doesn't show in his expression is evident in his eyes, but he does not speak.

"You okay?" I ask.

"Not even close."

"Yeah," I say softly, and this time I am grateful for his bluntness. What's the point in pretending? None of us are okay. What the hell would it say about us if we were?

After a few seconds, he takes a shuddery breath and pulls free. He swipes an arm across his eyes, and that's that.

We join the group and form a loose circle, Naomi chewing her lip.

"We were talking while you were up there, right?" she says.

"Okay," I say, urging her to continue.

"We just…I don't get where everyone is. Wouldn't someone be expecting *one* of us?"

"Supposed to be eating pancakes," Hudson reminds her.

"Like I said, my parents are out of town," Quincy says. "Their flight was delayed from California, so they're probably waiting on a red-eye right now."

"But they'll look for you when they land?" Naomi asks.

He nods. "Sure, but it's a five-hour flight, and last I heard, they expected a takeoff at ten."

"What about you, Summer?" Hudson asks.

There's a faint hardening of his tone. Does anyone else notice? No one seems to react; they're all just looking at Summer, who shakes her head. She had declined pancakes, come to think of it. Wasn't a surprise since she usually gets dropped off by her parents, but now it begs a question. Where the hell *are* her parents?

"Don't your parents usually pick you up?" I ask her.

"Yes, usually," she says, her eyes brimming with tears and cheeks flushed. She doesn't just look frightened now—she looks ashamed. "There's a church camp. In Pittsburgh. Mom was excited for me to go. We've been saving money. I was going to take the bus tonight."

"The 12:04?" Naomi asks. She's got family in Pittsburgh, so I know she's there often.

Summer nods. "Yes. It was all planned. I was going to call home in the morning when I got to the station. The camp sends a van to pick up kids at the bus station and airports."

"But won't someone notice you didn't show up to the bus?" Quincy asks.

"I don't know," she says, sniffing. "It's a Greyhound. Do they track those tickets?"

"Track the tickets? Shit, girl, you'd be lucky to get a seat belt." Naomi sighs then. "Cara's home, but she'd just go to bed. She knew about IHOP, so she won't have any reason to stay up."

I nod, but I don't add the other part. That, yes, my sister will fall asleep. She's always been an early-to-bed, early-to-rise type. But Cara is also a nightmare type. As in, she's had them almost every night since the gas station. Most nights, she'll launch out of bed screaming, sending me bleary-eyed into the hallway to find her. I touch her sweat-soaked arms and reassure her that it's okay, that we are okay. It's never about the words. My rules include a soft voice and gentle touch—barely a person at all, just a safe warm presence to lead her back to bed.

"So what are we supposed to do?" Quincy asks, and for the first time, he doesn't sound calm or calculating. He sounds afraid.

Naomi doesn't have a smart-ass answer for once. She has a thousand-yard stare that matches Summer's. Even Hudson seems subdued. His fingers tap at the sides of his pants, but other than that, he is bizarrely still and quiet. They're all still and quiet.

Because they're in shock. This horror is fresh and new to

them, and they have no idea how to make sense of the world anymore. Tonight does not fit into the fabric of their universe.

But it does fit into mine.

I inhale sharply, wishing to God I had some other role to play in this nightmare because I've never wanted anything less than to take charge of a situation like this. But situations like this don't seem to give a shit what I want.

"First, I think we should stay together," I say.

A strange thump sounds overhead, and we all flinch, looking up. The balconies stretch into darkness. At the ceiling, I can only make out the edge of the large skylights, the moon having now moved across the left panes.

A door opens and then closes. I whirl, trying to spot the noise. My heart is a hammer tap-tap-tapping at the center of my chest. Where is Clayton? Where did that come from? We look at each other and at the balconies. We search and cower and wait, but nothing happens.

There are no more thumps or bumps. The same hollow quiet descends. I scan the balcony railing above, and a strange prickly feeling moves up my back. If Clayton comes back down those stairs, we could be cornered here. It's darker on this edge of the atrium too, with fewer lit pathways to provide light. If Clayton wants to come back for us, we're making it easy. We'll never see him coming.

I know you know what happened that night, but there are things I should tell you. I had a secret I never shared. And I knew someone else's secret too—the secret that set this whole thing in motion.

CHAPTER 16

I TURN AWAY FROM HUDSON AND NAOMI, KEEPING Summer in my peripheral vision. Her rocking sets my nerves on edge, but what the hell about this night isn't doing that? No one is calm right now, and no one is looking inclined to take over from the gentle suggestions I've offered.

Which means I'm going to have to keep going. And since I don't know how to pick a lock or disassemble giant sheets of plywood that appear to be covering the exits, there's only one strategy I know.

"Let's just think for a second," I say. "Even if no one is looking for us, someone must be looking for Hannah or Lexi. Or, hell, even Clayton. At this point we should have been home from pancakes, so someone could come while we're trying to think of an escape route."

"We hope," Naomi says, not sounding so sure.

To be honest, I'm not feeling confident about a rescue, but we need to regroup before we run off on a wild-goose chase. And there's another part of this I don't want to lend voice to. I want to know where Clayton is. If we're quiet—if we are all watching and listening—then we'll find the monster before he jumps out of the closet.

I take a few steps away from the stairs, trying to assess the mall. It's still hard to orient myself with all these slabs of plywood and giant plastic sheets draping everything like an old house with the furniture covered up at the end of the season.

"Maybe we should stay somewhere safer," Naomi says. "Like not in the middle of the open where you're standing."

I shake my head. "In the open is good. I don't want to be caught in a corner."

"But he could be watching us from somewhere we can't see," Quincy says. "Doesn't that bother anyone?"

"Doesn't bother me," Hudson says with a shrug. "Asshole doesn't have his gun. If he comes at us again, we'll pound him."

"Yeah, he's twice your size, hotshot," Naomi says.

"It's a numbers situation," Quincy says. He pushes up his glasses. "Five to one isn't bad odds."

I notice Summer still sitting on the bottom step. Her arms are wrapped around her knees, her pale, pale wrists showing from beneath her long-sleeved cardigan. She's still rocking, but barely now, her body twitching back and forth. Back and forth.

"Come on," I say. "Let's get ourselves in a back-to-back position."

Quincy's brow furrows. "So everyone faces away from everyone else?"

"Yeah, like musical chairs or something," Naomi says. She nods, looking steadier. "I get it. We can see whatever's coming."

I nod. "Exactly."

We arrange ourselves twenty feet from the stairs, almost smack-dab in the middle of the atrium. We are back-to-back, and from my position, I can see the dry streambed and four of the little bridges that cross over it. The edge of the stage and a couple rows of sunken seats are visible from here too, and to my left, Quincy will have a better view of the rest of the stage. Naomi is after that, and Summer is directly behind me, facing the area just left of the stairs. Which leaves Hudson on my right. I can't see any of them, but I feel them moving now and then.

It feels incredibly exposed. But I know what it's like to be crammed into a cubby. To feel my sister's panicked breaths on the back of my neck. To hear terrible sounds and have no idea what they are. I will choose exposed every time if it lets me see what's happening. And from here, I see everything, so I stay silent, and the others follow suit.

We sit in silence and watch.

And listen.

And wait.

"This is so damn creepy." Naomi's voice makes me jump on the plastic chair I've dragged over. I force my shoulders to relax.

"What do you think he's doing right now?" Quincy asks softly.

"He could have left," I say. "Maybe he climbed up and found a second-story fire escape. Or maybe he went to the roof."

"You think he got out?" Summer asks, her voice soft and afraid. She's directly behind me, but she's so quiet, she sounds like she's a football field away.

"Maybe," Hudson says. "Or he could be plotting which one of us he's going to kill next since he's obviously gone completely psycho."

"Shut your mouth about things like that," Naomi says.

"I agree," Quincy says from somewhere off to the left. All their voices are strange and disembodied, their words floating behind me in the darkness.

"It doesn't make any sense though, does it?" Quincy asks. "I mean, why would he do this?"

"Well, for starters he's an asshole," Naomi says.

"But I thought people who kill usually have motive," Quincy says. "Not that it's valid, of course, but in their minds, there is some logic."

"For killing Lexi and then Hannah?" Hudson asks. Even though I can't see him, I hear his fingers drumming against the sides of his chair. "What the hell did either of them ever do to him?"

"I don't know," I say. What I don't say is that Hannah provoked Clayton by turning his own gun on him. Because it doesn't matter what Hannah did. He had zero justification to hurt her. He barely ever spoke to her.

But Lexi feels different. Clayton was almost friendly with her. He certainly liked her better than the rest of us, but how much? Was it more than any of us realized?

I take a breath. "Do you think there was something going on between Clayton and Lexi? Something we didn't know about?"

"I'm not sure," Naomi says. "But she could calm him down quick as can be."

"Lexi had a calming presence in general," Quincy argues. "And that doesn't logically explain Hannah, does it?"

"Hannah…" I shake my head, my eyes going hot with the sting of tears. "She went after him. I don't know what she was thinking."

"She was thinking she had to go after him," Hudson says. "She was convinced, and I think maybe *someone* convinced her."

I hope Summer doesn't put two and two together with what Hudson is implying.

"It's nasty," Naomi whispers. I feel a tremor run through the chairs as she shudders. "Can you imagine being with someone like that?"

Hudson snorts. "Because he's a gym rat? Or because he's a first-class douchebag who's apparently even shittier to his wife than he is to us?"

"Like I said…gross," Naomi confirms.

"I couldn't agree more," I admit. "He makes my skin crawl."

"I say no way did she go there," Hudson says. "Clayton is vile, and Lexi was a badass."

"Except do we really know that? None of us can be sure of their relationship. She wasn't exactly easy to read," Quincy says.

He's right. Lexi kept to herself, and while I couldn't imagine her with Clayton, she also never seemed as uneasy around him as some of us. And none of us knew her well enough to be sure.

"It's possible they were romantically involved," I admit. "Ava said something about finding out 'who she was,' which had the distinct whiff of a woman who'd been cheated on."

"Do you think it could have been a sex thing?" Naomi asks. "Clayton is nasty, but he's got that blond, white pretty boy thing going on."

I shudder, because as true as it is, it's a revolting thought. "I don't know. Clayton is just so…"

"Repugnant?" Naomi asks.

"Foul," Hudson breathes.

I shiver again. "Yeah, like she said. I can't fathom being interested in him."

"I feel like I should have been paying better attention," Quincy says.

My laugh is sharp, echoing off the balconies above. I look around, feeling Clayton's eyes. Is he up there right now? Lurking somewhere in the darkness? Thinking of him up there makes me second-guess myself. How long do I want to wait here knowing he could be watching? How long until someone comes?

Goose bumps prickle up my arms, and I rub them with both hands.

"I hate this," Naomi says. "I don't know how much longer I can just sit here."

"I keep thinking of that saying about offense being the best defense," Quincy says.

"We can't sit here all damn night," Hudson says.

"Well, we can't go after Clayton," I say. "He's killed two people, and he didn't need a gun to do it. From here we can see him coming."

"I don't want to hunt the guy down," Naomi says, "but I want to get the hell out of here."

"I hear your point, Jo," Quincy says. "Isn't there a way to do both? Can we get out of here without necessarily putting ourselves in a corner?"

"If we stay together, we can still keep watch and we can handle him if he manages to sneak up on us somehow," Hudson says. "He's a fitness freak, not a pro fighter."

Quincy sighs. "But the goal isn't to handle him, it's to escape, right?"

"Yes!" Naomi says. "Let's just go."

I squirm in my seat because I'm not convinced. Every door we've seen is behind wood or down a corridor, and while I want to get out, I don't want to give him the chance to sneak up on us.

But is that all it is? Or am I back to that same girl I was all those years ago, my hands over my sister's eyes and my body still as stone?

"I'm ready when you are," Hudson says. "Beats the hell out of sitting here like fish in a barrel."

"But as soon as we move, we give him the chance to sneak up on us," I say. "We should all vote. What do you think, Summer?"

She doesn't answer. I don't hear her back there squirming or thinking on it either.

"Summer?" I ask.

"Um…" Quincy's voice is low and concerned, and I spin around in my chair. Summer is not on her bench. And she is not on the stairs. My eyes sweep the area to the left and to the right. I spot padded benches, the edge of Hannah's feet when I crane my neck far enough. I look farther to see a covered kiosk, the empty planters by the stairs.

"Summer?" My voice is loud and sharp, but it doesn't matter. There's no one there to answer.

Summer is gone.

CHAPTER 17

WE BOLT OUT OF OUR SEATS LIKE THEY'VE BEEN LIT ON fire. We search around the general area, looking in ridiculous places. Behind a kiosk. Under chairs. As if she's going to pop out with a laugh and confess she thought a little hide-and-seek would be fun.

"What the hell?" Naomi says. "She was just here."

"Is she hiding?" Quincy asks, his voice high and nervous. "Or maybe hurt? Do you think she could be hurt?"

"I—I don't know." I scan the second-floor balcony, looking for movement. Clues. There's nothing. I turn back to the mall, which is a yawning, shadowy cavern. Could she be out there somewhere? Could she really have slipped past us? My eyes drag to the stairs by Hannah's body. She could have gone up the stairs without us noticing. In truth, the plastic-draped storefronts and skeletal remnants of this mall could be hiding anything or anyone.

"She can't have just disappeared," Naomi says.

"Funny, 'cause it sure looks like that's exactly what happened," Hudson says. He looks unsurprised.

I open my mouth, but there's nothing to say, so no words come. Hudson meets my eyes, and there's no missing the told-you-so look he gives me.

"We'll find her," I say. "She can't have gone far."

"Summer!" Naomi shouts.

I grab her arm. "Don't. Don't yell."

"Why not? You just yelled."

"Yes, but calling someone's name once or twice could be anything," Quincy says. He's pacing now, scanning the shadows around us. "We don't want to announce that she's missing."

Hudson exhales heavily. "He's probably watching us and has already heard every word we've said."

"He could have seen her leave," Naomi whispers. "She could be in real danger."

"Naomi's right," Quincy says. "We have to find her."

But Hudson narrows his eyes and makes no move to look around. "You know, anyone with a speck of common sense would be scared shitless to go off on their own. Unless..."

"Unless what?" Naomi asks.

Sound overhead cuts us off. A door? I'm not sure. I crane my neck, but it's so dark up there. I can see the second floor some, but the third? Anything could be up there—anything or anyone.

"Did you hear that?" Quincy whispers.

I nod, but all is quiet now. Still, none of us speaks. Something in the air has changed.

My skin prickles with that wordless feeling that danger is near. I search for a flicker of movement, but there is nothing. Everything is still. Quiet. There is—

Something moves.

My pulse skitters like tires on black ice, and then the rhythm catches. I lock my gaze on the space where I think I saw something. "Did anyone see that?"

"See what?" Hudson asks, but even he keeps his voice low. So he senses it too.

I strain my eyes and ears. My heart thuds so hard, I feel it in the tips of my fingers. We turn in circles, staring up into the darkness, waiting for something to happen.

"I think we should go," Naomi says. "I have a bad feeling."

"What do we do about Summer?" Quincy asks. "We can't leave her."

I think of Cara's little-girl arms around my neck, all those years ago. I think of her eyes so round and frightened when I pushed her deep into that space beneath the counter. When I held my finger to my lips and tried to keep her safe.

Some part of me feels like I should have kept Summer safe too, and maybe I would have, but Summer didn't stay still or hidden like Cara. Summer didn't listen; she ran.

"We'll have to come back for her," I say. "We can try the food court. There might be a way out."

"It's behind the stage, right?" Quincy asks.

I nod, and we fall into a line and start moving through the atrium. The stage is maybe fifty yards away diagonally. We cut through the mall with our eye on the hazy plastic curtains barely visible behind the stage. That's where the food court should be. Even with everything boarded over or draped like a haunted house, I can still make sense of this part of the building. The stage is in the center of the mall, a giant half circle between the long-gone Macy's on the right and the food court on the left. The audience would sit on one of four rows of sunken carpeted stairs, all angled to allow a good view of whatever singer or marching band was putting on the show. Sometimes, I'd listen too—usually lurking with my Auntie Anne's pretzel at one of the tables set far back from the stage seating.

We hesitate at the kiosk for Christmas ornaments and face creams, pressing ourselves to two of the sides. I pause, listening for Clayton. For Summer. For a miracle rescue I don't have much faith in. We have to cross one of the bridges to get to other side of the mall, but before I can debate which one to suggest, Hudson leads the charge, marching right for the fancy arched bridge that empties directly at an entrance to the stage seating.

The others quickly follow, so I bring up the rear. Halfway to the bridge, I hear a tapping and a creak, up on one of the balconies.

I can't place it, but after a few seconds of silence, it starts again. A creaking, clattering noise. Like bottles rattling on a tray.

It's just a sound. There is nothing inherently dangerous in what I hear, but it sets the hairs on my neck on end. I stop.

"Wait," I say.

Because there was nothing sinister about the jangling bells over the convenience store door either.

There was nothing evil in the heavy footsteps that approached the counter.

There was nothing deadly in the hissing sound of my sister's dress when I pushed her under the counter and climbed in after her.

Quincy stops mid-step and cocks his head. "Do you guys see—"

A long, high-pitched scratching interrupts him. It's like a fork scraping a porcelain plate but louder. Longer. Something's happening. Something is coming. My lungs shrink and my muscles tense.

"It's up there," Hudson whispers, and that horrible nails-on-a-chalkboard shriek continues.

I nod and swallow even though my throat feels parchment dry. It's definitely above us, but it's not the second floor. It's higher. The third floor. The noise goes and goes until my teeth ache and my ears ring. Naomi covers her ears with her hands. Quincy grunts miserably. And the sound scrapes and scrapes.

And then it stops.

The silence is so sudden and shocking that I hold my breath, my whole body tensed and waiting. But nothing happens. The quiet continues, and we stay frozen in place, the bridge no more than ten feet away. My knees wobble, and a cold sweat has broken out on my back and under my arms.

"Let's go," I whisper urgently. "Move. Move fast."

"Look out!" Quincy shouts, and then he's backing up, his neck craned. He's watching something, and then I see it too. Something is falling from the balcony. My eyes rush to track it, but it's falling too fast. It hits with a splintering crash, and we cringe together, our bodies curling toward one another. Safety in numbers.

"What the hell was that?" Naomi asks.

I cannot answer. I am staring at the thing that hit—a wad of broken glass and gold pieces and parts. Whatever it was, it landed ten feet away from us. We're lucky it didn't hit us.

Crash.

This time we don't see it coming. It hits the roof of the kiosk we just left, and we shriek and jump back, but it's not done. There's more. Something else hits the steps leading up to the stage. The carpeted stair seats. The floor just behind us.

Whatever plan we had now vanishes. We run like hell, sprinting to the bridge and toward the wall on the closer side of the stage. Things are crashing left and right, raining down from somewhere above.

We don't stop. Something else explodes just behind us. There is glass and noise, and we hurl ourselves over the bridge, heading to the right side of the stage because cover is the only thing that matters now. We are mice running from a raptor. We knock into piles of construction debris and stumble down and then back up some of the sunken stage seats. We run until we're under the cover of the second-floor balcony, until we're pressed against the rough black wall, my cheek brushing the prickly plastic leaves of a fake plant.

Three stacks of rusting chairs to our left provide meager shelter, but I still see glass raining from above. Something crashes on the swirling carpet inches from Quincy before he ducks behind the stacks of chairs with us. It's barely ten feet of shelter. Hardly enough for the four of us, yet what choice do we have but to ride it out?

Crash. Into metal bars that form the shell behind the stage.

Crash. Into a table.

Things continue to hit. With horror, I watch one of the objects fall. It explodes, leaving nothing more than glittering shards, one that juts up from a circular glass base. I realize what it is. It's a drinking glass. Looking around, it looks like most of these things are drinking glasses. Where the hell would Clayton find something like that? Because this has to be him. Another glass lands next to my foot, and I yelp and lift my hands to shield my face.

Glass rains down over and over and over. And then it ends.

Time passes while we breathe and tremble against the gritty surface of the wall. Slowly, I uncover my ears, not remembering when I covered them in the first place. There is quiet for the span of a breath. And then another. And then I hear the muted rhythm of footsteps far above. Someone is moving fast.

Where the hell are they going? Who is it? Clayton? Summer? My head hurts from trying to pick apart all these noises. We are not creatures made for the darkness, and my senses ache for a reprieve.

Naomi whimpers and moves like she's going to run, but I hold her arm. Not yet. We have to listen. We have to be smart, or he'll kill us. He'll kill us all.

A door opens and closes, and there are distant bumps and bangs. I don't know where they're coming from. It could be a stairwell. Furniture in one of the offices on the third floor. The only thing I know for sure is that it proves this wasn't some bizarre failure of an overhead lighting fixture or a nameless poltergeist whirling glass from the balconies.

These glasses were thrown. We were targeted.

We cling together, braced for what happens next. But nothing comes. The atrium is eerily quiet, except for an occasional tinkle of glass or creak in the giant skylights overhead. I look up to see the moon, full and bright in the lower edge of the middle skylight.

"What is all this?" Naomi asks. "What was he throwing?"

"Glasses," Hudson says.

"Why would there be glasses upstairs?" Quincy asks.

"For the banquet rooms," Hudson says. "They had two or three event spaces and enough coffee cups and glasses to hydrate an army."

I look across the floor and spot the round edge of a glass bottom. The carpet glitters with shards like it's been raining diamonds. All is still quiet above us. I feel the muffled thump of my own heart. A high-pitched whine behind my ears. Everyone is ashen and shaky, but we're okay. We're alive.

Except that's not really true, is it?

Five of us are alive. And currently, one of those five is missing. I stare into the darkness. "I don't know what we should do about Summer."

"Jack shit, that's what," Hudson says. When I shoot him a look, he shrugs. "What the hell do you want to do? She took off."

"She's probably terrified," Quincy says.

"He's right," Naomi says. "It's not like she's a *worldly* sixteen-year-old, right?"

No one argues with Naomi, and no one spells out the facts any further. We all know Summer's...sort of different. Naomi thinks it's because she's never around other people her age. I think it's more than her parents' isolation-based homeschooling methods, but now doesn't seem like the time to pick her apart.

"What if she didn't run away from us?" Quincy takes a deep breath. "What if Clayton took her?"

The idea slithers through me, cold and sickening. Clayton creeping down the stairs. Clayton plucking her out of her chair, his thick arm around her waist. His hand over her mouth.

"Without her making a single sound or screaming?" Hudson scoffs as if that's all the answer he needs.

Naomi chews her lip. "Yeah, I feel like we would have heard something."

Hudson throws up his hands. "Except she obviously didn't want us to hear."

"Do you have a problem with Summer?" Quincy's voice is hard and flat. "You seem perfectly comfortable with her being alone."

Naomi clucks softly. "Yeah, you're throwing nothing but shade at that girl. Why?"

Hudson shrugs. "She was the physically closest person to the two people who died tonight."

"Wouldn't that be all the more reason to be worried about her?" Quincy asks.

"Yes," I say. "Especially since she's the one who pissed off Clayton earlier. Remember the whole soda machine debacle?"

"True," Naomi says, looking distraught.

"It's just weird," Hudson says. "I'm not saying she's an accomplice or whatever, but it's weird for her to run off."

Is it, though? When we're terrified, there's nothing left but instinct. Some fight. Some run. Cara would have run. If I hadn't stopped her and tucked her under that counter, back by the cleaning rags and the extra boxes of receipt tape—what would have happened to her?

"She's a kid," I say, and I mean Summer, but I'm picturing my sister's face. "She's alone out there somewhere in the dark. Shouldn't we do something?"

Hudson cocks his head. "Like what? You can't fix everything for everyone."

"What's that supposed to mean?" I ask, tensing.

Hudson watches me in a way that makes me wish I hadn't asked. Not because he's right—he's not. Not quite. But it shows me he's been paying attention to me.

"It means you're going to be a kick-ass doctor," Naomi says, sounding defensive.

Hudson smirks. "Guess you are going to fix things."

"That's really cool," Quincy says.

"Yeah, she's a rock star," Naomi says.

My tongue feels thick and dry, and my cheeks burn. I don't want to talk about me or my plans. Me wanting to be a doctor isn't cool. I'm not a good person or a Florence Nightingale type. What if they knew the truth? That I don't feel like I have a choice. A doctor might have saved my dad. Maybe could have saved Lexi. When I'm a doctor, I'll know how to stop my worst nightmares from happening.

That's the truth. That's why I want to do this. I have to know everything I can about saving a life. Because I can't stand being the helpless, frozen little girl who let my dad die.

"Jo?" Naomi's voice is a worried squeak. It's the way you'd say someone's name if you saw an oncoming train, or if you realized your plane was about to crash.

Naomi raises a finger to point at me. But then it's not at me; it's at something above and behind me. I turn around, my eyes catching movement on the second floor, back behind the railing. Someone is there, just above us, but they are too far from the railing to see them clearly. The shadow steps forward, and I see the drape of a long skirt, the silhouette of stringy hair and slender elbows.

She stands at the railing, looking down at us, and I don't know if it's the mild expression she's wearing or the shock of seeing her up there, but chills roll up my spine.

"Summer."

Local News

CITY IS CONSIDERING LEGAL ACTION
AGAINST PDG DEVELOPMENT

According to City Attorney Debra Mitchell, the City of Sandusky is considering legal action against PDG Developers, the managing firm responsible for the unsafe conditions at the site of former shopping mall Riverview Fashionplace. Four residents were found dead at the former mall, and widespread reports cite conditions inside the building and inaccessible exits as a factor in the victims' deaths. Ms. Mitchell did not provide specific comment but advised that this topic will be discussed in executive session at the city council meeting on May 26. Council meetings are open to the public but executive sessions, which are allowable under Ohio's Sunshine Laws under certain circumstances, are closed meetings.

CHAPTER 18

"WHAT ARE YOU DOING UP THERE?" NAOMI SOUNDS AS astonished as I feel.

"Are you all right?" Quincy asks. "Are you hurt?"

Summer doesn't answer right away but waves her hands like she wants us to stop talking. She looks around, clearly nervous.

"Why did you leave?" Hudson asks. There is no question about how Hudson is feeling. He doesn't trust her. And the way Summer's face pales tells me she knows it.

Summer's gaze suddenly shifts across the atrium, to the third-floor balcony. Does she see something? I turn but spot nothing and can't help but wonder if Hudson is right. Is she playing with us? Is she in on this?

But then I hear a faint clamor across the atrium—up high where she's looking. We crouch, but there's no movement in the shadows. No more sound to track either. I slowly stand in time to spot Summer watching that space where I heard the sound. She moves backward, not walking or turning, just melting into the darkness like a phantom.

"I think you scared her," Quincy says when she doesn't return.

"I don't think *we* scared her," I whisper because I know who scared her. That noise we heard is Clayton. And she heard it too.

Summer reappears, her face pale and distorted by the strange moonlight above. She lifts her hands to the railing and peers down at us. No one speaks. I'm not sure any of us knows where to start.

"He's on the third floor," she whispers.

I take a step closer, trying to make out her expression. It's hard to see much beyond her strange and ghostly coloring.

"Are you okay?" I ask softly. I ignore the scoff I hear behind me. I know it's Hudson. His opinion is clear, and mine isn't made up.

My dad always told me you catch more flies with honey, and other than that one night when the honey got him killed, he was right.

She nods and her head adjusts. I think she's trying to meet my eyes, but it's hard to be sure from this distance and in this light. Overhead, the moon is shifting, now only visible on the bank of skylights on the right.

"You shouldn't be up there alone," I say, still softly.

"She chose to be up there," Hudson says.

"Be quiet," Naomi tells him.

"Why did you run away?" Quincy asks. "We were worried about you."

Before she can answer, I hear another noise higher up. The third floor again. My shoulders tense as I strain to make sense of the noise. It's a door opening and then closing.

"Clayton just stepped into one of the stairwells," Naomi says.

"Are you sure?" I ask.

Naomi nods. "Positive. I saw him for a second."

Summer's shoulders and arms have gone tight, her grip lethal on the railing. Her feet shift like she is poised to run. Is that what happens next?

"Summer, wait," I whisper.

She looks down at me, her tangled hair swinging free. Her face is positively skeletal in the darkness, her eyes black smudges.

"Go to the arcade," she whispers.

"What?"

"The fire alarms in the arcade—I see lights on them from up here. They're working, but I can't get inside."

A short bang on the opposite side of the atrium makes us jump. It's Clayton; we all know that. But this time, he's not two floors above.

"That was the bottom floor, wasn't it?" I whisper.

Hudson pushes his way in front of me, and I almost shove him back, but then I hear the way he's breathing—fast and shallow. He's just as frightened as the rest of us, and maybe being in front is the way he handles it.

"That was down here?" Naomi asks, her voice trembling.

Quincy swallows hard and adjusts his glasses. "I think so."

"So Clayton is down here, and we have no idea why," I whisper.

Hudson's hands curl into fists. "Maybe not, but he's definitely up to something."

My worst fear is unfolding in real time. We stopped watching, and now Clayton could be anywhere doing anything.

When I turn back to the balcony, there's nothing but shadows behind the railings. Summer is gone.

"Damn it," I say.

"Where the hell did she go?" Naomi asks.

"Summer?" Quincy calls. His voice is shrill with worry. "Summer?"

"Quiet down," Hudson says. "We don't need his attention."

"She's frightened, Hudson," Quincy argues.

Hudson says, "We're all scared."

Goose bumps rise on my arms, and I spin in a slow circle, searching the darkness for a flash of movement, the barest hint of a sound. My body is coiled tight and ready to react, but nothing happens. Long minutes pass, but there is no more Summer and no more noise. Until this moment, I never believed fear could be boring, but there's something about this that's horribly monotonous.

My mind flashes to an old memory of my dad, bearded and humming at the gas station counter. Mom was on an international flight, and I was laboring my way through a math sheet while Cara played with a stuffed rabbit. For a long time, those were my favorite Sunday afternoons, just the three of us stocking bags of chips and playing all our favorite music while customers poured in and out for lottery tickets and cigarettes.

That day, Dad was filling up these cheap backpacks, the kind with a simple rope cinch that doubled as straps.

"Who are those for?" I ask.

"People having a hard time."

"Like people doing three-digit subtraction?" I shake my homework sheet at him, and he laughs, scooping me up and popping me on the counter.

"Difficult as it is to believe, kiddo, some people are facing harder things than that."

"Bunny works hard," Cara says from the floor where she's constructed a maze of empty boxes for her stuffed bunny, Mr. Fibbs.

"Daddy means real hard things," I say. "Like Mr. Galtry who comes in for coffee."

Dad nods slowly. "Like Mr. Galtry. Do you want to see?"

He puts a sack on my lap, and I search through the contents while my legs swing. It doesn't seem too exciting to my nine-year-old self. A travel toothbrush and a pack of baby wipes. Granola bars and cheese and crackers. But then I pull out a word-find magazine and a pen.

"How will they know all the answers?"

"You don't have to have all the answers," he said. "Figuring it out is the fun."

"But how do you figure it out?"

"You just keep trying. Over and over until something works."

"Jo?" Naomi's voice brings me back to the present.

I look around at the darkness. "I haven't heard anything in a while."

"Not in eleven minutes," Quincy offers instead. "I checked my watch."

"'Course you did," Hudson says, eyes still closed.

"Don't be snarky," I say.

"I'm not," Hudson says. "I'm just sick of being here. I don't feel…" He rubs his temples.

"I get it," I say. "This sucks."

Quincy steps away from the wall tentatively. "Well, at least we aren't currently dodging glass objects being thrown from the third floor."

"We need to be careful about that," I say, looking up at the dark balconies. "We're lucky no one got hit."

Naomi nods. "It doesn't mean our luck will hold."

"Especially not if he's smart enough to get closer before he throws," Hudson points out.

"If he's closer, he could do some real damage," I say.

"So, when we move, we need to do it quickly," Quincy says.

There's a pause while we all consider our earlier experience. I really believed we were safe in the open. If we'd stayed there, he could have found us and thrown something. I think back to the noises I heard before the glasses rained down. He must have been dragging something closer to the railing. We did get lucky, and we can't count on that luck to hold.

"Moving targets are harder to hit," Quincy says. "Statistically speaking."

"So we move," Hudson says. "Any ideas on direction?"

"Summer said something about alarms in the arcade," Naomi says.

"Got zero shits to give about what she said," Hudson says.

"But she's trying to help. The arcade might have power backups or something, right?" Quincy asks. "It's possible their alarms might be working."

The Arcade is a three-story monstrosity at the north end of the mall. Once upon a time, it was a department store that tanked, but as long as I can remember, it's been a massive video game complex with glow-in-the-dark miniature golf, laser tag, and tenpin bowling. The Arcade was hands down the coolest part of the mall, but even it couldn't stay open when the stores all closed.

"I say we follow our own plan," Hudson says. "We can look for alarms in the food court. Which is closer to us anyway."

Hudson is right. We're in the center of the mall, maybe twenty yards from the food court. The arcade is at the far end of the mall, opposite the theater.

"Which one is the food court?" Quincy asks.

"Right there." Hudson points at the side of the stage, and he's right—the food court is close, but to get there, we have to go back out in the open. I liked being in the open when I knew Clayton was far away, back before he started throwing things. But now

152 | NATALIE D. RICHARDS

he's back on this floor. He could be close enough to grab us, and I would have no idea.

"So you want us to just run for it?" I ask.

"Pretty much," Hudson says, and he's rubbing his temples again.

I hate the idea. We have to cross a section in front of the stage, so we'll have to step down into the seating area in front of the stage, a place where our visibility will be complete shit and he could probably sneak up on us easy as pie. Then again, our visibility is shit now, and if there are working alarms in the food court, then it's worth the risk.

"What if he moved closer like you said?" Naomi asks. "What if he starts throwing glass again?"

"Our best bet is to keep moving fast," Quincy says, pushing his glasses up. "It's hard to hit a moving target, remember?"

"And what if he attacks us?" Naomi asks.

"Then it's just like Hudson says," Quincy says. "There are four of us. He's not Superman."

"Okay, then we'll move fast," Naomi says. "Straight down the stage seating and back up the other side, right?"

"I think that's right. Hudson?" I ask.

Everyone turns, but Hudson doesn't answer. He's turned away from us, his shoulder pressed to the gritty outcropping. He looks very still other than the strange off-beat tap-tap-tap of two fingers against his thigh.

"Hudson?"

He doesn't answer, just stares off into nothingness, his lips moving over and over like he's rehearsing lines before stepping onstage. Or like he's completely paralyzed with fear. Has the shock finally gotten to him?

"Hudson!" I take his shoulders, and for one second, I feel like the world is sliding sideways because he is so stiff, his whole body tense under my hands. Even when I position myself directly in front of his face, it's like he's staring right through me.

And then his arms soften, and he lets out a shaky breath. His eyes shift, and I know he's seeing me. Intense relief washes through me, and my hands shake where I'm holding his arms.

"Are you okay?" I ask. "Did something happen?"

His hands are trembling, and his forehead has gone shiny with sweat. He shakes his head and looks around like he's confused. Then he laughs. "Fine. Sorry. Totally spaced out there."

Worry curls in my middle. That wasn't spacing out. That was something very different, but what? Dehydration? Exhaustion? Fever? He doesn't feel warm through his sleeves, and the idea of touching his neck or face makes me nervous.

"Should we stay here?" I ask. "Maybe you need to rest."

Hudson steps away from the wall, pushing past me. "No. I've got to get out of here. *We've* got to get the hell out of here. Right now."

CHAPTER 19

WE PAUSE AT THE EDGE OF OUR LITTLE CHAIR-STACKS shelter. Beyond it I can see four tiers of stair seating encircling the stage. Unless we want to climb and go around the outside of the sunken seating area, we'll have to descend on this side, cross the ground in front of the stage, and then ascend the other side, closer to the food court.

"See any other option but to go for it here?" Hudson asks.

"Not a single one," I admit, and so we go.

We cross quickly and uneventfully. Our feet patter against the carpet, and my knees crack when we make our way down each step, but then we are crossing the floor, the stage looming dark and tall to our right. My whole body is pulled tight, braced for Clayton to dart down the stairstep seats or leap from the stage. But we cross without incident and climb back up, just a few feet from the plastic sheets across the food court entrance.

Naomi reaches the plastic first and slips inside. The entrance isn't open as I expected. Instead, the rolling metal cage is down over the wide threshold. I run my fingers along the cold metal with a sigh. "Now what?"

"There's a door," Quincy says, moving past me. There are two sets of glass doors, actually—one on either side of the caged main entrance. Naomi pulls on the doors and shakes her head.

"Yeah, they're locked," she says.

"How do we get in there?" I whisper, feeling frustrated.

"It's not locked. The locks are drilled out." Hudson points at a large hole I hadn't noticed below the right-hand door. I push again, but the door doesn't budge.

"Look at the top," Quincy says.

Hudson reaches up, feeling around the top edge of the frame. He stops moving, and his eyes light up. Then he wiggles something, and the sound of scraping metal grates at my ears. "There's a pin at the top," he says.

Hudson grunts and manages to yank the pin out. The door swings open a little, and Hudson holds up a large metal bolt.

"They just had it propped closed. I bet a bunch of the doors are like this."

We push the door open and slip inside. The darkness is all but suffocating. Whatever meager light we had in the atrium isn't making its way in here.

Panic flares through my middle. I have no idea what I did with my flashlight, but then a beam illuminates the room. It's Quincy holding a flashlight. He tucks it quickly under the hem of his shirt to mute the brightness and then hands me a second flashlight.

"Is this mine?" I ask.

Quincy nods. "You put it down earlier, but I thought we might need it."

"Smart thinking, Diaz," Hudson says.

"You can take mine," Quincy tells him. Hudson accepts it without question.

"There's paper over most of the windows and plastic behind the main entrance," Naomi says. "I think the light will be okay."

She might be right, but Hudson and I both keep our flashlights low and covered all the same. We gather in a loose circle looking wary and exhausted inside the entrance where a hostess station lived once upon a time.

Heaps of restaurant detritus are stacked as far as the eye can see: tabletops against a wall, stacks of chairs, random piles of gleaming stainless steel counters or industrial pans. It's hard to sort it all out. It's even harder to see where the restaurants themselves are, though I can see bits of counter here and there and a stack of large hanging menus leaning in one corner.

"They were in the middle of renovating this whole food court when the mall went belly-up," Hudson says. "They thought new food options might help, but no dice."

"Is your family working on the project?" Naomi says.

He shrugs. "*Working* is a stretch. My dad does the financing. But he talks about the construction side all the time. He obviously ended up in the wrong career."

"Why didn't he pursue construction?" Quincy asks, frowning.

Hudson smirks. "Because good Indian sons go to college so they can support their family. Or that's what his mother always told him."

My foot kicks into something hard, a precarious stack of metal supports. This entire food court is in shambles. It's like a bomb has gone off.

"We need to be careful," I say.

I point at the general disaster area we're entering. There are tabletops and broken pieces of chairs heaped on every side. Rows of stools stacked three to four high sit next to a pile of busted drywall and a heap of miscellaneous wires and light fixtures. I also can't make out any exits from here, but there must be some. Maybe through one of the kitchens?

There are several sheets of drywall and plywood leaned against the different restaurant counters, and scarier still, I see a few slabs stacked on the top of some of the higher piles, remnants from windows or tables, I guess. We can probably move all that, but it's not going to be easy. And getting back there quietly without killing ourselves is going to be a challenge.

I clear my throat and nod toward the mess at the back of the food court. I turn on my flashlight to better illuminate the area. "The stockrooms, bathrooms, and offices are probably all down that hallway. Which is completely blocked off with plywood."

Hudson exhales hard. "Getting more convinced by the minute that a chainsaw would solve all our problems."

"Let's try to check behind the counters," I say. "There might be other exits."

Hudson and Naomi start off to the right, and Quincy tries to pick his way to the left, where there are fewer obstacles to deal with. I follow him.

"I think I see a light," he says.

I swing my flashlight toward Quincy and see him walking toward a huge stack of plywood, one with two or three pieces of glass stacked on top.

"Quincy, be careful," I say. As if on cue, Quincy trips. He catches himself but wobbles left to find his balance. His hip bumps the pile, and my breath catches as it shifts. There is a hissing scrape, something heavy sliding across the top of the pile. Quincy puts his arm out to steady it—and then the whole thing collapses.

My hands fly up to protect my head as a shower of wood and metal and glass rains down. It feels like an endless cacophony of splintering crashes, but it is over in the span of a breath.

The silence is as sudden as the noise, and wherever Quincy was before, he's gone now. I pull a breath into my tight lungs.

"Quincy!" Hudson and I call his name together, but I am closer. I am right here, staring at the rising plume of dust where he was standing.

"Where is he?" Hudson shouts. "Do you see him?"

"I—"

The wreckage shifts on the ground, and Quincy lets out a raspy cry. It is unlike any noise I have ever heard him make. And it tells me something is terribly, terribly wrong.

The secret I knew is about the two of them. I had seen them a few weeks earlier in the locker room. They moved apart quickly, trying to hide what they were doing, but I knew. When you're quiet, you see lots of things people try to keep hidden.

CHAPTER 20

"OH SHIT." QUINCY'S VOICE IS WRONG. TOO HIGH AND TOO breathy. "Shit, shit, shit, shit."

My heart leaps into my throat. It isn't just his voice that's wrong. Quincy never swears. Not ever. Not when he saw Lexi. Not when he saw Hannah. He is quiet and calm and composed. And now he's groaning and swearing, and he's not getting up from the floor. I can't quite see him through the scatter of miscellaneous construction debris, but I know he's hurt.

"What happened?" I ask, spotting his silhouette through shifting pieces of wood and trash.

"Don't, there's glass," he says, and then he makes a terrible, animalistic sound of pain.

My stomach twists itself over and over. I want to cover my face and curl into a ball. I want to disappear right out of this room, this mall, this entire moment in time. But I can't. I can't keep freezing when terrible things happen. If I'm going to save people, I have to learn how to *move*.

"What did you hurt?" I force the words out, and they are wooden and strained.

He doesn't answer, but he shifts, and I realize he is curled over on his side. He's moving, but he isn't trying to get up. He's writhing in pain.

My throat tightens, and I use my foot to carefully push some of the boards and glass out of my path. I see a dark drop in the beam of the flashlight. Blood. Oh God, he's bleeding.

"Where is he?" Naomi asks. "Is it bad?"

"You're all right," I say automatically, ignoring Naomi to focus on Quincy. In truth I have no idea if he's all right. My gaze follows the first drop of blood to the next. Memories flash through my mind. Plastic lighters next to smears of blood. My father's gurgling breath. The smell of copper and salt. My hands—still sticky from the Lemonheads we ate—pressed over my sister's eyes.

That's how my dad died. He bled out on a dirty floor while I covered Cara's eyes and turned to stone.

Move. You have to move!

My heart pounds so fast and hard I feel sick with it. But I force my feet forward inch by terrifying inch.

"I'm almost there," I say, my knees knocking harder as I carefully move things out of my way. "Almost."

"What happened?" Naomi asks.

"A pile of shit fell on him," Hudson says. "Is he trapped?"

"I don't think so," I say. But he's injured. How badly, I can't tell, so I keep it to myself.

Hudson's moving this way. I can see him through the murky light. "Is he all right?"

Quincy groans, and I'm closer now. Almost close enough to reach him. I crouch low and try to assess him through the scatter of wood and glass and random old restaurant menus.

There are stools and chairs and tabletops. At first I can see nothing but restaurant detritus. Behind the black pole of a table base, I see a terribly jagged hunk of window glass.

And more blood. So much more blood.

Hudson's flashlight beam darts around like a disco ball. He makes no effort to cover it. "Where is he? Where are you?"

"I'm fine," Quincy says with another groan. He is absolutely not fine. In first aid class, one of the first things I learned is that you can bleed a lot more than you'd suspect before you're in trouble. And I still think this is too much blood.

"We're fine," I say, willing myself to believe it. "Everything is fine."

I don't think I've convinced anyone, but there's no more time to worry about it. I push a stack of small round tabletops out of the way. Broken glass litters the floor like glitter, and streaks and blobs of crimson stain everything in sight.

"I need a broom," I say. "Something I can move this glass with."

Quincy is now sitting awkwardly in that glittery mess, one knee up and one leg bent to the side. I can't tell where he's bleeding because his shirt is dark.

I smell salt and old pennies. I see my father again—mouth open and eyes losing focus. I shake my head because I am not nine years old, and this is not my father, and there are things I have to do. I have books and certificates and more than thirty hours of first aid training, and it is time to use them.

I try to look for Quincy's wound again and realize his shirt isn't dark like I thought. It's pale blue, but the entire right sleeve and part of the right torso are soaked dark with blood. Did he fall? Did something fall on him? I try to remember the moment just before the pile collapsed.

He tried to steady it with his hand. His arm stretched tight to hold it in place.

I crouch, and Quincy rolls his head to look at me. "Jo?"

I have never wanted to disappear more in my life. Adrenaline pushes through my veins, contracting every muscle. I wrench my mouth open, but no sound comes out. I can't do this. I absolutely *cannot*.

"Jo!" I whirl at the sound of Hudson's voice. He is shoving something between two of the piles beside us. A piece of cardboard? "Try this for sweeping the glass."

Sweeping the glass. I can do that. I take the cardboard, and the simple task shifts me into gear. I can sweep a path to him, so I do. I can lay down the cardboard to sit beside him. So I do. And I can look to see where he's hurt.

"I'm going to take a look and help, okay?" I say, my voice shaking.

There is something on his bloody sleeve—something he's holding. I scooch close, ignoring the blood on the tile, the sour, salty smell that hangs heavy in the air.

Quincy looks at me with glazed eyes. There's a smear of blood on his glasses. On his cheek. His fingers move near his bicep, feathering over whatever is on his sleeve. I move my flashlight to see better, taking care not to scare him with the light, but his pupils are blown wide. He's going into shock. The symptoms come back to me—bullet points on a dry-erase board. And notes I'd furiously scribbled in my notebook.

The vibrant red of his sleeve is ghastly under the direct light, but it's the triangular glimmer of glass jutting out of his sleeve that turns my body to ice. Quincy has a large hunk of glass wedged in his bicep. The giant shard that fell didn't just cut him—it impaled him.

He is bleeding profusely, and if he takes that glass out, he may very well bleed to death.

Quincy grabs the glass as if he can feel me staring at it. My throat squeezes like it's caught in a fist. "Quincy, whatever you do, don't—"

Quincy yanks the glass with a terrible cry. The jagged piece drops with a clatter, and blood gushes from his arm. I lunge for him, pressing my palm directly to the wound even as he cries out and writhes underneath me. I do my best to hold him fast.

"Oh shit," Naomi says, and I hear her quickly backing away.

Quincy is squirming. Twisting. "I know it hurts," I tell him. "I know, but you have to be still."

"I can help," Hudson says. His feet shuffle behind us. "Do you need me to hold him?"

"Quincy!" My tone does nothing. He is absolutely not listening to me. His breath has turned fast and shallow, like a panting dog. And his hands are shaking.

"Quincy," I repeat, shifting to my knees for better leverage and finally getting a good angle on the wound. Quincy is backed against a stack of heavy wallboard. He has nowhere else to go, so he goes still and then limp.

I press hard, having no choice but to use my bare hand for now.

"Tell me what to do, Jo," Hudson says.

I keep the pressure on the wound. "I need you to wedge my flashlight into that chair so I can see. And then I need you to find a first aid kit. There has to be one in one of the kitchens."

I hope.

Hudson is already moving. He props the light and rushes to search the kitchens. I hear rustling, banging, and swearing.

Quincy makes a mild sound of protest. "I'm fine."

Things definitely don't look fine, and worse still, I don't know if I can make this fine. Is it even slowing? I can't tell. There's no way to quantify the blood drenching everything in sight, but it's so much. Too much. I have to slow it down.

"Just be really still, okay?" I say again, forcing a smile I'm sure is weak as hell. My hands are shaking, and I feel queasy and terrified. But I do not ease the pressure on his arm—not even for a second. "Once Hudson stops messing around, we'll get you patched up."

But Hudson isn't messing around, and we both know it. He swears again in one of the kitchens. I hear him stomping back our way.

"Want the bad news or the worse news?" he asks.

"Just spit it out."

"The kitchens are empty—there are no emergency exits, just signs sending us to the hallway."

"The one that's boarded over," I guess.

"That's the one."

"The T-shirt kiosk," Naomi says. "It's the one diagonal from the weird one that sold creams, right?"

I'm confused, and my hands are sticky. I need supplies, not riddles.

"What the hell are you talking about?" Hudson asks.

"Even without a first aid kit, if we can find some clean T-shirts…"

"That will help," I say. "Clean cloth will definitely help."

I want to tell them to rush, but Hudson is already halfway through the food court, and before I can say a word, he is pushing through the plastic with Naomi.

"Alone at last," Quincy jokes.

We laugh, but then his face pales, and his eyes roll up. I start to say his name, but it is too late. Quincy is unconscious.

CHAPTER 21

"QUINCY?"

His head lolls to one side, and fear scales my spine with icy hands. My vision blurs, and all I can see is my father, the pool of blood beneath his outstretched arm. The strange shift in his eyes when his last breath was exhaled.

This can't be happening again.

Daddy? Daddy?

I shake the memories back and push my hands harder against Quincy's arm—hard enough to jostle him. Hard enough to hurt. He gasps, and his eyes fly open.

"Stay with me!" I say. It's a thing TV doctors say, but not everyone agrees it's medically necessary or in some cases even the best course of action. But I say it again anyway. "Try to stay awake, okay?"

"Yes," he says, nodding a little. "I can do that."

He hisses when I slightly adjust my hand on his wound.

"I'm sorry," I say with a wince. "I need to keep the pressure on this."

"Did I get all of the glass out?"

"I'm not sure. I honestly haven't looked." I don't add that it was the most dangerous thing he could have possibly done; it's too late to bother with that now. And unless my eyes are deceiving me, I think the bleeding has significantly slowed.

"Doesn't this bother you?" he asks, his eyes drifting vaguely over my body.

I look down and take in the carnage. Blood stains my jeans, and my hands and arms are a grisly mess. It should bother me, I think, but I'm shocked to find it doesn't. Maybe because this time I'm not watching it happen. I'm fixing it. Or, at the very least, I'm trying.

"Not really," I say. "Is that weird?"

"Oh, I didn't mean it like that," he says. "Are your parents doctors too?"

I shake my head. "No. Uh, my mom is an airline attendant. She travels a lot."

That's putting it lightly. My dad was the glue that held our family together. Without him, the three of us drift along, Cara and I together and my mom floating in and out on weekends and slow travel times. It's not a bad relationship, per se, but we mostly communicate through text messages and Post-it Notes on the fridge.

"And your dad?"

My heart sinks. "My dad owned a gas station. I lost him when I was nine."

Quincy's face contorts. "I'm sorry, Jo."

"It was a long time ago," I say. Because nine years is a long time. Even if some days it feels like seventy years won't be enough to make me stop missing him.

"My brother died when I was seven. Diabetes."

I'm afraid to meet his eyes now. It's easier to talk about my father's death with people who don't understand. There are polite ways to talk about it. You use words like *lost* or *passed* because *dead* and *died* make people squirm. They'll inevitably tell you they're sorry, and then you'll assure them that *it's been a long time* or *he didn't suffer* or whatever other bullshit line works. You can always find a line that will hit the brakes on the whole topic. People who haven't lost anyone are happy to pretend death doesn't exist at all.

But talking to someone who's grieved? It's harder to hide in that conversation.

"Was your father sick?" he asks.

I swallow hard, my throat dry. "It was... He was shot."

I do not explain that I was eating Lemonheads when it happened. I don't explain that when the bells jangled overhead, I didn't think anything of it. I don't tell him what it felt like when Dad pushed at me—when he whispered to get my sister. To hide.

Are we in big trouble?

I didn't understand until I heard the men. Until my dad opened the register drawer and told them it was all okay, that they could have it, that it would be—

He never even finished his sentence. They shot him three

times, took the money, and ran. And I sat motionless in that small space beneath the counter.

My hands covered Cara's eyes.

My knee pressed into the side of the safe.

My body and mind and soul turned to stone.

"It was hard," I say. I hated myself, is what I mean. I've wondered forever if there was some way I could have changed it. If I had known to put pressure on the wounds. If I had at least called 911. I could have tried, but I did nothing. I was paralyzed.

"It's hard when you're young," Quincy says. "I'm sorry it happened to you."

I smile weakly, noticing the sickly yellow color he's turning from losing so much blood.

I need clean cloth and bandages. We need a real doctor. What we don't need is a deep examination of the fact that tonight wasn't the first time I witnessed a murder. We don't need to ponder why I've seen two people die without doing a single thing to stop it.

"I'm very glad you're here," Quincy says, casting a lightning-quick glance at his arm. "You seem like you know how to handle this."

"A little. I've taken all the first aid classes I could find."

"I wholeheartedly agree with that decision."

I laugh again and decide it's time to check the wound. "Why don't we elevate this arm now that you seem a little steadier? Let's use these chairs. We can prop your arm up before I cut away the sleeve here when they get back."

Which had better be soon. We need supplies. This is like trying to treat a wound on a Civil War battlefield.

"I will try. I'm not sure how much I can help," he says, but I've already eyeballed it, and I know the seat of the chair should be a good height for how he's sitting.

I help him maneuver his arm onto the padded seat, and though he grits his teeth and breathes hard, he doesn't cry out. After he's situated for a minute or two—long enough for his heart rate to slow back down—I slowly lift my palm from his sleeve.

It's impossible to see what's happening. Everything is a sticky, bloody mess, but even with him covered in blood, I can see there is a three-inch jagged gash in his arm. It's deep too, but nothing is spurting, so thankfully he didn't hit a major artery that I can see.

Still, this is not a situation that can be left as is. He's going to need stitches. And in the meantime, I need to do something to keep the wound a little bit closed.

"Do I get to keep my arm?" he asks.

I chuckle. "Pretty sure your arm is safe, but you lost a fair bit of blood. It's not gushing or spurting though, so I don't think you hit an artery. Which is a miracle, really. Are you feeling dizzy or faint?"

"No."

"Can you still move your fingers and your thumb on that arm?"

He flexes them experimentally, and blood oozes from the wound.

"Okay, never mind that. I guess I still have some medical things to learn."

"You'll have plenty of school to teach you. Twelve years of it, I think."

I laugh and hear the patter of footsteps. My laugh cuts abruptly to silence, my eyes searching the darkness near the entrance. I wish I'd thought to turn the flashlight off, or told Hudson to signal if it was him. Then the plastic rustles, and Hudson's dark, shaggy head pokes back into the food court. He's holding a box.

"How is he?" Hudson asks.

"Alive," Quincy says.

"Tell me you found something helpful?" I ask.

Hudson moves carefully closer, and I look up, accepting a first aid kit, a couple of bottles of water, and a stack of T-shirts.

"That kiosk was a bust, but there was a gift shop with the same kind of locked gate. As soon as we pushed out the pin at the top, we got right in."

"Where's Naomi?"

"I'm over here," she says, sounding a bit sheepish. "I'm going to keep a lookout."

"We..." Hudson trails off, and Naomi coughs. I look up just as they look away from each other. Hudson crouches near Quincy and me and continues, "We heard something on the second floor, so I threw a shark."

"You threw a shark?" I ask, using the water to rinse the worst of the blood off my hands before opening the first aid kit.

"It was one of those big bathtub toys from the gift shop," Naomi says.

Hudson nods and takes the water to help me rinse my hands better. "The shark worked fine. I just needed something to distract anyone that might have heard us."

"Where did you throw it?" I ask.

He shrugs. "At a wall near the south side of the mall. Between here and the theater."

"And that helped how?" I ask.

"Yeah, it was a weird idea," Naomi says. "But it did make a hell of a noise. So whoever we heard was definitely led in the wrong direction."

Hudson holds the first aid kit and keeps it steady while I carefully wipe my hands with an alcohol wipe.

"Wicked papercut, man," he says.

Quincy's laugh is more of a cough, but it's good. We could stand a lighter mood. I use a bottle of antiseptic wash to irrigate Quincy's arm as well as I can. He hisses but bears through the pain pretty well. I empty the entire bottle, hoping to God it will catch any gross germs my dirty hands pushed into the wound. When it's empty, I carefully pull on the sterile nitrile gloves. I hardly think I've done an operating-room-worthy job of keeping things clean, and he'll definitely need antibiotics and stitches, but it's better than nothing.

"Perhaps I am mistaken, but gloves seem a little silly now, don't they?" Quincy says. From my questioning look, he waves at them vaguely with his good hand. "You already have blood on your sleeves and your pants. I'm sorry about this, by the way."

"This isn't for my benefit. It's for yours. I should have tried to find some antibacterial gel before I touched your arm in the first place."

"It seemed that time was of the essence," Quincy says.

"We brought shirts just in case there wasn't enough gauze," Naomi says from her safe distance. She jiggles another wad of T-shirts folded over one arm, and I raise my brows. Exactly how many shirts did they pilfer from that gift shop?

"Those are going to come in handy soon enough. Quincy, let's go ahead and get this arm bandaged better. What do you think?"

"I think I wish I could stop reliving how it felt to pull that hunk of glass out."

"Oh my God," Naomi says, sounding faintly ill.

"Dude." Hudson cocks his head. "That's some hard-core shit."

"It was indeed hard-core," Quincy says, his smile weary.

"Here," Hudson says, and he reaches forward to take Quincy's glasses before cleaning them with the hem of his shirt.

I watch, transfixed as he carefully replaces them. "Better?"

"Yes, thank you."

"You are full of surprises, Hudson," I say, and he laughs, his cheeks looking a little darker.

"That's truer than you know." He winks, and I turn back to Quincy to start cleaning up.

I clean the worst of the mess and am pleased to see the wound isn't bleeding much. If I remember the class right, I think it's better to leave it open if the bleeding slows, so I carefully open sterile gauze pads and start layering them on.

"Should you use some of those tape things?" Hudson asks. "To close it up?"

"I don't really know," I say. "I think they're for small cuts."

Hudson arches a brow. "Wouldn't exactly call this a small cut."

"It's perfectly fine if you'd like to keep all these little details to yourself," Quincy says.

"Sorry," I say. "You're doing great. Pretty soon, you'll see no blood. Only bandage."

"Unless I look down for even a moment at my shirt."

"Yes, unless you do that."

I carefully layer the last gauze pads before fixing everything in place with long strips of medical tape. I wrap them in the crook of his elbow and closer to his armpit then sit back, shucking my gloves with a contented huff.

"I think it's pretty good, but maybe avoid using your hand to keep the wound from reopening," I say.

"Turn your flashlights off," Naomi says abruptly.

Something about her tone makes me instantly comply. I shift to flick off the power on the light Hudson wedged in the chair. Hudson already has his flashlight off, so the darkness returns, thick and surprising.

"What is it?" Quincy asks softly. His voice feels closer in the dark. "What's happening?"

"What do you see, Naomi?" I whisper.

My eyes slowly adjust, and though it is very dark in here, I see dim light coming from the front of the food court. Naomi is carefully tucked behind the half-open door, and she's peering through a gap in the plastic sheeting. Her shoulders are tense, and her hands are balled into fists. I'm sure she's watching something. And I'm just as sure that whatever it is, it's very bad news.

CHAPTER 22

"WHAT'S OUT THERE, NAOMI?" HUDSON ASKS QUIETLY.

"Clayton," she says, keeping her voice to a whisper. "He's on the second-floor balcony. He's looking for something. He has a little flashlight. Like the kind from key chains."

Hudson slips through the shadows until he's very close to Naomi's position. He's nearly a foot taller than her, so I'm guessing he can see through the same gap she's viewing. And Quincy and I are back here in the dark, seeing nothing. Knowing nothing.

"He's heard something," Hudson says. "One of us or maybe Summer."

I think of Lexi's tangled hair. Hannah's twisted neck. Is Clayton really going for another victim? Why is he doing this? Why won't it stop? My head feels buzzy and strange. "Where is he headed?"

"Can't tell yet," Hudson says. "Best get up just in case, but be quiet about it."

"He's in the stairwell," Naomi breathes.

I help Quincy to his feet as quietly as possible. Together, we pick our way carefully across the restaurant until we're a few feet behind Hudson and Naomi. They're standing at the edge of the plastic sheet that separates the remnants of the food court from the rest of the mall. Any moment now, Clayton could burst out of the stairwell on the ground floor. I try to remember exactly where it is. Twenty yards north of here? It might be even less.

He could have seen us come in here, or he could have heard Quincy earlier when he fell. But he wouldn't approach us, would he? There are four of us. He can't possibly be that stupid, right?

Quincy stays just to my left, close enough that I can feel him shaking. Is it because he's still in shock or because he's lost a decent bit of blood? I'll need to keep an eye on him.

"Where did he go? Do you see him?" I ask, my voice whispery and frightened.

"We're watching the stairwell door," Hudson murmurs.

Naomi takes a sharp breath. "He's on the third floor now. I just saw him. We're okay."

"We are, but she's not," Hudson says, pointing.

"Oh shit." Naomi's voice is tight. "This is not good. *Not* good."

I'm done being lost in the dark with my heart hammering and an injured person a few feet behind me. I push my way to the door and hear Quincy slowly following. Just a little closer, and my vision improves infinitely thanks to the light in the mall.

I scan the shadows and darkness on the third floor. For a

while, it's nothing, just endless smears of black and gray, until I spot a small white light moving up and down. Up and down.

Clayton.

A shudder rolls through me as I watch that glowing tip travel along the balcony. And then all is dark again. It must be one of those push flashlights—the kind you have to hold down to keep lit.

"Summer is on the third floor too. She just opened a door," Naomi says.

"Is she okay?" Quincy asks. "Is she safe?"

"She went into the stairwell," Hudson says.

"What's she doing?" I ask.

"I think she's running." Naomi turns to me, and I can see the horror on her face. "Jo, I think she's running from him."

"We need to do something," Quincy asks, surprising me. He's just behind me now, his face pale and shiny with sweat. But he looks alert and doesn't seem to be shaking.

"We can't. She's in the stairwell, but we don't know if Clayton's seen her. We could make it worse if we draw attention."

"Then Hudson was wrong," Quincy says, his voice steady.

Hudson doesn't move, but Naomi turns to face us. "Wrong about what?"

"About her being involved," Hudson says. I hear the slightest edge of tension in his words. "If Clayton's chasing her, she's innocent, and she's alone out there."

"Maybe we should have done something," Naomi says, sounding stricken.

"Like what?" Hudson asks. "She ran away. With zero explanation."

Naomi shakes her head "Yeah, but no one can *explain* how people react to a mess like this. That's animal instinct shit."

"Be quiet," I say, but it's not because I don't agree. It's because I want to know what's happening, and they are being too loud for us to hear.

Maybe there's something we can do now. Summer's a kid. A panicked kid who tried to help us. And now she's out there alone with a killer.

A door bangs open, and I scan the balconies, spotting that pinprick of light again on the third floor. Did he open a door? Is he moving?

"Second floor," Hudson breathes. "Summer's on the second floor."

It feels like the whole world is collectively holding its breath. Waiting to see what will happen next.

Summer emerges from the shadows. She is fifty yards down the balcony from us and headed north, toward the center of the mall. Which is exactly where Clayton is standing, one floor above.

My heart pounds, and my chest aches. I have to do something, but what? Splitting up is not an option, and Quincy is in no shape to run after her. So what options do we have? My feet feel glued to the floor. My eyes know where to find the monster now, and I can't pull my gaze away from the small white light he's holding.

When Summer is close, the light goes out. There is only

darkness above her, but I know what's hiding in those shadows. She's still running, and I hear the soft tread of her steps from here, so there's no chance Clayton won't hear it too.

I see a flash of long hair on the second balcony. A slim arm. Summer is running *directly* beneath him now. My heart thumps, and my hands roll into fists. I don't know where he is. I don't know what he—

"Summer." Clayton's voice is an awful singsong greeting, a sound that scrapes layers of the quiet away to leave all our fear exposed.

Chills run the length of my body, and Summer halts midstep. She whirls, her knotted hair flying around her. Every fiber of my being is telling me to crouch. To hide. But I am done being that girl.

I'm trying to choose the best move when a shadow peels away from the others on the third floor. It's Clayton. He suddenly hurls the top half of his body over the railing, and then the small flashlight flicks on, the beam illuminating his features from below.

It's horrific. His perfect white teeth are bared in a parody of a smile. Every plastic inch of him turns me cold with fear.

He changes his angle, crouching to reach through the railing slats. My stomach tumbles, but his fingers grasp at nothing. He can't reach down far enough to do whatever the hell he wanted to do. But then a *clang, clang, clang* rings out in the quiet.

We all flinch, but none of us like Summer, who cowers instantly on the balcony. She crouches away from the railing, but she is right below him. And she is frozen. Clayton's smile gleams in the distance, and my stomach clenches. I have to do something.

I have to stop him and protect Summer and keep Quincy safe, and it's too much. There are too many things, and my brain is tugging me to that safe sluggish place. I feel trapped in wet cement, but I am fighting. Scanning the mall for a weapon. An option. Something I can do.

Clayton slaps the metal bars again; this time the sound is different. Harder. Summer yelps and he laughs. Throws back his head like someone would do onstage in theater, like her terror is the greatest punchline he can imagine.

Naomi shifts and brushes the plastic. Noise ripples through the sheet.

Clayton's laughter fades in an instant, and my skin goes cold. Did he hear that? Is that possible? His face is lost in shadow again, but I sense him watching us. Impossibly, I feel his eyes on me.

I know it isn't possible. We're behind the plastic. He can't see us, but I think he heard. He knows where we are now. There can't be any question about that. Before, when Quincy fell, Clayton might have been in a stairwell or at the opposite side of the mall. We may have gotten lucky then, but this time, he's right across from us, and I'm sure he heard that noise.

For a moment, there is nothing but stillness and quiet. Stillness and quiet. And then I see Summer. She stays away from the railing, but sometimes I catch a flash of movement or a change in the shadow. She is moving south, and Clayton is matching her pace. He's chasing her one floor above.

He's almost to the emergency stairs. One flight down and he'll be on her. She won't be fast enough to get away from him. She'll die while we watch.

I move toward the gap in the plastic. And then the words burst out of me. "Get the hell away from her!"

My whole body jerks in shock. I whirl around, as if I'm not quite sure that just came out of me. Hudson's expression matches everything I'm feeling. Quincy's too. Only Naomi looks unsurprised—maybe because she looks terrified.

"Shit," Hudson says. No whispering this time.

I turn back to my peephole to the atrium. Summer is gone. Maybe she ran. Maybe she's hiding. But Clayton is staring our way again, hands on the railing, his face pushed out to catch the moon from the skylights. He is an equation of ugly angles in this light. I see the shine of those white teeth again. And hear him laugh.

"Wait your turn, Jo," he says.

A wave of cold runs through my body as my mind wraps itself around those four words. And then Clayton melts back into the darkness. A few seconds later, I hear a door open and then shut.

Clayton is back in the stairwell. And he is coming for us, one by one.

CHAPTER 23

SOMEONE TUGS MY ARM. IT'S HUDSON.

"We're going," he says, and without giving me a moment to think or breathe or respond, he pulls me forward.

He ushers Quincy and Naomi ahead, and we all head south against the wall, plastic to our left, a wall to our right, and a murderer somewhere we cannot see.

"Where are we going?" I ask, but Hudson is moving fast. He's laced his fingers with mine, and I am a rag doll, being pulled along for the ride. He moves faster until he is just behind Naomi.

"We have to get the hell out of here," Naomi says.

"I know. You don't think I know that?" Hudson asks.

"We should have told them," Naomi cries.

"What are you talking about?" I ask, but Hudson tries to move faster. I yank back hard, looking behind us. "Slow down! Quincy can't do this."

Hudson ignores me, so I jerk my hand free from his grip. "Stop!"

"It's okay," Quincy says roughly. He's catching up quickly, but it's clear running is not in the cards. But he gives a thumbs-up with his good arm. "Everything's okay."

"Like hell it is!" Hudson says.

"What the hell has gotten into you?" I ask.

"He found the gun," Hudson says. "Clayton. He's got the gun again."

My throat goes dry. I look at Naomi because I want her to shake her head or laugh or explain what he really means. But she looks at me, tight curls flying in every direction, her dark eyes soft and warm the way they are when Cara cries.

"It's true," she says.

A door bangs open, and we all turn. It's the other side of the mall, over the bridge and across the bone-dry river. *Clayton.*

Hudson turns, his finger pressed to his lips in warning. His eyes are nearly black, or maybe that's just the shadows. But he takes my hand and cocks his head before he starts out.

"Gift shop," he whispers.

Naomi nods and beckons Quincy closer, and we move quickly and quietly. I feel the desperation in Hudson's grip, though. And I see it in Naomi's eyes. They are afraid in a way they weren't before.

Which tells me Clayton does have that gun. Somehow they saw it, but when? When I was helping Quincy?

How were we so stupid to not find it ourselves? Except we weren't stupid. That gun fell near Hannah's body. None of us had the stomach to go poking around her looking for it.

But Clayton did.

Footsteps patter closer, and Hudson pulls me behind a pillar before going still. Quincy and Naomi join us, and I can hear the shudder and wheeze of our collective breathing. I can smell us too, layers of sweat and popcorn and blood. And licorice. Hudson always smells a little like licorice.

The muffled footsteps grow louder. He's close. Chills roll through my body when I spot Clayton on one of the bridges. His meaty hand drags along the railing. Halfway across, he kicks one of the broken glasses. The shards tinkle when they hit the streambed below. And then I see something in his other hand, something dark. It's the gun.

My stomach crumples, and Hudson tugs me along. We walk past three stores that are boarded over or closed off with roll-down grates. One store still sports the classic Hot Topic black paint and white stenciled letters. Hudson stops just past the Hot Topic, where I can see an open store, one with a single glass door partly open.

Plastic sheeting hangs from the balcony overhead, creating a tunnel of sorts. Hudson releases my hand and slides through a gap in the plastic, careful not to brush it as he slips inside the tunnel and to the open door. Behind us, I hear clattering and banging in the food court. Someone swearing. My heart is beating in my throat as I, too, move inside the plastic and follow Hudson through the door.

Naomi follows my path quickly and quietly, but on his turn, Quincy stumbles, brushing the plastic just beyond the glass wall.

The sheet ripples and hisses. It sounds like someone's tearing the sky in half to my tuned-in ears. I lunge for Quincy through the open door and pull him inside, my heart racing.

The banging in the food court is totally quiet now.

Did Clayton hear that?

Does he know where we are?

Is he coming for us?

Quincy's coppery skin has paled to a sickly yellow, and his eyes look sunken. His shirt is still soaked through with blood, and worry curls on top of the fear filling my chest. He shouldn't be running like this. He should be resting.

"We need to stop," I whisper. "Quincy—"

Hudson shakes his head and pulls the door until it's barely cracked. He stays at the narrow opening though, his face hard and eyes fixed on the inch-wide gap.

He's watching for Clayton. Waiting for him, maybe.

I flex my fingers and look around. Small emergency lights cast a faint glow around the store. Round racks that must have once held T-shirts are now empty. Most of the display units are empty too, but there are a few items remaining. Loads of T-shirts with an ugly Riverview logo on the chest. There are stacks of expired calendars and seat cushions with various Sandusky and Lake Erie sayings on them. In the corner, I spot a heap of the plastic sharks Hudson mentioned and an empty cooler for drinks. It's like the store was closed for the weekend, not forever. Even the register is still sitting on a counter nearby.

"Is he coming?" Naomi asks. She's standing at the front near Hudson now.

"Don't see him yet."

I move quickly to Quincy. "How are you feeling?"

"I'm a little queasy but fine."

I check his arm, happy to see the bandage is still clean and white. So far, so good on that front. If we can just find him some water and maybe a snack, it might help, but nothing will help like getting out of here and getting him real medical help.

I glance past the register counter and wonder if we should check for a door in the back.

"You can't hide forever!"

Clayton's voice is clear and crisp and not nearly far enough away. All the hairs on my arms stand upright as I look to Hudson. He is dark and motionless at the entrance, his face pressed to the gap in the open door.

"What's behind us here?" I ask softly. "Could there be an exit?"

"I don't think so," Quincy says. "There's a long access hallway behind these. Mostly storerooms. Clayton sent me here once when we were out of register tape."

"So he knows about the hallway?" Naomi sounds worried.

"Relax," Hudson whispers. "He doesn't know where we are. And most of the hallways are blocked."

"How did you know he had the gun?" Quincy asks.

Naomi's face crumples a little. "I saw him." Her eyes glaze

over like the words alone have taken her back to that moment. "I heard someone when we were looking for a first aid kit and thought it might be Summer, but it wasn't. He was over by the stairs—not far from Hannah."

"Picking around her body like a vulture is more like it," Hudson says, his voice full of cold fury. "Probably knew the gun wouldn't be far from her."

"I didn't think he'd go over so close to her. It's…horrifying."

"But the son of a bitch is a psychopath who doesn't care," Hudson says. "Look, we don't have time for this. We need to—"

Naomi's hand flies up. "He's back out in the atrium."

My body should have run out of adrenaline, but it's an endless supply, and her words send it firing again. It pushes through every beat of my heart, fizzing into my fingers and toes. I spin slowly, staring at stacks of T-shirts and decks of cards and dozens of things that can't help us at all. There's a door to the left that leads to some side entrance and an opening in the back. I point at it.

"Is that the way to the hallway?" I speak as softly as I can.

Quincy frowns. "No, I think the side door connects to the hallway."

Naomi steps back and bumps a table. An old sign holder at the top bobbles and then falls to the ground with a loud slap. We all freeze, looking at one another in the darkness. For one moment, our expressions are blank, and then panic rolls through us like a wave, rising in my chest and throat and falling over Naomi's expression.

Hudson's hand flies up, palm spread wide to cut us off. "He heard it." He barely breathes the words, so I don't have to ask if Clayton is close. The stiffness of his shoulders and the tendons corded on his arms make the answer clear. "He's coming. He's coming for us now."

If I had told someone that day, maybe he'd have been fired and everything would be different. If I'd pulled that secret out into the light, Clayton wouldn't have been there at all. And if he wasn't there, they'd all be alive.

CHAPTER 24

AT FIRST THERE IS NOTHING. HUDSON'S HAND TREMBLES where he's holding it up to keep us quiet. Naomi grips a pillar inside the gift shop, her dark fingers turning paler at the knuckles from the tightness of her grasp. Quincy breathes in shaky pants.

Hudson lowers his hand slowly, but his palm still faces us, holding me from speaking, holding us back like we're eager to lunge forward. Something shuffles against the plastic across the front of the store. Panic squeezes my heart like a fist. A shadow appears so suddenly, I nearly scream. It's a hand brushing the outside of the plastic sheeting. And then I see his silhouette—the breadth of his shoulders and clean line of his jaw. Clayton.

My whole body tenses, my tongue like sandpaper against the roof of my mouth. He's going to push through that plastic and find the door, and we'll have nowhere to hide or run. But Clayton keeps moving, his shadow traveling south toward the theater. He's going to walk right past us.

Maybe he didn't see the gap in the plastic, or maybe he doesn't know exactly where we are. Maybe his ears are playing tricks on him.

I hold my breath until my chest burns, until I am sure I will pass out. And then—*whump!*

He punches the plastic—a lightning jab that makes me jump. Naomi slaps her hand over her mouth, and he punches again. Again. He cannot see us. If he saw us, he would lift the plastic and find the door and God knows what. No, he's playing this punching game to scare us out. It's the way you stomp in a cabin, trying to frighten any mice back into their holes.

We don't dare move. We hold ourselves as still as possible while he walks another few feet. Punches again. Heads to the edge of the store, his footsteps sure and steady. He pivots with a sibilant hiss of his boots against the tile floor. And then his shadow is gone. His footsteps are muffled, like he's walked into the wall just south of the gift shop, but that's not possible.

Is it?

"Where did he go?" Naomi whispers.

I look at the door on the side of the gift shop feeling sick with fear. Is he in the service hallway Quincy mentioned? Is he in another store or maybe wandering south, headed for the theater?

"Maybe we should go out the front," Quincy whispers. "We could run for it?"

"You can't run, period," I say, and I nod at an opening in the back of the gift shop. "What if there's an exit in the back?"

"Might be," Hudson whispers, rushing back. He weaves around the shirt racks and display tables toward the opening.

I follow, but Quincy and Naomi stay near the front, looking nervous. When I hesitate at the doorway, Naomi shakes her head.

"No way," she breathes, glancing at the side wall. "I don't want to get cornered back there. He's in that hallway. I'm sure of it."

I join Hudson at the opening and flip on my flashlight when we enter the darkness. There's a time clock and a human resources poster and a small grubby table for breaks. There's one other notable thing about this area of the gift shop—the emergency door with a sign reading: EXIT TO LOT.

I feel nearly giddy crossing the room to that door. This is it. There's no construction in here. There's no plywood or plastic over anything inside this store. I hold my breath and push the silver bar, and the door pushes open a crack. I see a sliver of night sky and feel a rush of cold air. Joy bursts through my chest.

Hudson holds up a hand. "Be careful in case—"

A bang interrupts him when the door slams into something hard and metal. I push the handle all the way in and open the—*bang*.

Whatever I hit before isn't moving and it isn't my imagination. I stare at the two-inch gap and push, but the door doesn't budge. I push my face against the crack, seeing the star-pricked sky and an overhead electrical wire. Below that, I see the edge of something large, green, and rusty.

"Something's blocking it," I say.

"I can see that."

I give the door an experimental push, but it doesn't give a bit. "What is that?" But then I shake my head because I don't really give a shit. "Just help me."

"I think it's a construction dumpster," he says. "It'll be too heavy."

"Just try!" I hiss.

He opens his mouth like he's going to argue, but then he shakes his head and moves in next to me. We both heave against the door, pushing until my breath burns in my lungs, and tendons tighten like ropes in Hudson's arms and neck. We might as well be trying to push over a brick wall.

I give up, sagging against the door with a loud exhale. I turn my face to that open crack, feeling the delicious cold air just beyond my reach.

"This is beyond reckless. Why are they locking us in like this?"

"Not trying to lock anyone in. They do this to keep people from getting inside in the first place."

"Hudson," Naomi says, her voice hushed and whispery.

Hudson swears again. "We've got to go."

I don't want to close this door. I want to feel this air and see the glitter of stars. We are so close. How can we be so close to being out of this place—being away from this night—and still impossibly far away. My heart clenches when I release the handle, letting the door shut with a quiet *click*. I turn, but Hudson is already waiting in the open doorway, his eyes trained on something in the dark gift shop.

I turn off my flashlight and pad forward to meet them. Naomi is ushering Quincy toward the far-left corner of the store. It's not the door we came in, but she seems determined to avoid the entire right side of the gift shop. Who can blame her? Clayton is in the hallway on the right side of the store. A single wall between us and that monster doesn't feel like nearly enough.

And then I hear something beyond that wall. I push my way in beside Hudson. Naomi is making small frightened noises in the back of her throat, and Quincy is breathing hard and fast, his eyes darting to the open door, even as Naomi tries to reach for the pin in the far-left doors. But those sounds don't scare me. What scares me is the quiet metal rattling. Soft, but insistent.

It's coming from the right side of the store—from Clayton, I'm sure.

It's coming from the door that leads to the service hallway.

I try to squeeze my way further into the store, but Hudson's fingers wrap around my wrist. I want to yank my arm free, but then I see the handle on the side door begin to twist.

There is a flap at the top for a padlock, but it's open, the padlock long gone. And the lock mechanism on this door isn't a dead bolt; this is like the bathroom door in my mother's condo— a single-button lock you can break through with a solid enough push.

The door handle jiggles, twisting one inch and then two before holding fast. My mind flashes back to the jangle of bells over another door. Clayton is trying to get inside.

CHAPTER 25

HUDSON LEAPS AROUND ME, PUSHING ME BACKWARD toward Naomi and Quincy. He hurls himself between us and the door, but there is no chance I'm hiding behind him. I'll never let myself hide like that again, no matter how desperate I am to do it.

"Go out the front," Hudson hisses. "Hurry!"

The knob stops moving, and I hold my breath. Maybe he's done. Maybe he's given up. Maybe he thinks he heard us somewhere—

Clayton slams into the door, and the whole frame shudders. A muffled *whump* comes again—another hit. Miraculously, the flimsy lock holds, but the wood frame beside it cracks. I redirect my light to see a fissure snaking beside the door handle nearly up to the corner of the doorframe.

"He's going to break it," I whisper frantically, pulling at the back of Hudson's shirt. "He's going to get in here."

Awful images flash through my mind. The black sliver of gun under Clayton's shirt. Hannah's twisted neck. Lexi's bruised skin.

My heart is pounding out a warning. It's everywhere, this racing beat-beat-beat telling me to find a small dark place where this night will never find me.

But I know now there are no safe places left. Maybe hiding saved my life, but God knows it killed my soul.

"Move," Hudson whispers, urging me backward toward the door.

Naomi grunts, struggling with the pin at the top. "This one's stuck!"

"Go to the other door," Hudson urges.

I follow his order, fumbling toward the front of the store and around a table of T-shirts. But Hudson doesn't follow me. He moves closer to the side door—closer to the door Clayton is trying to break.

"Hudson!" I whisper, my voice desperate.

"Hurry your fool ass up!" Naomi says.

"Go," he repeats. He points at the glass door that will lead us back to the mall—but he doesn't look at us.

The handle rattles again, more urgently. Clayton slams into it again, and I flinch. Another impact and this time Hudson crouches, his palms pressed into the edge of the display table near him.

Rattle rattle—crack!

The frame splinters, and I see the side door shift and push. It's opening. *Oh God, the door is opening.*

"Hurry!" Hudson shouts.

It is like running in the ocean. My legs are impossibly heavy, and my eyes will not let me look away from the side door as it pushes open. A muscular arm snakes through the gap, and I see something hard and black gripped tightly in long fingers. Panic needles my spine and neck.

"He's got the gun!" I shout. "Hudson, run!"

But Hudson doesn't run. He pushes slowly forward, shoving the display table into the door, not slamming it shut, just pushing enough to slow Clayton's entrance. Naomi and Quincy are moving past a T-shirt stand to get to the front door. I steer around a display to reach them, trying to hurry. My feet slap the tile hard. The sound is like drumbeats. Like cymbals. But it doesn't matter if Clayton hears me now.

Naomi and Quincy are at the front door, but I hesitate. I don't understand what Hudson is doing. Clayton is halfway inside now, his gun hand hidden but his other fingers wrapped around the edge of the door. He is lurching, the door banging into the table Hudson's holding. What is Hudson doing? What the hell is he planning?

Then Hudson eases his grip, letting Clayton push the door farther open. I see the gun again, and then his arm and his blond hair. My throat squeezes, and then Hudson explodes forward.

He slams the display table into the door, pinning Clayton to the wall with a bang. Something clatters to the floor, and Clayton grunts. He is stuck there, scrabbling at the ground and kicking at the door when Naomi takes my hand and pulls me.

"Come on!" she says.

"Not without Hudson," I say.

Bang!

I whirl to see that Hudson's game is up. The side door is wide open and Clayton is inside. Just like that.

Hudson's one display table away and Clayton is already leaning down. He's going to shoot him—I'm sure he'll shoot him, but then I see Clayton crouch, his giant shoulders working as he gropes around on the ground.

He's looking for something.

Realization spikes through me. "He dropped the gun!"

Hudson doesn't miss his chance. He shoves the table with a grunt, but this time Clayton is ready. He catches it with both hands. I sprint to Hudson's side. Clayton is so close, I can see the whiteness of his teeth when he pushes the table back at us. My head hits a display stand, and I taste the metal sting of blood and fear on my tongue.

Clayton cuts across the side wall, moving toward the entrance. He kicks something and then reaches, metal skittering on the ground. It's the gun.

"He's trying to get the gun!" I shout.

"Stop him!" Hudson says.

Quincy darts for the front, pushing over a stand for hanging clothes. It knocks into Clayton, blocking his path and spilling metal hangers onto the concrete floor.

Like a display case of lighters.

Are we in big trouble?

My sister's voice echoes in my ears, but this time I do not want to hide. I want to fight.

Clayton hurls a handful of hangers and Quincy dodges, bumping one of the pillars with a cry. Clayton returns to his frantic searching.

"Go! Right now!" Hudson's voice thunders, and he shoves me backward, toward the front of the store. Away from Clayton— from all this. But I am not going to freeze. I'm not going to run. Not this time.

I grab a folding chair and hurl it at Clayton. He lurches out of the way so that it only clips him on the shoulder before crashing into the wall.

"Go," Hudson says. "Get them out!"

Naomi. Quincy. I turn in time to see Naomi throw a snow globe. It hits Clayton's fingers where they are curled over the table. He roars, "Bitch!"

Fear grabs me in the middle. Hudson is right. I have to get them out of here.

I kick at the toppled T-shirt stand, shoving it into Clayton's shoulder, and then I move past Hudson, grabbing Naomi. "Come on. Hurry!"

She throws something else and then lets me pull her away from the table and away from Clayton as Hudson begins to fire hangers and boxes and anything else he can find at Clayton. We scramble for the front of the store, for the door that will lead us back to the mall.

Halfway to the door, I see Clayton rising, the gun in hand. I sprint forward, snagging hangers as I run, throwing them as fast and hard as I can. I'm at Hudson's shoulder again, and I heave the big display table at Clayton with all my weight.

"Stay back!" Hudson screams, and then his arm is around my waist, hauling me backward.

I kick another chair in Clayton's direction, and then my feet are back on the ground, and I am sprinting for the door. Quincy is already there, holding it open. Naomi joins me, and together we retreat to the mall.

I turn, waiting for Hudson, but there is still an endless loop of banging and crashing, punctuated by an occasional cry or moan. My heart climbs into my throat—into my mouth. Where is he? Where is Hudson?

"Hudson!" I shout, my throat thick.

"Jo, come on!" Naomi cries. She's already several yards ahead of me, but I don't know where she's running. Where the hell can we go?

"Hudson!" I repeat, and I bolt back to the gift shop. The plastic is in the way, so I'm not sure where the door is, but I hear them fighting, and then something changes. There is running.

The plastic bursts open, and a tall streak sprints out of the west side of the gift shop opening. I see long limbs and blond hair. Clayton. He doesn't even look at me—he bolts north as fast as his legs will take him.

He's running away.

Hudson stumbles out after him, nose bloody and face flushed. He's holding a step stool in one hand. The look of rage on his face is like nothing I've ever seen. The promise of violence lingers in every heaved breath.

"You better run!" he screams in Clayton's direction. "You come near us again, you're the one who dies!"

But he's talking to an empty atrium. Clayton has disappeared into the darkness.

Half a minute later, I hear the soft noise of a door being carefully opened and then shut. We circle together in the quiet of the atrium.

"Did he get the gun?" Naomi asks.

"Yeah, he got it." Hudson swipes at his bleeding nose with the back of his hand. "I tried."

"It's okay," I say. "As long as you're okay, it's fine."

"He didn't shoot," Quincy says. "Why wouldn't he shoot once he had the gun?"

Hudson holds up the stool. "Because I jacked up his hand."

"Are you all right?" Naomi asks.

"All good," he says, but as calm as his tone is, there's no missing the dark, hungry look in his eyes.

"At least you won," Quincy says, but Hudson shakes his head.

"Didn't win shit," he says. "He'll find a way to use that gun."

I swallow hard, and I can't disagree. Every cell in my body reminds me he's already killed two people tonight. And now he has even more reason to want us dead.

MARCAIN THEATERS PRESS RELEASE

Official Statement on Riverview Theaters Tragedy

Marcain Theaters extends its deep sympathies to the families of the victims found dead at Riverview Theaters on April 8. We are and will continue working closely with local and state authorities on the investigation of this terrible tragedy. Marcain is heartbroken to have lost four team members in this incident, and our condolences and thoughts are with their families and loved ones during this terrible time.

CHAPTER 26

I LOOK UP AT THE TIERS OF BALCONIES OVERHEAD. THE moon is no longer visible, but it must be nearby because there's still a hazy glow drifting in from the skylights A few hours ago, I would have loved it out here. I can see the whole mall—every inch of railing around the balcony. But now I notice other things. The gloom behind the balcony railing. The shadows around each kiosk. The planters concealing the edges of the bridges. There are a thousand places for Clayton to hide.

And not just Clayton.

"Where do you think Summer is?" I ask.

"I don't know," Quincy says. "But right now, I think the best way to help her is to get real help as quickly as possible."

"Yeah, I'm with you," Naomi says. She looks up at the skylights. "So how the hell are we getting out of here?"

Everyone avoids eye contact, and no one responds. Maybe we all want someone else to take charge. Or maybe we just can't stand looking at each other anymore because of all the things we've seen together. Being silent is familiar and welcome, but I can't let myself be comfortable. Somehow there is a tendril of reality left in me and I have to hold that tight for all of us.

I know even the most horrifying things have their limits. This nightmare will end. And I want to be sure it ends with the five of us alive.

"I think we have three possibilities," I say, surprised that this time my voice doesn't shake. "We could try the other side of the mall to see if any of the back entrances behind the stores are unblocked. We didn't remove any of those pins, so we can get inside stores we didn't check earlier."

"What else?" Hudson asks.

Everyone is watching and waiting, and there is still an instinct to clam up. To shift the conversation to someone else. But then I see Quincy's blood on my shirt, and I remember that I've made different choices tonight. I have not been helpless.

"Our second option would be the roof. There is probably a fire escape."

"And the third option?" Naomi asks. "Because I think we'd be damn fools to get ourselves stuck between a man with a gun and a four-story jump."

"Good point," Hudson says.

"Our third option is to check the alarms in the arcade. The ones Summer said were working."

Naomi pulls her bottom lip between her teeth, and Quincy

frowns. It's clear they don't hate that idea. But they're both looking at Hudson because he was so against it before.

"Are you still worried about this?" I ask.

Hudson's face gives nothing away. He looks up at the balcony and then down at all of us. Then he nods across the river. "Let's try the other side first."

"And if that doesn't work?" Naomi asks.

"One bridge at a time," Hudson says. And then he points at the nearest bridge, a simple wooden platform that arches over the dry streambed.

Dread weighs down my feet with every step, but we move fast across the mall, and our trip is uneventful.

We assess the stores systematically, moving north. Half the stores are locked with security gates, but most with the glass doors and display windows are only locked by the bolt at the top. We release every one and check the store inside each time, one of us keeping watch while the others check the interior.

Thankfully, this side of the mall is much cleaner. Most of the stores are completely barren, with nothing more than a few built-in shelves and framed-in dressing rooms. Most of the stores have emergency exits, but every last one of them is locked tight or boarded over. After we've checked the fifth store—given the faint smell of raspberries and freesia in the air, I'm guessing it must be a former Bath & Body Works—Hudson waves us into a store so stripped down and nondescript, I don't have a hope of figuring out what it is. We find an alcove near the door and gather in a loose circle. My legs send a wave of relief through me when we sit.

"Haven't heard a thing from Clayton," Hudson says. "Any of you?"

"Not a thing," Naomi says.

"Maybe you hurt his hand badly enough to frighten him," Quincy says.

"I don't care about Clayton. I want to know why all the damn exits are blocked," I say. "What the hell could anyone possibly steal?"

"Not about stealing," Hudson says. "It's about squatting. People who don't have anywhere else to go know a good place to stay warm and dry when they find it."

"Yeah, God forbid someone stay warm and dry," Naomi says.

Hudson puts up his hands. "I'm not preaching the glory of the method, but it's a big deal on construction sites. If a squatter gets injured, it could be big trouble for any of the contractors involved."

"Still, there has to be a better way to deal with that problem," Quincy says.

"Oh, you mean like safe, affordable housing? Better job training? Budgeting assistance?" Naomi's face tightens. She's talked about going to college for social work, but this is the first time I've ever seen her talk about it like this.

"Not sure we can resolve societal problems *and* survive this nightmare," Hudson says, rubbing his temples.

I nod with a sigh. "He's right. This is ridiculous, but right now we've got to focus on getting out."

"I am tired," Naomi says. "It feels like it's late enough that someone should have come looking for us."

"Like I said, we can count on my parents whenever they land. So maybe four or five," Quincy says. "I honestly don't know."

"Well, I was supposed to stay with you and Cara," Naomi says.

Hudson nods at me. "Is your mom in town?"

I smirk. "Is she ever?"

Naomi chuckles. The answer is no. Mom has run into Naomi exactly once in the months she and Cara have been dating.

Honestly, I'm not even sure where she is. Guam? Or maybe Hawaii? It's probably on the fridge, but I don't always bother to check that. I know it isn't normal. We don't bake cookies or talk about crushes or shop for prom dresses. It's not that she doesn't love us. She always stocks the fridge with our favorite foods. She leaves notes on the bathroom mirror and twenty-dollar bills in our coat pockets. She loves us. But I look just like our father, and Cara has his taste in music and his sense of humor. Maybe it's too much. Maybe some losses are always too much.

"Well, don't look at me," Hudson says. "Dad works like eighty hours a week. He wouldn't notice. Mom works nights, so she usually leaves before I get home. She's off at five or so."

"But if you're not home by then?" I prompt.

He nods, his fingers going to his temples. "She might..." Hudson's eyes lose focus and mouth goes slack.

"Hudson?" I ask.

He does not respond, but his eyelids flutter as if he's just waking up or maybe walked into a very bright room. I repeat his name, but he doesn't answer. His flashlight slips from his fingers. It hits with a thunk and then Hudson sways on his feet, slumping sideways into the wall.

CHAPTER 27

"HUDSON!" I LUNGE FOR HIM, FINDING HIS FACE WITH MY hands.

"Did he faint?" Naomi asks.

"Let me get the light," Quincy says. He maneuvers the flashlight awkwardly with his uninjured hand, but the shadows make it hard to get a good look at Hudson.

I turn his head to the side and feel for his pulse. His heart thumps in a reassuringly steady rhythm against my fingertips. His breathing is normal too, but he's completely limp.

"What's going on?" Naomi asks. "Is he okay?"

"He may have fainted," I say, but I don't think so. I remember his weird spaciness earlier. There's something going on with him. I try to remember any conditions they talked about in my first aid classes. "Does anyone know if he gets low blood sugar? Does he have diabetes or a blood pressure disorder?"

"I have no idea," Quincy says.

"Hudson," I say softly, jostling his head gently in my hands.

I've never been this close to him, and it feels strange to have my palms on his jaw. My pale fingers stand out on his brown skin, as does the simple silver chain that disappears under his T-shirt.

I run my finger down the chain because I think I've seen ones like this before. I am just hooking my finger underneath it when he rouses with a groan. He shifts immediately, trying to sit up.

"Go slow," I say. "Nice and slow."

He slowly rotates his head to look at me, seeming puzzled by my presence or maybe by his position. His hands come up to cover mine, and heat rises in my cheeks.

I pull my hands free, and he blinks as if seeing everything for the first time.

"I think you may have passed out," I say. "Has that ever happened to you?"

He scrubs a hand roughly through his hair. It's clear he's still hazy on what's going on. I take his arm again, pressing two fingers to the pulse point on this wrist. I don't remember how fast it should be or how slow, but it is steady. I'm sure steady is good.

"Hey," I say gently. "Has this ever happened to you?"

"What's that?"

"You passed out, I think," I say. His pulse feels a little fast, maybe? I don't know for sure. He could just be alarmed by seeing me looming over him when he woke up. I lean back to give him a little more space. "Are you feeling okay now?"

"I'm fine," he says softly.

I settle onto my knees, putting even more distance between us.

"Do you have any blood sugar issues?" I ask. My gaze drifts to the metal chain again, the one that disappears beneath his collar. I realize with a start what it looks like—it's a medical alert necklace.

"Sugar?" he asks.

"Yes, are you a diabetic? Or do you suffer from fainting spells?"

He drags his hand over his face, looking more alert and more like Hudson. So, more annoyed than he looked thirty seconds ago.

"I'm fine. It's fine. What are we doing here just sitting around?"

"Trying to figure out how to talk you into checking the alarms in the arcade," Naomi says.

"Right," he says. "So what'd you come up with?"

"Not much." Naomi cocks her head. "Did losing consciousness jostle your opinion?"

Hudson snorts, but then frowns. "How long was I…"

I shake my head. "Not long at all. Less than a minute."

"Okay," he says, like the timing matters. "Yeah, it's fine. I'm all good. What were we talking about?"

Quincy and Naomi exchange looks with me, but my astonishment comes out in a hard laugh. "All good? Hudson, you *literally* passed out mid-sentence for no reason."

"I feel fine," he says.

"Then why did you pass out?" Quincy asks.

"Yeah," Naomi says slowly. "Because that doesn't seem fine."

"It seems concerning," I say.

"I don't know why! We haven't eaten, so maybe something with that."

I start to argue, but he cuts me off. "I said I don't know! But if you're so damn worried, let's find a way out of this shithole so I can get to an urgent care or something. So do you have some sort of plan?"

He's hiding something. I feel it in the marrow of my bones, but I don't know how to keep pushing. Everything about Hudson right now makes it clear he doesn't want to talk.

"We had concluded none of us have anyone looking for us right now," I say. "And that since the emergency exits are a bust, we maybe want to think about the arcade."

"I still don't love following Summer's advice," Hudson admits. "Just think it's weird that she hasn't tried to hook back up with us."

"But he was hunting her," Naomi says. "For all we know he actually found her and finished her off too, right?"

Quincy's brow furrows. "I can't think like that. She could be hiding. She's smart and quiet—she might be okay."

"What about the roof?" Hudson asks. "They may still have the fire escapes intact. They'd be harder to access from the ground so they probably wouldn't be considered a risk."

"There should be fire escapes," Quincy says. "It would make sense in case of fire and for mechanical purposes."

"Yeah, I don't think so," Naomi says. "After what happened to Hannah, I'm not going near the edge of anything."

Hudson runs a hand through his hair. "I get what you're—"

"Shh!" I hold up my hand to stop him. I heard something. A voice, I think.

"Did you hear something?" Naomi asks.

"I thought I heard someone cry out," I admit.

"I might have heard that too." Quincy frowns. "I hoped maybe I was imagining it."

We listen for long minutes, and there are faint creaks and thumps and random noises, but nothing that brings a clear image to my head. Nothing that tells me what we should do next or where we should go.

I sigh. "I'm sorry. It could have been nothing."

But it wasn't nothing. It was a voice. A scream, I think. But now it's gone.

"We should get moving," Hudson says.

"Could we do one thing first?" Quincy asks. Even in the dim emergency lights, I see his face flush. He looks over at a built-in shelf where I see a few heather-gray folded shirts, remnants of a long-lost store.

"You want a souvenir?" Naomi asks.

"No," Quincy says, and then he fingers the hem of his shirt. The blood-soaked fabric is turning brown at the edges. If I had to guess, I'd bet it's stiff, sticky, and absolutely miserable.

"Gotcha," I say. "Maybe Hudson can help."

"Help with what?" Hudson asks.

I nod toward Quincy. "I think we've got to figure out a different shirt."

We flip through the T-shirts, and while a few are probably big enough, one look at the neckhole makes it clear it will be tricky to navigate without moving his arm a lot.

"I don't think I can quite manage that," Quincy says while we all stare at the shirt. "Never mind. This is fine for now."

I touch the edge of his shirt with two fingers. It's a grotesque mixture of sticky and hard, and I recoil almost the instant I touch it. He absolutely cannot sit in that shirt for another minute.

"God, I can't even watch you touch it," Naomi says.

"If you three wanted me to strip, you just had to ask," Hudson says, but his grin isn't smug when he starts unbuttoning his white-and-gray flannel. He's got a gray T-shirt underneath, one with bleach stains on the hem that remind me of the streaks in his dark hair.

"Do we have scissors?" he asks.

"I'll check the back room," I say. It's a simple task. There is a row of cabinets across one wall. The drawers are mostly empty, other than a few outdated-looking cords and a couple of manager-issue coupons. In the back of one drawer, I find a cheap box cutter.

"This is about the best we've got," I say.

"It'll do. Thank you." Hudson takes the box cutter and waves me off.

Naomi and I walk over to the plastic covering the door to give them privacy. While we listen to the careful snips and muted conversation between the boys, Naomi's frown deepens.

"I'm worried about Cara," she says out of nowhere.

I think of my sister's terrified eyes under the counter. Her arms, small and shaking around my neck.

Are we in big trouble?

"She's probably asleep," I say.

"But she has nightmares," Naomi says. Seeing my expression, she rolls her eyes. "I know her too, Jo."

"I know you do. I know that."

"I know what she's been through—what both of you have been through."

I swallow hard, thinking of Cara's dark eyes when I pushed her under that counter. That *pop, pop, pop*. And the sound of my father falling.

I don't say anything. I'm not sure there's anything to say to Naomi's statement.

"We have to make it out of here for her," she says.

"We will."

"I don't think this is over," Naomi says. "I don't think he'll let it be over, but we have to end it. We have to get out because she can't handle…"

"I know she can't." My heart feels swollen and tender—too inflamed to fit inside my chest.

"I think we've about got it," Hudson says.

The boys are admiring their handiwork and Quincy's new shirt when a new sound rips through the night. There is no mistaking the sound this time. It is Summer, and she is screaming.

CHAPTER 28

"WHERE DID IT COME FROM?" HUDSON ASKS, BECAUSE there is no need to ask whether we all heard that scream. Goose bumps have sprung up on my arms, and I rub them hard, looking upward.

"It's upstairs somewhere. Up high, I think."

Another distant scream and I startle, searching the balconies. A door opens and slams. There are noises. Thumps. Scrapes. Shouts. Summer is in trouble. Somewhere up there, she needs help. We have to find her. Right now.

"I'm going up there," I state, willing my body to follow the command of my words.

"Up where?" Hudson asks.

"Where do we go? Where is she?" Quincy asks, desperately scanning the balconies.

Summer screams again, and a door slams. Panic courses through my body like an electric current, and my feet want to stay put. My body wants to go still, but I move all the same. I burst out of the store into the mall. For a moment there is quiet. And then footsteps. It's the third floor, and it's muffled like the sound is coming from inside one of the offices. And soon, there is no sound at all. It's like a shade has been pulled over the scene, leaving an empty stage behind.

The white belly of the streambed stares up at me. The stage looms in the distance, empty and silent. There is nothing.

"They must be in one of the offices," Quincy says, brow creasing in concentration. Still trying to find the logic in this madness.

"Or they're on the roof," Hudson says.

Quincy is breathing hard, and glass crunches under Hudson's foot. I turn in a slow circle, straining my ears to pick up any other hint of noise, but there is nothing.

"Do you hear anything?" I ask, hoping someone else has picked up something.

"Nothing," Naomi says. She, too, is slowly rotating, staring at the balconies overhead. "It just stopped."

The quiet stretches and stretches. I stare at the brightest star outside the skylight, wishing it could guide us home. And then a dark smear blocks it out.

I startle and Naomi gasps. Another shadow darts across the skylight. It's like a static shock, jangling through every nerve in my body.

"Shit, they're really up there," Hudson says.

"What are they doing? Is Summer hurt? Is she safe?" Quincy still wants the logical answers to impossible questions.

"I can't tell," Naomi says.

We watch and we wait and we—

Pop. Pop.

I know that sound the way I know my sister's voice. It is followed by a noise that makes me think of a bird hitting a window. But this is much louder and larger than a bird.

"What was that?" Naomi asks.

"Is something up there?" Quincy asks. "Is someone here to help?"

Chills slither up my arms and legs, but I don't know how to answer. There was real hope in Quincy's tone, and I don't think I have whatever it takes to rip that hope away.

"We need to stay quiet," Hudson says, and then he gestures toward a pole, shepherding us back into the shadows behind an old information kiosk. Hudson keeps his eyes trained on the stairwell door and bumps his hip into the kiosk. Something falls off the kiosk shelf, but Hudson ignores it, motioning to everyone to listen.

They do as they're told, but I'm not listening. And I'm not looking at the skylight to see what hit the glass. I'm staring at the thing that fell off the shelf—a blue plastic lighter. I blink once and I am dragged back nine years, to the worst day of my life.

There is a shift in my father's face. I see it from below, from the floor behind the counter where I am sitting with Cara. I look up from the box of Lemonheads we're sharing. I'm offering a candy to my father, but he's ignoring me. His attention is locked on something outside.

"Daddy?"

He inhales sharply and looks at me. It's fast, his gaze shifting to me for one anguished second, like he doesn't have time to linger. And he doesn't. He doesn't have any time at all.

His palm is on my head and then my shoulder. Urgent and half-distracted. "Get your sister and get under the counter, Jo. Hurry."

For one fraction of a second, I think it's a game—a silly, strange hide-and-seek—but I push Cara into the little cubby beside the safe. I push her all the way to the back and climb in after, and then I see my dad kick Cara's coloring book and our box of Lemonheads beneath the register. Out of sight.

Bells jangle over the door.

Cara's arms lock around my neck.

My dad's greeting trembles.

"Are we in big trouble?" my sister asks.

Daddy offers them the money. He tells them it will be okay. But it is not okay.

Cara squirms in front of me when we hear the pops. One, two, three. She wants to get out—she wants to run, but I hold her back, I clamp my hands over her eyes as lighters spill and my father falls. I don't want Cara to see, but I can't make myself stop watching. I can't move at all. I stare at the pool of blood spreading from my father's body. And my childhood bleeds out too, dying with my father on a dirty linoleum floor.

I didn't tell because I was angry. And I was angry because my secret is that I was in love.

I can't believe you didn't see the look all over my face. I saw how bright and interesting she was every day, but I never told her. What I saw didn't change how I felt; it only made me sure my feelings didn't matter. So I held back and kept quiet, and now she's dead and I'll always have to live with wondering if I could have stopped it.

CHAPTER 29

WHEN THE MEMORIES FADE, I PRESS MY BACK INTO THE giant pillar stretching from the floor to the underside of the balcony. I have a flash of the mall from before, the way the water gurgled over the rocks, and teenage girls used to linger on the bridges with iced coffees and too much lip gloss. It was a little cheesy, sure, but it was never frightening. Now it's the setting of a nightmare, from the bone-dry riverbed to the drawn security gates and gauzy plastic curtains hanging from the ceiling.

Except it's more than a nightmare landscape now: it's a grave. A dark whisper in my mind tells me that this grave has just claimed another member of our group. The dull thump and crack of something hitting the skylight echoes in my memory.

Of course, we can't be sure of what hit until someone checks the skylights. Naomi, Quincy, and Hudson seem content to stand by this kiosk forever. The exhaustion must be taking its toll. Dark circles ring Hudson's eyes, and Quincy is slumped against the pillar near the kiosk. Even Naomi looks ashy and sluggish. And in that moment, I know I will be the person who does the checking.

And why not? I held my sister's hand and stepped around my father's blood. I kept her eyes covered until the policeman scooped us up and whisked us away. He rushed us to the relative safety of his warm cruiser, but it was too late for me. I'd already seen everything.

"I'm going to check the skylight," I say. They look at me in horror, but I nod. "I think what we heard was a gunshot. Two gunshots, actually."

"Yeah, it was," Naomi says softly. Her chin trembles. "My uncle used to go target shooting. He took me to the range once. I couldn't remember at first where I'd heard that sound, but then…"

I nod and square my shoulders. "Something hit the skylight after the gunshots. I think we all know what that means, but we have to check."

"What are we checking for?" Quincy asks.

"A body on the glass," Hudson says. His voice is rough, and he doesn't look at anyone.

"Whose body?" Quincy asks. When no one answers, he stiffens. "Summer's body?"

He sounds like he might be sick, even as he says it. His mouth opens, but he doesn't speak again.

"It could be something else," I say, though I don't really believe that. "I'm going to check."

No one argues, and of course they don't. No one wants to

face the truth that every heart eventually stops beating, or that life is not forever. They've seen it tonight, sure, but all of this is still tucked under a thick layer of mind-numbing shock for them. But I've stepped through that safe and hazy veil, into the weeks and months and years after the shock wears off. In my mind, I've watched my father's eyes gloss over a thousand times. I've seen his chest stop rising and his skin go gray over and over in my memory. No matter how much I don't want to do this, there is nothing waiting for me on those skylights that will be worse than what I've already seen.

I force myself to start toward the large arched bridge ahead of me. I'll have a good view of all four skylights from there, so I know it's a good spot. Nausea is rolling through my stomach in hot, terrible waves as I get closer, and my palms are slick with sweat. More than anything in the whole world, I do not want to look up.

But I do.

I check all four windowpanes and find them all dark. The moon is gone now, and we are left with four slick black pools. I can't see anything. Anything could be up there. Anything or nothing.

"I can't see," I admit.

Hudson steps away from the pole and joins me in six long strides. He looks up but soon shakes his head. "It was easier when there was movement to follow."

I try again, my eyes tracing the dark rectangles of skylights.

It's too dark to make them out clearly and certainly too dark to see anything outside them save a few of the brighter stars. "We need to find out what's up there."

"How?" Quincy asks. "The flashlights would reflect off the glass."

"Yeah, well there is no way in hell we're going up to the roof to see if Clayton's still hanging around," Naomi says.

"If it's Summer and she's still up there, she could be alive," I say. "She could be hurt and needing help, and if there is any chance of saving her, I have to try."

I know if she's dead seeing her body will haunt me, but nothing haunts me more than the things I didn't do.

"I'm going up in case I can see any better," I say.

"I'll go too," Quincy says.

Naomi scoffs. "You want to go up there? You're the damn fool who keeps telling us we should stay together to stay safe."

"This is what dumbasses do in horror movies," Hudson says. "Splitting up means people are going to die."

"No, being stupid is how people die," I say, and then I wince thinking of Lexi and Hannah. "I mean, being stupid is how people die in horror movies. And, Quincy, you trying to climb stairs with your arm is definitely not smart. I want the three of you to stay together, and you can watch me."

"Watch you die too?" Hudson asks. He sounds furious.

I shake my head before anyone can start poking holes in my half-baked plan. "We heard the gunshots, and we heard something hit the roof, but we haven't heard any of the stairwell doors, right? Clayton hasn't opened a door, because we would have heard it."

After a long pause, it is Quincy who sighs. "She might be right. We would have heard a door open. He couldn't have gotten back into the first floor without leaving a stairwell or walking down the main stairs, and we would have seen that from here."

"So we're counting on that son of a bitch not finding a quiet way inside," Naomi says. "And how am I going to explain this to your sister if we're wrong, Jo?"

"You're not," I say. "Because you're going to watch me every step of the way. If he starts shooting, I'll run along the wall. It's hard to hit a moving target, and a hell of a lot harder if that target is in the dark, right?"

No one is buying it. Everyone is fixated on what might happen, but my mind is set. My father died the last time I chose to do nothing. If I'd done CPR faster, maybe I could have saved Lexi. If I'd bolted up those stairs after Hannah, maybe, just maybe I could have saved her too. I didn't let myself freeze with Quincy. I forced myself to move and he's here—alive and breathing. Maybe I don't know what will happen if I go up those stairs, but I know that when I do nothing, people die.

"Look, I'm done talking about this," I say. "We left Summer. She was scared, she ran, and we all assumed the worst. Now she may very well be shot and completely alone. I am *not* leaving her up there if that's the case."

For a few seconds, everyone is silent and still. Waiting for someone to break the silence. And then Hudson heaves a sigh.

"I don't know what part of this is dumbest," Hudson says. "You thinking you can fix whatever the hell happened up on that roof, or me insisting on being the one to go with you."

I open my mouth to refuse his offer, but he holds up his hand. "Enough. You go and I go with you. I swear I'll tie you to one of these pillars if you try to go up there on your own."

"Fine," I say.

"Fine," he repeats. Then he shoves his streaked hair out of his eyes and looks south, toward the large open staircase that leads to the second floor. Hannah's body is beside that staircase, but I know it's our only option if we want to be sure to avoid Clayton.

"Promise me you are not going out on that roof," Naomi says.

I tilt my head to look at her because she knows I can't make that promise. If I spot Summer and she's in trouble, I'm going out on that roof. I'll have no option. So I offer the only thing I can. "I promise I will make it back down here in one piece."

"Can you explain it again?" Quincy says. "What's the plan, exactly?"

I point up to the third-floor balcony, waving my finger back and forth to a stretch that is faintly illuminated by fading emergency lights.

"Do you see that part of the balcony? Hudson and I will take the open stairs and follow that portion of the railing. We'll move until we have a better view of the windows. If you see anything, you can flash your light. Once for 'everything's fine.' Twice for 'come back down.'"

"And three times for 'he is right behind you,'" Hudson says, tapping his foot. Naomi's scowl makes it clear his joke has fallen flat.

"Three times is for 'hide.' From here, you can see the stairs and the balcony. You can see us the whole way, and we can see you."

"And what happens if you need to go up to the roof?" Naomi asks. "You'd have to enter one of the stairwells."

I wave at Hudson. "Then we do that whole one-bridge-at-a-time thing Hudson was talking about."

"What if he's just waiting up there on the roof?" Quincy says.

"I don't know," I admit. "I don't know what I should or might do. But I know I can't live with myself if I don't try."

CHAPTER 30

HUDSON AND I HEAD TOWARD THE STAIRS. HIS STEPS ARE almost silent across the tile, and when we reach the wide carpeted stairwell, I can't hear him at all. We hug the farthest edge of the steps, to keep every possible inch of space between us and Hannah's body. I'm not sure it makes a difference. As I follow him up the stairs, my eyes drift to the right over and over. I don't know what pieces of this night *won't* stay with me, but I know the shape of Hannah's shoe soles will be burned in my memory forever.

Still, I force my eyes ahead, watching Hudson climb steadily and swiftly up the staircase. At the top, he pauses. He looks left and right and waits. My ears strain for any noise, but there is nothing. No hum of a heater, no creak or groan of a large building settling in the wind.

I glance down, toward the fountain near the stage. That's where we stationed Quincy and Naomi, but their flashlights stay dark, so they are just two more shadows in a black sea. We walk a little ways down the balcony so we're closer to the skylights overhead. I can make out the frames better from here, but the glass is still dark.

"Can you see any better?" I ask.

"Not yet," Hudson admits.

We retrace our steps and start up the stairs to the third floor. The stairwell here is still open, but it's narrower. It's hard to imagine a three-floor mall in Sandusky, Ohio, and it's equally hard to imagine businesses clamoring for offices overlooking Macy's and Cinnabon.

Maybe it's the fatigue setting in, or the lack of dinner since we missed our IHOP plans, or the endless waves of stress rolling through all of us since we found Lexi dead. Either way, by the time we reach the third floor, I am winded, and my legs feel heavy. I follow Hudson down the hall, but my face feels a little buzzy and numb. Am I dizzy?

I'm definitely dizzy.

A couple of minutes later I have to stop. I reach for the railing to steady myself, and Hudson grabs my upper arms.

"Hey," he says, holding me still. Had I been swaying?

"What's going on?" he asks.

"I think I should sit," I say softly, but he's already pushing me down gently. I turn to sit on the worn carpet.

"Put your head between your legs," he says.

I do it, feeling my lips and cheeks tingle as I force myself to slow my breathing. To let my body catch up. "All we need is for both of us to pass out."

Hudson chuckles, and his arm bumps into mine. He pulls away, and my skin feels cold at the absence of his warmth.

"Hey, about that passing-out thing," he says.

I look up, expecting to see his face above me, but my eyes are quickly drawn beyond him, to the skylight that is now only twenty-five feet or so away. This time, the view is much different. I inhale sharply. "I can see the skylight."

Hudson drops whatever he was talking about and looks up. It is still dark, but being closer is making it easier to see. The silver frame of the window is clear, along with the long fracture that stretches diagonally from the center of the pane to the southwest corner.

I can see the sky beyond it too: tiny, barely visible stars interrupting the velvety black. The glass is perfectly transparent, cleaner than I'd expect, except for one long smudgy streak just beside the crack.

"Hudson," I say, and my voice sounds strained.

He follows my gaze and, after looking for a second, turns on the flashlight, directing the beam to the glass. The light creates a reflection, just as we expected, but I can see the glass just a little bit more clearly. And I can see the smudge near the crack isn't brown or black or gray. It's red.

My breath comes out of me all at once. "I think that's blood."

"Shit."

My stomach rolls, but I can't look away from the glass. I squint, trying to make out some shape in the darkness, some clarity beyond the red streak. Is there anything up there? Is Summer up there?

"Turn off the light," I say, feeling steadier.

He complies, leaving us in an abrupt darkness. I keep my eyes trained on the skylight. The smear of blood is still visible, a darker smudge in the charcoal pane of glass, but there is nothing else. No body.

Nothing is up there.

"I don't see anything," I say. "I mean there's blood, but there's no body."

I look down the center of the atrium, and my stomach shrinks. It's only three stories, but they are big stories. The world below seems impossibly small. The streambed bisects the mall like a long crooked bone. Plastic sheets and giant slabs of plywood cover half the storefronts. This place isn't just empty. It's lifeless. A carcass of a mall.

I turn, my hand on my suddenly uneasy stomach.

"Got a thought you want to share?" Hudson asks.

I shake my head. "I'm honestly trying to think of what we should do now."

"Well, no one's up there, so we're back to where we were, right? We head to the arcade."

"I don't know. Someone obviously did fall on that window. Probably Summer."

"Probably," he agrees. "But she got back up."

"Maybe. She might have only managed to crawl off the window. She might be too hurt to open a door."

"Or she might have climbed down a ladder," he says. "The point is, if she's not on that glass, then she's mobile. Which means there's a good chance she's reasonably okay. The best thing we can do now is to get the hell out of this building. Even if we have to light a fire or break a window or what the hell ever. We need to get out and get real help."

"Okay, I hear you. But are you willing to believe Summer and try the arcade?"

His eyes narrow. "Willing to try the arcade, yes. But I don't know what to believe about Summer. I'm not saying it makes sense. It's not fair, but I don't trust her. I don't want to lie about that, especially not when it comes to you."

I feel my face scrunching up. "What does that even mean, when it comes to me?"

Before he answers, a sharp, shrill scream rises from the atrium floor. I whirl to the railing, my heart flying into my throat.

"Run!" Naomi screams. "Run, Jo, he's coming!"

CHAPTER 31

I SEE ONE OF THE FLASHLIGHTS FIRST, THE ONES THEY were supposed to only turn on to signal us that Clayton was near. But this beam isn't shining up—it's directed in a narrow arc right along the floor, the beam flickering and weak. The batteries must be going.

"Naomi?" My voice is small and hollow. I can't see her. I can't see anyone.

"He's coming up the stairs!" she screams. "Run! Now!"

"The north stairs!" Quincy says. "He's—"

A door slams open. It is an interior stairwell, and it's not far enough away. I don't know if he knows where we are or if we can make it back to the steps we climbed before he finds us. Even if we make it, I don't know that he won't be fast enough to catch us. Or that he won't shoot us.

Hudson doesn't ask questions. His hand is on my arm, and he is moving so fast, he's all but dragging me. We're heading back the way we came, past a cart half-full of drinking glasses, past a rip in the blue carpet, and then past a door that reads STAIRWELL.

I twist around to look behind us, but it is just darkness. Shadows and stillness and—

Wait. Movement catches my eye, maybe forty yards behind us.

My heart is in my throat. I'm tripping over my own feet. "Hudson. He's—"

"I know," he says. Almost growls it. And then he is steering me against the wall of offices, where it is dark. So dark, I can barely make him out in front of me.

"I don't know if we can make it in time," I whisper.

Hudson doesn't answer, but he suddenly grabs my arm and hauls me toward an office door. At first, I want to warn him these doors will be locked, but then I realize the door he's at is slightly ajar. He pushes the door wide enough to tug me inside. Then he pulls it shut slowly. So slowly.

It's too dark in here to see much. At first I can't even tell where the furniture is, but the window is easy to spot, just left of the door. The glass is bare, the curtains pooled in a twisted heap on the floor. I take a breath that smells of old carpet and faintly of mildew. I do not want to be in this room.

But out there, a killer is searching for us.

I look behind us, my eyes adjusting enough to make out two desks and an ancient-looking phone with a missing handset. There are no other doors. No windows to the outside world. It is only marginally larger than a prison cell, and just as terrifying. If Clayton finds us here, we are as good as dead.

I open my mouth to speak, but Hudson raises his hand to stop me. He cocks his head like he's heard something, and then I hear it too. It's a voice. Clayton's voice.

I press my ear to the door, and Hudson is right there beside me, his eyes feverish in the darkness. He moves the metal stopper slowly from the frame to rest against the door. As if a lock will solve things when there's a plate glass window ten inches to our left and a gun in Clayton's possession.

My insides wobble at the sound of footsteps moving closer. And then, without warning, Clayton's voice comes again, much closer.

"No one else has to die."

It is not what I expected him to say. He doesn't sound like a maniac. He sounds exhausted and maybe a little desperate. He sounds too much like the rest of us. "I just want to talk. That's all. We can find a way out of this together."

He pauses, but I hear his footsteps drawing closer. Closer.

"I never wanted to kill them! This whole thing was... Jesus, Summer was just..."

Summer? The smear of blood on the glass. My heart sinks. Did she die up there, alone under the stars? I think of her looking up like my father, her eyes seeing nothing.

"You can't hide and pretend you're innocent." Clayton is so close now. I feel his steps outside the door, the way a bridge shivers when a jogger moves over it. Clayton suddenly roars, "You know they're all dead because of you!"

My next breath is sharp enough to sting. *Dead because of you.* I don't understand. It's an impossible, nonsense thing, but it *feels* right. My father on the floor. Lexi under my hands. Hannah tumbling over. I didn't stop any of it. If I had made different choices. If I had moved faster—done something—

"But we can fix this," Clayton says more softly. He is *right* outside the door now. "Come on, Jo, I know you want to fix this. I know you didn't mean for this to happen."

Jo. Not Hudson and Jo, just Jo. Naomi only called my name. Clayton doesn't know Hudson is with me. He thinks I'm alone.

"Come out, Jo!" Clayton roars.

He is past the door now, on to the next office. To the next window. My knees are going to give. My heart pounds harder and harder until I think it will hammer its way out of my chest—until he will hear it right through this door. Clayton screams my name again, but Hudson pulls me in, pushing one of my ears to his chest and cupping his hand over the other.

He holds me while Clayton rages on, his voice muffled and blurred. He holds me though I make no move to return his embrace. My tears soak his shirt and drip off my chin and Clayton's voice slowly grows quieter. His words blur around the edges, and then turn to murmurs, and finally fade to silence.

I slowly lift my head and listen. For a while there is nothing, but then a distant *shhhunk-click* interrupts the quiet.

"That's the south stairwell door," Hudson says calmly. "The stairway he used after he pushed Hannah. You're safe."

I shake my head and sniff, swiping my face with the backs of my hands. Hudson quietly pulls open the door a crack, and suddenly I can see everything.

Once, Dad and Mom took Cara and me to Mammoth Cave in Kentucky. After the quick tour, Mom and Cara went back to the hotel to nap. But Dad and I took the longer tour. The part I remember best was being in this massive cave—bigger than any auditorium I'd ever been inside. The guide turned out all the lights and talked to us in the darkness for a couple of minutes before lighting a match. That single flame was so powerful, I felt like I could see for miles.

That's how the light is now. Meager as it is, it illuminates every part of Hudson's face, including the scar above his ear and the hollows under his cheekbones. He tilts his head, and I can tell he's looking me over. Assessing the damage, I guess.

"I'm okay," I say. "We need to check on Naomi and Quincy."

"Jo." Hudson's voice is soft. And then I feel his hands, those big palms and the calloused fingertips, on either side of my face. "I know what he said. It was insanity. You didn't do any of this. You know that, right?"

I nod, but I can't force any sound out of my mouth. My eyes are hot with tears, and my throat is growing tight. I'm desperate to push him away. And some small part of me is even more desperate to pull him closer.

"You didn't hurt anyone," he says, as if he's seeing right through me, to the guilt weighing like bricks on my shoulders. "Tell me you believe me."

"But people always die around me," I say, my voice cracking. "It keeps happening."

"This has happened before?"

I want to change the subject. I want to talk about Quincy and Naomi and how fast we can get into the arcade, and how we can get out of here. But when I open my mouth, it's the truth that comes out.

I tell Hudson about Cara.

I tell him about my father.

I tell him every terrible part.

And all the while, he holds my face and looks me in the eyes. And when I am done—when I am crumpled and crying against his chest again—he doesn't say a word. No platitudes or promises that everything will be okay. No apologies for sins he did not commit. Hudson allows the truth to sit, and it lets the air out of the room.

After a while, I swipe my face with the hem of my T-shirt and face the window. Hudson squeezes my shoulders gently and lets me go. My eyes feel gritty and hot, and I am tired in a way I can't ever remember being tired before.

"We need to find Naomi and Quincy," I say. "We need to see if Summer was right about the alarm."

"I'm ready when you are."

We are quiet in the hallway, but I know Clayton could sneak up on us. He could wait in the darkness or move quietly and carefully. He could make it so we'd never see him coming.

A shiver rolls through me at the thought, but I keep moving. A few yards from the stairs, Hudson stops, and then I see something at the bottom. Movement. Someone is waiting for us.

Before adrenaline can fire again, I spot the telltale silhouette of Naomi's tight curls. My whole body relaxes as we slip down the stairs to meet her. Quincy is nearby, and we move to the west side of the mall, back into the ancient Bath & Body Works store. Every breath smells sickly sweet, vanilla and honeysuckle, but it is dark and tucked away under the balcony which feels safer.

Inside the store, Naomi gives me a quick hug. "Thank God he didn't find you. He didn't, right?"

"No," I say, and I feel that awful pressure again, that invisible weight crushing the center of my chest. "What happened down here? You screamed. It was terrifying."

"We were watching you, scanning the balcony and the stairs, just like we agreed," Quincy says.

"Yeah, but little did we know his psycho ass was creeping around too," Naomi says. "We damn near ran him over."

"What?" I ask.

"He didn't see us behind the kiosk where we were waiting," Quincy says. "And we didn't see him crossing the bridge or coming up on the other side of our kiosk."

"We saw him once he was maybe ten feet away," Naomi

says. "I tried the flashlight, but it would not come on, and he was getting closer."

Quincy nods. "It was like he'd seen you. He was heading straight for the open stairs."

"He was getting so damn close, and I just—I screamed." Naomi shakes her head. "I'm sorry. He was heading right for you guys, and it flipped me out."

Quincy nods. "Especially when he turned and took the north stairwell, the one that opened right next to you."

"That bastard was running up those stairs. So we just started screaming like banshees."

"We heard that part," Hudson says, rubbing his temples.

"It worked," I say. "You did good."

"I panicked," she says. "But, hey, it kept you alive, right?"

"Did you see where he went?" I ask. "We were hiding in one of the rooms."

"I saw him enter the south stairwell," Quincy says. "I haven't seen him since."

"I think he's scared," Naomi says.

I ask, "Why do you think he's scared?"

"Did you hear him?" Naomi asks. "He was ranting up there. He's desperate to blame this on someone else."

"I think she's right," Quincy says. "I don't think he can get out either. He's as trapped as we are, except we will eventually be rescued. He'll be arrested. He's probably more panicked about getting out than we are."

"I don't think he wants out," Naomi says. "He wants to kill us."

"Doubt that was his plan," Hudson says. "His wife showed up losing her shit. Then his girlfriend heard and probably lost her shit too—"

"Don't call Lexi his girlfriend," I say. "We don't know what that was about."

"Whatever, I'm just saying: in his eyes, this all happened *to* him. The way he was talking up there..." Hudson shakes his head. "He thinks he's just reacting to all of this."

My skin prickles, remembering his words upstairs. "He did say he didn't mean to kill them."

"Like that makes this okay?" Naomi asks.

"No, but maybe Hudson's right about him not setting out to kill anyone. Things like this make a person feel unhinged," Quincy says. "I mean, I feel a bit crazy."

"Yeah, me too," Naomi says. "But funny enough, I'm managing not to kill anyone."

"Because you're not violent," I say. "You aren't always looking for someone to punish."

"Or someone to blame," Hudson says as he rubs his temples. "He doesn't think any of this is his fault."

"Then he's psychotic," Naomi says.

Quincy nods. "That much seems clear."

I sigh. "At this point, he might be trying to kill us all because we're witnesses."

Hudson groans like this whole line of conversation is physically painful.

"True," Naomi says.

And then a sudden *whump* right behind me makes me jump. Naomi gasps and I spin to face the source of the noise.

"Hudson?" Quincy asks, his voice tight with worry.

But Hudson is gone. There is a fraction of a second when I believe he has vanished or run away like Summer did earlier. Then I see him on the ground on his side. His legs and arms are stiff. His left leg jerks over and over, his right fingers splayed and spasming.

In an instant all the pieces of a very terrible puzzle click into place. The loss of consciousness. The spaciness. I suddenly know exactly what's wrong with Hudson.

"Did he pass out again?" Naomi's voice is nearly a whimper.

I am already on my knees, pushing a chair clear of his head.

"Get everything away from him," I say. "I think he's having a seizure."

GRIEVING PARENTS JOIN FORCES IN FUNDRAISING

Elle and Henry Price met Shawna and Bethany Kohler under the worst imaginable circumstances: their daughters—Hannah and Alexis, respectively—were both victims of the infamous Riverview Theater murders. "It started with lunches," Bethany said, when asked about their friendship. Elle added, "We were just shattered. Our lives were in ruins, but Shawna and Bethany understood. They'd lost their daughter too."

Shawna soon suggested turning their coffee and dinner meetings into fundraisers for silent sufferers, and Henry, a web developer, launched an event calendar. "So much suffering is silent," Elle added. "Heart conditions, grief, mental health disorders—no one sees those things, but they need our help." The couples have raised funds for grieving siblings and for seizure disorders, raising over $12,000 total in just two months.

"People want to help," Shawna said. "They just don't know where to start. So we picked a spot and started with a single step." When asked if they'll continue the monthly fundraisers, Shawna said no. "Someone came to us with an amazing new idea. We don't want to give it away, but we can't wait to support that. That's what's next for us."

CHAPTER 32

QUINCY QUICKLY OBEYS, PUSHING A TABLE AND ANOTHER chair away. I move behind Hudson, remembering the class, all the tips and tricks and things I should remember when someone is having a seizure. He is still spasming. His skull thumps the ground once. Again.

I cradle my hands behind his head, and the next time he seizes, he hits the padding of my palms instead of the hard floor. It is better but not perfect.

"Do we have anything soft? Like a towel?" I ask. There is a veneer of calm over my voice, but beneath that I'm roiling with terror. Still, I can hold it at bay. I can keep moving even with that fear rising. Maybe for now that's enough.

"We could go get T-shirts," Quincy says.

"Should we get a spoon?" Naomi asks, her voice shrieky and strained. "For his tongue or something?"

"No, just give him a minute." His head bashes my hands three more times before the twitching stops. I feel the change in his body, his neck softening under my fingers. His body goes limp shortly after. I leave one hand cradled under his head and hook my thumb under the collar of his shirt to pull out the silver chain I saw earlier.

A medical identification tag flashes at the end. I turn the metal disc over to read it:

Hudson Kumar

Seizure Disorder

On: Topamax—Allergies: Penicillin

"What's happening?" Naomi asks. Her voice is growing shriller. "Is he breathing?"

"Is he okay?" Quincy asks.

"He's okay. It's passed, I think. Can you just…"

"Let's give them some space," Quincy says. "We'll keep watch."

"Good idea," I say. "Not too far."

Quincy is quick to comply, leading Naomi to the edge of a built-in planter by one of the pillars. I refocus my attention on Hudson and try to slow my breathing.

His head is heavy on my palm, and leaning over him like this is sending a dull ache through my lower back. But I stay still and steady. Quiet and calm. His chest rises and falls evenly, his long dark lashes fanned out perfectly against his skin.

I feel him moving before I see it, his head shifting against my palm and then his arms reaching slowly. His eyes flutter open, but I can tell his gaze is drifting. Unfocused. I can tell, too, the moment clarity returns. His pupils shrink and sharpen, and his mouth thins.

"You had a seizure," I say softly. "You're okay. You're safe."

A crease forms between his brows, and he struggles to sit up. He makes me think of Cara when she was little. She used to wake up from naps shaky and confused, like the whole world was strange and unfamiliar.

"You're safe," I repeat. "You had a seizure, but it's over now."

"Yeah, I know," he says and then shakes his head. "About the seizure, I mean."

"Really? Because it was quite a surprise to me."

My voice is gentle, but a flush darkens the skin around his neck, so I know he catches my meaning. There are some medical conditions you shouldn't hide. Food allergies. Narcolepsy. Seizure disorders.

Across from us, Naomi cranes her neck to see how things are. I give her a thumbs-up but then hold up my hand to ask her for some time. She nods and returns to whatever whispered conversation she's having with Quincy.

"I read your necklace," I say.

"Right," he says.

"I didn't need to read the necklace to figure out you were having a seizure. That much was pretty clear. But when you passed out earlier, was that passing out or another seizure?"

He holds my gaze for a minute, like he's not sure he wants to tell me. I guess he wasn't the open book I thought. Maybe we all have our secrets.

"That was a seizure too," he says all in an exhale. Then the words tumble out one after the next. "I actually think I might have had one much earlier, but it was very small and short. I don't think anyone noticed."

I think of him earlier when he'd spaced out in the little alcove. Maybe that's what he was talking about.

"Have you always had them?" I ask.

He shakes his head. "There was a car accident. I was eleven, and my uncle was driving. A semi jumped the divider on the highway, and my uncle tried to swerve out of the way..."

His words fade, and I understand the quiet pause. Some details are too horrible to fill in.

"I'll take it the accident was bad?"

His laugh is gentle. "Very. It gave me this"—he points at the scar cutting through his brow—"and a side of seizure disorder."

"And your uncle?"

He shakes his head. "He wasn't wearing a seat belt. Didn't make it."

"I'm so sorry."

"Why? Did you jump a divider in your semi?"

I snort. "I can barely back into a parking spot. I think semis are out of the question."

Hudson moves to sit up further, and I wait to see if he needs help, but he doesn't. And then he touches the back of his head gingerly. He grimaces, and I feel my chest squeeze.

"You hit your head on the floor," I say. "I tried to get there—"

"Jo?"

His eyes are so warm, and his smile quirks up a little higher on one side than the other, and I realize with a shock that he's attractive. Like, not just attractive in the general sense but attractive to *me*.

"You do realize you're not responsible for the whole world and everyone in it, right?"

It's my turn to blush, a flash fire running up my neck that is undoubtedly turning my cheeks bright scarlet. "I know that."

"Do you?"

I shake my head and retreat to old habits, pivoting to a new subject. "Has this ever happened to you at work?"

"Once, but it was mild. Dumb shit that Clayton is, he assumed I'd snuck in my phone and was nodding along to some music."

We laugh, and when we stop, I bite my lip and look down. "Why didn't you ever tell me?"

"Well, I don't tend to lead with it when I introduce myself to pretty girls."

My cheeks feel hot again, but this is a different feeling, one I don't want to examine too closely. I look to the right, where he'd fallen, and frown. It's the second time he fell tonight. The third seizure.

"Wait, you said you only had one at work. Like ever?"

"Think so."

"You had three tonight. That sounds bad."

"Because my dumb ass forgot my medicine," he says. "One

dose would be fine normally, but I missed in the morning, and since I'm stuck here, I couldn't take the evening dose either."

"Two doses is all it takes?"

"Maybe. Maybe not. But when you add in a metric ton of stress? It's a recipe for bad things."

"Do you think you'll have any more?"

His mouth twists, and I see the worry behind his gaze now. Or maybe not worry, but something else. Is it guilt? Maybe shame?

I reach for his hand, giving his fingers a squeeze. "I just want to be ready so I can help. I don't want you to fall. I feel like you're in too much danger as it is."

"Don't be so dramatic, Jo. You act like there's a murderer on the loose."

We share a grin that feels good, even if I know it's lunacy to laugh about something like this. But then his smile fades, and this time it really is worry in his eyes. "I'm not sure I've ever had so many in a row like that. Not since the beginning. After the accident."

"Is there anything we can do to keep them at bay?"

"You mean like remove the stress of trying to get the hell out of here before something happens to you?"

I shake my head. "To me?"

But Hudson looks right at me. His dark eyes are crystal clear, and it's instantly obvious that his words came out exactly as intended. "Yeah, Jo. To you. Two years and you really haven't figured me out?"

His honesty is like nothing I've ever seen. He doesn't look away and laugh it off—he lays the words bare and holds my gaze. I'm the one who breaks away because I don't know what to do with this information. It's just one more surreal thing to add to the pile.

So I look at my folded knees and tuck my hair behind my ear, and finally, I manage to find my voice. "Well, I guess we have to make sure nothing else goes wrong."

"Things are starting to turn around."

I look up then, ready to argue, but maybe he's right.

Hudson is alive. He didn't bash his skull into the concrete floor. Or not to a point of serious damage, I don't think. This crisis didn't end in tragedy. He is here. Living and breathing and sort of flirting with me, which is weird, but overall... This is a turn in the right direction.

Hudson says, "Let's get to the arcade before that dick decides to come out of whatever shit pit he's hiding in."

I gesture for Quincy and Naomi to come over, and we scoot closer to the shadow of one of the kiosks. Overhead, the faintest trace of indigo is visible through the skylights. Dawn is coming. Help cannot be far away.

All we have to do is stay alive.

CHAPTER 33

"I WANT TO DO THIS CAREFULLY," I SAY. "I DON'T KNOW where he is, and I don't like it."

"Maybe he found a way out," Quincy says.

"I hope to hell not," Hudson says. "I want that asshole to rot for what he's done."

"Yeah, we all want that. And the faster we get someone here, the better," Naomi says.

"We need to pull an alarm," I say. "We need to get into the arcade."

"That entire end of the mall is boarded over," Quincy says. "I saw it when you were upstairs getting Hudson. There's plywood nailed across the entire building, from the old Starbucks all the way across to that hat store."

"Lids?" Naomi guesses.

"Yes, that one."

"Summer saw the alarms from the second floor. Was there an entrance up there?"

"No idea," Hudson says. "I don't remember one, though."

"Let's just go up," I say. "Summer saw the alarms up there, so obviously there's some way in, right?"

We debate the pros and cons of the different stairwells. The south stairwell is out, because that's the one Clayton took after he hunted for us on the third floor. It's possible he could still be in there. The open stairwell is an option, but I don't like the idea of climbing in a way that gives Clayton a clear, open shot if he did manage to sneak back out into the atrium. So we take the north stairs.

We ease the door open, and then, once we're inside, we close it with excruciating care. We are so quiet that I'm only sure the door is latched when I notice the complete absence of light. By wordless agreement, we do not use our flashlights. We climb in absolute darkness, inching our way quietly up the stairs one step at a time. I feel my way along the cold metal handrail, and then, at the second-floor landing, my hands sweep in front of me, brushing Naomi's hair, and then Hudson's T-shirt, and finally the rough brick of the concrete wall.

Hudson finds the door first and opens it quietly. We slip into the hallway, snaking our way along the wall, careful to stay in the shadows. The carpet swallows the sound of our footsteps, and all is quiet in the mall below. Sooner than I expected, we find ourselves at the northernmost edge of the mall, with enormous windows overlooking the arcade.

Driftwood letters hang above the boarded-over entrance,

spelling out the name—POSEIDON'S PLAYPLACE. A golden trident punctuates the space between the words, and I remember the arcade's theme. Riverview Fashionplace soothed shoppers with the gurgle of water, but Poseidon's Playplace enticed visitors with pirate music and undulating lights that made you feel like you'd slipped under the ocean waves.

Once upon a time, the place was pretty cool. Now it is a monstrosity. Empty tenpin lanes line the left wall, and graduating platforms rise like theater balconies on the back wall. Most of the first floor was devoted to arcade games, but they're long gone. Half the carpet is ripped up, and electrical wires jut from holes in the floor like long twisting worms.

There were bars inside the arcade too—nothing like liquor to keep the parents shoveling game money into kids' hands—and they now sit empty and dark. Tridents still perch on every wall, directing guests to different areas. Massive mirrors reflect endless images of each other. My eyes lock on a strangely untouched section—a pair of whack-'em games situated on either side of an oversized sledgehammer pad, the giant bell as gold and shiny as it was the first time I saw it.

"Why does this look creepy as hell?" Naomi says.

"Because it's basically a half-demolished abandoned indoor carnival," Hudson says.

"I agree," Quincy says. "It's quite disturbing, isn't it?"

"Maybe," I say, but then I spot a red light. A soap bubble of hope inflates in my chest. "But it's also going to be our salvation."

I point to the thing I've spotted at the far wall of the arcade, a small steady light barely visible through the window. Then I see another behind the whack-'em games, and my soap bubble feels stronger.

"Those are fire alarms," Quincy says, his voice low with wonder. "Summer was right."

"Correction," Hudson says. "Those look like *functioning* fire alarms."

A soft, grateful murmur moves through our small group, but then Hudson moves to the edge of the balcony, looking straight down at the expanse of glass wall. "One problem, Jo. How the hell do we get in?"

"I don't know yet," I say, turning around. The windows don't have latches or hinges, and there isn't an entrance here. The mostly glass expanse looks to be an impenetrable fortress. I scan the arcade's interior walls and notice a narrow metal walkway flanking the east and west sides of the room. Catwalks connect the walkways across the middle of the arcade. Maybe for access to the overhead wiring or the lighting systems. Maybe for something else. I don't really give a shit what the real purpose is. If those walkways are accessible from this floor, then we might have a way inside.

I walk back and forth along the glass, trying to get a better angle on the metal walkways. It's hard to see them clearly, but my further inspection makes it clear they provide access to the enormous overhead lights, dark bowl-shaped lamps dangling over the arcade from their spider-silk wires.

"What are you looking for?" Hudson asks.

"Access points," I say. "Do those walkways just dead-end into this wall?"

I walk to the farthest possible edge, trying to see the wall. I can't get the right angle, but if I crane my neck, right at the last pane of the window, I can see the edge of a doorframe and a spray-painted stencil that reads ELECTRICAL ROOM.

"There's a door up near the top," Quincy says. He is pressed against the glass now too, one cheek mashed against the middle pane. "I can see it over there. Something with an *E*."

"Electrical Room," I say.

I twist myself around to look at the stores we passed on the balcony. They were easy to ignore because nearly every opening was gated closed. But this part of the mall was a dead zone for me long before anything shut down. I remember a blur of boring stores. A mattress shop and an optometrist with rows of eyeglasses. An overpriced massage spa with new age music perpetually floating out. There's nothing helpful here, but I bet the third floor is a different story.

"I bet there's a door to the electrical room upstairs," I say. "I remember people wearing Poseidon staff shirts used to mill around up here."

"So there might be a way inside from the mall?"

I nod. "I think so."

"That means we need to go up?" Naomi asks, looking dubious at the idea.

"Can't think of any better options," Hudson says.

"Okay, but what if we didn't keep moving around?" she asks.

I tilt my head. "I'm not sure what you mean."

"It's almost dawn, and we know someone is coming soon," she says. "Cara will wake up or Hudson's mom will get home. We could barricade ourselves in one of the offices and wait for someone to find us."

"I thought of that too," Quincy says. "But I'm concerned that searching a building of this size might take more time than we think."

"Plus, we won't be their first priority," Hudson says. "When they come, they'll start with the theater."

"Which means they'll find Lexi," Naomi says. Her voice grows soft and sad as she puts together the terrible truth. "They'll be focused on investigating a murder."

Several murders, actually.

There's another problem with waiting. I glance at Quincy's arm and then at Hudson. I can still feel the weight of his head against my palm, and I still have Quincy's blood on my clothes.

"I think Quincy needs to get to a doctor about his arm," I say. "And Hudson's had some weird things too."

He shoots me a surprised look. Maybe he's grateful that I didn't spill his secret. Or maybe he's annoyed I mentioned him at all.

We decide on the same stairwell that took us to the second floor. It's nearby, and we haven't heard any indicators that

Clayton is close. Right now, those are the best conditions we're likely to get.

Inside, the stairwell's darkness is suffocating. We bunch into a group, hesitant to move. Hudson tries his light, but the beam flickers in and out.

"Just turn it off," I say softly. "Everybody grab the handrail. We did the dark before, right?"

Hudson flicks off the light, and we are plunged into darkness so thick I feel I might choke on it. I wait for a moment, remembering to use my hands. To move slowly.

"It's...really dark," Naomi says. As quiet as she is, her voice still echoes off the bare concrete walls.

"I know. I just want to save the batteries in case we really need them," I say.

"Are we ready to move?" Hudson asks, his voice a low and reassuring murmur above me.

"We'll go slow like last time," I say.

We climb in unison, ascending the steps in a slow, easy rhythm. It is the same as the first climb, but uneasiness begins to build in my chest, growing stronger with every step. My body tenses, expecting the third-floor door to fly open, for Clayton to come barreling down. But we reach the final landing without incident.

"Everyone okay?" I ask, my voice shaking. I am winded and unsettled by the darkness and our closeness. I smell the cocoa butter of Naomi's hair and hear the faint ruffle of Hudson pushing his hands through his hair. Quincy, as usual, is still, but I think I can feel him shifting on his feet beside me.

"Can we get out of here?" Naomi asks quietly.

"I'm trying," Hudson says, and I hear him feeling around the smooth metal door until the telltale metal jiggle of a door handle meets my ears.

He twists and grunts.

"Is it locked?" I ask because it shouldn't be locked. Do the stairwell doors even have locks?

"No, it's just really stuck."

"Here, let me try."

"Sure, Jo, I'm sure all ninety pounds of you is going to manage—"

A distinct *cha-chunk* beneath us cuts Hudson off. I suck in a tight breath. Maybe I was wrong. Maybe I imagined it. But then I hear the unmistakable sound of heavy feet below. Someone just stepped into the stairwell.

How do you believe in your own goodness when you know something like that? Maybe one day I'll learn to make peace with what I did. Maybe we all have to make peace with that night, with the fact we're here and they're gone.

CHAPTER 34

NAOMI'S HAND REACHES FOR MY WRIST, AND HER fingers are cold on my skin. She is not breathing. None of us are breathing. We are all hoping, wishing, praying for him to change his mind—to turn around.

Clang!

Clang!

Clang!

The noise is so sharp and loud that it hurts my ears. He's hitting the railing with something, and I have the same feeling that I had when he punched the plastic. We are rabbits hiding in the dark. And Clayton is a hunter trying to scare us out of our holes.

Fear curls cold fingers around my spine. We have to get out of here. Ten minutes ago wouldn't be soon enough. But if we move a single muscle, he will hear us. A hiccup, a burp—*anything* could give us away and send him bounding up these stairs in the darkness. He could use whatever thing he's banging on the banister to beat us to death.

Or Hudson could drop into another seizure.

Or Quincy could pass out from blood loss.

Or Clayton could shoot us dead.

Because Clayton has already killed three people. He has less than nothing to lose by adding us to the list.

Hudson tenses behind me, and my gut tells me he is going for the door. He's going to try to push it open, but Clayton hasn't moved. He might not have heard us. Maybe he'll give up and turn around if we wait. Just a little longer.

I reach for Hudson, curling my fingers in his shirt and stretching until I am very close to his face—to his ear, specifically. He smells like licorice and boy and popcorn.

"Wait." I breathe the word so softly I'm not sure he's heard me. But his body relaxes the tiniest bit, and he remains still. Naomi and Quincy are also still—we are clustered together hoping for Clayton to change his mind.

Clang!

I flinch. We all flinch, but we all stay silent. And then I hear the door handle release, the door swinging shut. Is he leaving? Did he really leave?

I sag in relief, dragging a shivering breath into my lungs. And then I hear the scrape and hiss of a shoe moving across cement on the bottom floor. A whine sounds behind my ears, and adrenaline is a starburst in my chest, a terrible zipping rush. Footsteps, first one, and then another, start making their way up the stairs.

Clayton is climbing the steps. He is coming for us.

Hudson does not need my direction. His body shifts, and I hear the door handle twist again. There is an awful scrape of metal on concrete. The door is open a couple of inches, murky light spilling through the gap. It is not enough. He is pushing with all his might, but the door gives little grunts of resistance.

I can't hear Clayton. I don't know what's happening, but I know we are running out of time. We can't fight him off in this tight dark space. We have to run.

I lunge for the opening in the door, wrapping my sweaty fingers around the outside edge. I cannot hear anything over my own heart and the metal-on-concrete scraping. I push until my arms shake, until my fingers slip on the frame. It is barely seconds, but it feels like minutes. Hours, even.

Naomi joins in, our bodies and hands mashed together. Clayton is climbing fast. He's coming for us. My heart beats so hard that my chest aches. There are elbows in my face, shoulders bumping my chin. We jerk in a steady rhythm, over and over and over and—

The door gives, wrenching open another seven or eight inches. It sticks again, but the gap is wider. Is it wide enough? It has to be. I'll make it wide enough.

Hudson squeezes through and reaches for me, hauling me into the hallway. My ear bumps metal, and my stomach scrapes the plate of the doorjamb, but I am out. I am out!

I reach through, finding Naomi's arm. She is small and lithe, and she slips through easier than either of us. I push her aside and reach for Quincy. Is there movement on the stairs behind him? Oh my God, I can't tell. I don't know what I'm looking at. I pull with all my might, and though Quincy is smaller, he gets stuck, more than once. His feet, his head. Hudson joins me, and we tug him together. Quincy spills out of the gap with a cry that cuts through my stomach like a knife.

He groans, hand grabbing for his injured arm. I am reaching for him, even as Hudson hurls his whole body at the stairwell door.

"Help me, Naomi!" he cries.

I can hear Clayton. His footsteps. His rasping breathing. Naomi rushes to push with Hudson, the door scraping. Scraping. I push too, until my palms burn and my wrists ache.

Quincy is on the ground now, his face twisted with agony.

"I'm so sorry," I say. "Quincy, I'm so sorry."

He shakes his head to dismiss my apology, but when he tries to speak, nothing comes out but a terrible low groan.

"Is there anything I can do?" I ask.

"The door!" Hudson roars.

I jerk my attention back to the door and see the tips of Clayton's fingers at the edge. My heart leaps into the back of my throat. We have to stop him!

Hudson jogs back a few paces and then sprints at the door with a cry. He slams his whole body into the surface and the door scrapes shut with a decisive bang.

"Hold it!" Hudson says, then he jogs down the hallway,

checking office door after office door. He finds one that's open and disappears inside, returning with the spindly arm of an office chair.

"It's not much," he says, cramming the bar under the thin gap in the door. "I have no idea how long it will hold."

"We can run for the other stairs," Naomi says.

I shake my head, looking around. "No. We've got to get into the arcade. We've got to pull that alarm. If we pull the alarm, the police will come."

"And if they don't come soon enough?" Hudson asks, panting.

"Get that shit out of your head," Naomi says.

I swallow. "If we find a way in, we can find a way to lock him out," I say.

"She's right," Quincy says. "We can figure it out. Let's go."

We race down the hallway. Or try to race. Quincy doesn't have much race in him, but he does what he can. At the north end, the arcade wall, I expect a locked door. To my surprise, we find an unmarked hallway to the right with several doors inside. I don't really care what those first doors hold. The third door in has two words stamped below the frame.

ELECTRICAL ROOM

There is yellow tape across this door, but when we tear it away, it is blessedly unlocked. Hudson pulls the door open a few inches to reveal a grated metal platform. Beyond it a narrow bridge stretches across a cavernous room. My chest feels warm and light. That's the catwalk we saw in the arcade. This is the room we were looking for.

We step inside and a stale, vaguely industrial smell engulfs us. Quincy is shuffling at this point. His lips look pale, and he is clearly in serious pain.

We gather on the small platform inside the door. The metal grate floor shudders beneath our feet, and I don't dare look down. Instead I look around. There are electrical panels and signs, and two yellow safety vests that lay in a heap near one corner. At another corner I see a stack of clipboards and an empty package of industrial light bulbs.

And then there is nowhere to look but down. The arcade sprawls below us, a nightmare of shadowy shapes. Seeing it from above brings my memories into focus. The arcade used graduating floors. The first floor was the largest, with the tenpin bowling, arcade games, and bars littered with yard games like cornhole and giant Yahtzee. The back third of the first floor is an elaborate underwater-themed miniature golf course with faux coral reef walls, fake shipwrecks, and Escher-like stairs that guide players 'round and 'round on themselves as they work through the holes. The third floor, which only extends thirty feet or so over the second floor, is entirely devoted to laser tag. It holds the same underwater theme, with giant gritty rocks and ledges perfect for hiding. I was a master at hiding in that maze.

Then, I guess I'm a master of hiding everywhere.

The miniature golf and laser tag weren't visible from our last angle. Now they cast monstrous shadows under the emergency lights. *The emergency lights.* These aren't just the ones on battery backup or auxiliary power like the other lights we've seen. These are brighter and more plentiful. Even the red EXIT signs are lit, though I see plywood nailed over the exit in each one. But best of all: there are windows—too high to serve as an escape, but through them, I can see the northern edge of the parking lot and a ribbon of interstate in the distance. A few cars zip along under the mottled predawn sky.

The world is still out there. Life has not ended, and seeing proof of it is enough to send a bubble of hope floating up through my chest. Quincy hisses in pain, and the bubble pops. We are not out of here yet. I turn to Quincy, who's reaching gently at his injured arm. He doesn't touch, but his hand hovers above the bandage as if he can will the pain to stop.

"Is it bad?" I ask.

He shakes his head, but a sheen of sweat has broken out on his face, and I can tell the pain is intense. I tilt my head to get a look at his arm and feel my stomach drop. A red stain is spreading through the white gauze. He's bleeding again.

"I see the alarm," Hudson says, pointing down to the ground floor. "There. Do you see it behind that round bar? It's glowing bright as Rudolph's nose."

I smile at Quincy. "Okay, so there's some good news."

"You have bad news?" he asks, looking wan.

"The bad news is you're bleeding again, and you've done enough of that today."

"Yeah, we need to hurry," Naomi says. "We need to hit that alarm."

Naomi eyes the catwalk warily. I don't think heights are her favorite, and looking at the walkway, I see why. We are three stories up. I can see stairs at the far-left corner of the third floor. The platforms are connected by long catwalks. Bridges stretched over certain death. Or at the very least certain fractured bones.

"I think we'll need to do it one at a time," Quincy says.

He nods to a sign next to the catwalk.

WARNING: 250-POUND LIMIT—ONE AT A TIME!

"How long is this walk exactly?" Naomi asks.

I understand her worry. I'm not easily unsettled by heights, but this catwalk is maybe eighteen inches wide. The platform is shuddering every time we move, so I can't even imagine what it will feel like to be on that bridge. Even looking at it makes me queasy.

"We need to head down about thirty yards to the second platform there." Hudson points to a small patch of metal platform that appears to be nine hundred miles away. Then he points to the left of that, where the next catwalk looks like a piece of dental floss stretched between two points. "Then we take the second catwalk to the stairs at the edge of the third-floor balcony."

"Right," I say. And then I squirm, looking at Quincy's arm. Thinking of the way Hudson dropped not even an hour ago. Something could happen up here. Something could go very, very wrong.

A faint scraping interrupts my thoughts, as if a stuck window is being forced open several rooms away. But that's not what it is.

"We need to hurry," I say, and no one disagrees. Because we all know what we heard. It was a door opening. More specifically, it was a killer getting out of that stairwell.

CHAPTER 35

"MOVE," HUDSON SAYS. "GO NOW AND GO FAST."

"Um. No." Naomi cocks her head at the bridge. "Since you're the only one of us who isn't a little freaked out about walking on that thing, you can go first to test it out."

"Clayton's in the hallway," Hudson hisses. "How long do you think we have?"

"Just go," I whisper. "Naomi, you'll follow him, right?"

"How is this even safe for workers to use?" Quincy asks, looking at the rickety handrails. "This feels like a significant fall risk."

"They probably used safety harnesses," Hudson says, and then he rubs the back of his neck. "Which we don't have."

Hudson takes a step onto the catwalk, and my mind flashes an image of him prone and twitching on the ground. There was no warning before his last seizure. He was talking to us, and then he was down. Hudson has had three seizures tonight. What if he has one now?

I grab his arm before he can take another step. "Wait."

But when he looks at me, I don't know what to say. He can't stay here. He has to go—we all have to go if we're going to make it out of here alive. But the idea of something else happening him is like a fist to my throat.

Hudson smirks at me, his bleached hair hanging in his face. His smile is lopsided. "Don't worry, Jo. I'll try really hard not to fall."

Before I can say anything else, he steps off the platform and starts his way across the catwalk. His first step sends us bobbling like a boat over a wave. It doesn't get much better. Every step Hudson takes makes the platform jump under our feet. Watching him cross, I grip the railing so hard the metal bites into my hands.

Naomi starts to softly pray, and I close my eyes too. For the first time in almost a decade, I want to believe there is someone up there looking out for us. Someone who wants to see Hudson get to the other side of this walkway.

He reaches the next platform without incident, and now I've got new worries to face. Quincy looks truly ill. His skin is some unnatural mix of gray and yellow and his forehead is shiny with sweat.

"How are you feeling?" I ask him.

"Not my best," he says. "I think you might be right about getting a doctor."

The red stain has spread to the edges of the bandage. He's

ripped something open again, and the bleeding isn't what it was before, but any bleeding isn't awesome at this point.

I force a tight smile. "Once you get to the other side, you can sit. We'll hit that alarm, and the rescue team will arrive in five minutes, I bet."

"Nine, probably," he says with a wan smile. "According to a recent news article, average response time in Sandusky is nine minutes. They're struggling with staffing."

"Nine minutes it is, then," I say. And then I approach him with a serious expression. "Quincy, please hold on to the railing every step of the way—"

A rattling interrupts me. It's nowhere near as distant as the last noise we heard. It's in the hallway, I think. Maybe one of the other doors. My heart skitters out of rhythm. I put my hand on Quincy's shoulder and whisper, "Go. Go right now."

Quincy looks gravely at the walkway and takes a step. His footsteps shudder through the metal platform. He moves his hands down the railing, and I see his arms shake.

Another faint rattle and thump sounds from the hallway. This one is closer than the last. Which means Clayton is closer. How many doors were before ours?

Two. There were only two. He's going to come here as soon as he realizes the room he's in is empty.

"Jo?" Naomi's eyes are round with fear. She's heard it too, but I see her freezing over, her whole body stiff as she stares at the door. Waiting for the devil to come through.

"Follow Quincy," I whisper desperately, looking around for something to hold Clayton off or slow him down. I spot a tub of random cables and detritus on the far wall. I rush for it, feeling the platform shudder as my knees shake. I hear footsteps. He's back in the hallway. We're next.

I spot Naomi out of the corner of my eye, still hesitating at the mouth of the catwalk. Beyond her I can see Quincy more than halfway across.

"Naomi, you have to go," I whisper. "Go now."

"He isn't across!"

"You have to go. Clayton is coming."

The footsteps are drawing closer. I haul an extension cord out of the box. My hands are shaking so badly I nearly drop the cord. I loop the plastic coated cord around the handle of the door and reach for the rail around the platform. I am not a Boy Scout, and I don't know knots, but I do what I can, looping and pulling and doubling the cord around the platform railing. I pull it as tight as I can.

"I can't do it," she says.

I turn to her then, noticing the way her body is trembling. She's afraid. And of course she's afraid—nothing about the past eight hours hasn't been completely terrifying. But right now, there isn't time for being afraid. There is only time to survive.

"Naomi, walk," I whisper. "Cara needs us to live. That's what you said, so walk!"

Naomi takes her first step onto the catwalk. Quincy is only

two-thirds of the way across, and he is moving slow. My heart thumps harder and faster. I am running out of time. *We* are running out of time.

Naomi takes another step and the doorknob twists. I whirl to see the door push open a single inch. The electrical cord pulls taut, and the door sticks. I bite back the scream building in my throat and will Quincy to move faster. Faster!

The cord holds. Maybe Clayton will walk right on past. Maybe he will give up. Maybe he will hear something else or Quincy's parents will have landed and called the police. I make a lot of desperate wishes, but I made wishes when my father was bleeding out too. Not a single one of those came true, so if I want to survive this, I'm going to have to fight.

I move for the mouth of the catwalk. Hudson is watching from the other platform, his eyes fierce and terrified at once. And then I realize his eyes aren't actually on me. He's looking at the door from the hallway to the platform, the one a mere ten feet behind me.

I turn and look over my shoulder just in time to see the door push again. Thick pink fingers poke through the gap, fingering the electrical cord tying the door shut.

Are we in big trouble?

Cara's voice is in my mind—in my ears from almost a decade back. I know the answer to her question. Yes, we're in trouble. We're in very big trouble.

CHAPTER 36

HOW MUCH IS 250 POUNDS? MORE THAN ME AND NAOMI, maybe. Less than me, Naomi, and Quincy, definitely. But when I see Clayton's fingers plucking at that electrical cord, my respect for weight limits vanishes. I silently urge Quincy to move faster. Every step he takes seems to come slower than the last, but I can't wait another second. I set my foot onto the catwalk and try not to think about weight limits or structural integrity or the noises coming from the door behind me.

Clayton is struggling with the cord. He's trying to open my makeshift lock. I take a tentative step onto the platform, and it groans in protest. Naomi freezes and the catwalk sways. Quincy is still a few steps away from the opposite platform, and the addition of our motion isn't helping. The metal beneath our feet jiggles and shifts.

I twist back to find it is not the only thing in motion. Clayton is moving too, ripping at the cord that's looped over the handle. He is going to get through. We have no time. My nerves are buzzing and jangled. The handrails feel rubbery underneath my grip, and my knees threaten to buckle with every step.

"Hurry, Naomi," I whisper.

I look down and instantly regret it. The miniature golf course is below me. Seussian bridges and otherworldly towers protrude from the floor. I envision a thousand ways to bash, break, or impale myself. My head swims, but I take another step. The metal beneath my feet groans and shudders, and Naomi begins to cry in earnest.

My head snaps up as Hudson helps Quincy off the catwalk, though his eyes are clearly on me. Quincy is pale and sweating, obviously much worse than he was before, and Naomi isn't moving. She hasn't taken a step. I try to find my voice, but my stomach and throat are squeezing so tight, it's hard to breathe.

And the commotion at the door is getting louder. I can tell there's more give now. My makeshift lock won't hold forever.

I do not look back, and I do not look down. I rush down the catwalk, ignoring every jump and wobble of the floor beneath me until I am right behind Naomi.

I nudge her gently. "Come on," I say. "We've got to go."

The catwalk groans and something pops. I swallow a cry and Naomi whimpers, and her fingers tighten on the rails. Quincy is fully off the catwalk now, and the loss of his weight only makes things worse. We are on a trampoline bobbling in the wind, and even Naomi's hitching breaths send us bouncing.

"Naomi, please," I say.

Naomi sobs, and her body grows tight and still. She is shutting down. She is me ten years ago, my hands over Cara's eyes and my body paralyzed by terror. But the time for gentle is over. We can't stop. We're not quite halfway across, and I know he will hear us. I know—

The door opens with a bang, and I turn around. Clayton is there in the doorway. He is so much taller and larger than us—his shoulders fill up what seems like every inch of space. For one moment, I think it is surprise I see in his face, and then a horrific grin stretches his mouth wide.

"Found you," he singsongs.

Terrible scenarios rush through my mind. He will shoot me in the back. He will shoot Naomi. He will shoot both of us, and it won't matter if the shot is lethal. We will fall three stories onto the sharp points of the Putt-Putt buildings and ridges. We will be broken and impaled. Naomi will fall, and I will fall, and this will be over. We will die here tonight like Lexi and Hannah and Summer.

But we can't. That can't be how this ends when we are so close. I can see the red glow of promised rescue on the other side of this arcade: one more walkway and down the stairs, and there's an alarm right there on the back wall of a platform that used to house ticket games and Skee-Ball lanes.

Clayton's weight shifts on the platform behind us, and pins and needles race across my skin.

"Naomi, move!" Hudson shouts. "Move right now!"

Crack! Crack!

I hunch over instinctively, and Naomi screams. The first thing I see is the shift in Hudson's face, the way all his features go slack. His expression is pure terror. Which tells me that crack I heard was the thing I feared. Clayton is shooting.

Crack! Ping!

"Run!" I scream.

She doesn't move. All I can see are her dark hands holding the silver handrails, her knuckles gone pale with the intensity of her grip. She is sagging and weeping, and I scan her body quickly, frantically searching for blood. A wound. Some evidence a bullet has found purchase. There is nothing.

"Please," I say, my voice cracked and flat. "Please, Naomi!"

Beyond her, Hudson is ashy, his arm stretched as far as he can reach onto the catwalk. The metal groans, and I dare a glance over my shoulder. Clayton is moving toward the mouth of the catwalk. He's trying to get closer, and when he does, those bullets will stop missing.

Crack!

Naomi sobs and releases the handrails. And then she sprints. She closes the distance to the next platform with hard, heavy steps that send me lurching up and down. I hold on tight and watch as Hudson pushes her behind him, yells at her to get Quincy, to keep moving down the next catwalk.

My joints are wobbly and weak, and my head throbs. The walkway gives a long croak behind me, and I feel my balance shifting. Clayton takes another step, and something pops beneath my feet. A bolt or a joint. Something is giving way. I think of his wide shoulders and thick arms. His bulk and weight—it's too much.

"Run for it, Jo," Hudson says. He reaches both hands to me. "It's going to give. Run!"

I take a breath and lunge forward. I'm braced for the gun to shoot again, but instead there is the shriek of buckling metal—a car crash in slow motion. Another pop beneath me, so hard it bounces my feet up off the walkway.

I land on my heels, and the walkway pitches hard to the right. Hudson bellows my name as my feet slide. My whole body is sliding, toppling. I wrap my arm around the handrail and try to move forward, and metal pops and groans with a bone-deep shudder.

Clayton screams as the walkway rips free from the platform where we started.

The catwalk is collapsing. All I can do is hook my arms around the handrail and hold on.

CHAPTER 37

THE CATWALK DOES NOT HIT. IT DOES NOT SNAP AND FALL in a spectacular bang. It is a pendulum on a string, swaying left to right.

Left to right.

Left to right.

The swaying slows, and the handrail digs into the crooks of my elbows, the pain reminding me I'm still very much alive. And I want to stay that way.

I open my eyes and look up. Hudson's face looms into view. He is stretched out over the side of the platform, so close I can almost touch him.

But almost isn't enough to get me out of this.

I squeeze both arms around the handrail and bicycle my legs, my feet banging against the metal walkway that is now sloping down. There is no foothold or rough edge to find. It's like going up the slide at the playground, only worse.

At the playground, if you fall, you will tumble in a sea of

giggles. You will land, feet first or butt first on grass or rubberized mulch six inches below you. But if I fall…

"Don't look down."

Hudson. His voice is unusually steady, like he's suggesting an option from the dessert menu. I look at him. A haze has dropped over my vision, and his face is the only thing I see clearly. Naomi and Quincy are blurry, but I see them hunched over Hudson's back. They're holding him over the edge. Steadying him so he can reach for me.

Hudson's shoulders and arms dangle, his hands stretching for me.

"Push me farther," he says.

"We can't," Naomi says. "We can barely hold you now."

"Jo." Hudson's face is red, all the blood rushing downward. He's trying to help me, but I'm just beyond his fingertips. "I need you to reach for me."

"I can't," I say. My arms are shaking, and my hands are slick with sweat. I know they will slip. If I unlock my arms, even for a second—if I move at all, I'm going to fall. "I can't."

"Bullshit. You hung on when Clayton fell," he says. "You're here for a reason. You're still here."

I swallow hard, my arms vibrating with the strain of my grip.

"You heard me. That bastard dropped like a stone, but you hung on, and it had to be for a reason. Now try! Try, Jo!"

Every ounce of my strength is directed at keeping my grip locked on to this handrail. I pretend I am gathering my strength, but deep down I know how this ends. I am watching Hudson's eyes, and I am waiting to fall.

Waiting to die.

"Jo!" Hudson shouts. "You're in big trouble, and you need to fight!"

Are we in big trouble?

Cara's baby voice flutters through my mind again, her small arms around my neck, her fingers sticky with Lemonheads. We *were* in big trouble that day. Sixty seconds after my sister whispered those words into my ear, our father would drop to the ground, shot three times in the chest. And sixty seconds after that, he would be dead.

But we would live.

We crawled out of that hole awkwardly, with my hands still over Cara's eyes and our universe shattered into a million unspeakable pieces. But we grabbed those pieces and cobbled something new together. We took what we could, and we moved forward. And every day that Cara and I are breathing, a little piece of Dad is alive too.

My arm slips an inch, the skin in the crease of my elbow pinching painfully. Every joint in my arms, from my fingers to my shoulders, is screaming with pain. But now I see Hudson is right. If I stay still, I die.

I need to move, not so I can save someone else. I want to save myself.

I grab my right wrist with my left hand and pull with my

abs, my biceps, with every muscle I have. I curl myself in on that railing, and when I look up to Hudson again, I reach. My fingers miss, and my right arm shakes wildly. My whole body trembles. I move my arm again, slapping the side of Hudson's wrist. And then I've got him, my fingers curling around his wrist in a death grip.

Hudson grabs my arm with both hands, and then he takes over. He hauls me upward with a roar, and then there are other hands on me. I smell cocoa butter and dried blood and licorice. I feel Naomi's nails and the brush of Quincy's hair and they are clawing, digging, grabbing at me. They pull me without mercy. Fingers pinch and my collar rips, but then I am up. I am on the platform.

I flop belly first on the metal grate, seeing a swirl of shadows and shapes below. We are a heap of arms and legs. We smell awful, and we look even worse, but I'm alive. I'm still alive. I push myself to my hands and knees, and everything in me wobbles. I almost topple before I'm even on my feet, but I catch myself.

"I'm okay," I say. I don't know who I'm telling, but the words feel good coming out of my mouth. "I'm okay. I'm okay."

"Thank God," Naomi says, sounding winded. She sinks at the back of this platform, as close to the walls as she can get. Quincy is beside her, looking ghostly pale.

Hudson pats me over, my hair, my shoulders, my hands. Then, he nods. "We have to hit that alarm, now. Can you do that with me?"

"Where's the closest one?" I ask.

"Down the stairs at the back platform, see?"

I follow the direction he's pointing and put together the full shape of the platform and walkways. The entire upper floor is surrounded by walkways shaped like a wide squared-off U. Small platforms punctuate both ends and both junctions. Or they did. Now one of the sides is broken, dangling from each platform uselessly. What we have left is half a square. The opposite wall of the arcade is fifty feet away. There are two doors that lead to the opposite platforms, with markings too faint and distant to read. Only a single set of stairs joins these walkways to the main floor, and it's situated at the second junction, twenty-five yards away.

The fire alarm glows like a beacon on the bottom floor. My chest feels swollen with something light and bright as I spot another fire alarm. And then another. And another on the back wall. There are at least four alarms down there. We are twenty-five yards and three flights of stairs away from ending this. And our biggest threat just fell three stories.

I search the shadowy floor, looking for Clayton's body. I search the strange slopes of the miniature golf greens and the oddly barren wires that used to tether arcade games to the floor.

"He's right there," Hudson says, reading my mind. He points to a lump of clothing beneath the first platform. The edge of two miniature golf holes is underneath Clayton, with a half-busted bridge spanning both. "He hit that bridge on his way down, but he hasn't moved."

My shoulders relax, and I glance back at the red light nearest to the stairs. It's an easy trip. Down the stairs and across two miniature golf holes. Then up five steps to the back platform wall. We can make this whole trip in three minutes, I bet.

"Let's get this alarm," I say.

"Ready when you are," Hudson says.

But neither Quincy nor Naomi shift from their perch near the corner. Naomi looks at the walkway and then back at me. The naked fear in her gaze is unmistakable.

"Yeah, I don't think I can mentally handle it after that," Naomi admits.

"I'm not sure I'll be able to do it physically," Quincy says. "Not without a bit of rest."

He looks terrible, and she looks petrified. Neither one of them can do this right now. We're on our own.

"You and me, then," Hudson says. "We'll hit that alarm and get some damn rescue-ranger white knight types to come and save the day."

"Hold tight," I tell them. "We're going to get help."

"Just cross that platform one at a time, all right?" Naomi says with a smirk.

I offer a weak laugh. "No problem."

Hudson starts out on the walkway first, and I call out after him when he's a few feet away. "Don't stop to wait for me. Just keep going until you're downstairs and you've hit the alarm."

He doesn't answer, so I wait at the edge of the platform. He is halfway across the catwalk when I hear something on the bottom floor. A soft shuffle. The barest scrape.

No. I'm imagining things. Seeing bogeymen in the shadows. There's noth—

A low whimper interrupts my thought. My throat constricts. Below me, I can't see the shadows moving, but I can hear it. Soft and indistinct, but real. I don't know specifics, but one thing is clear—something is moving down there. Some*one* is moving.

I swallow hard and check Hudson's progress. Two-thirds of the way across.

"Everything good?" Naomi asks.

"Totally good," I lie.

And then there is a low, pained groan, faint but unmistakable. Naomi sucks in a tight breath behind me.

"Jo?"

"I know," I whisper. "I heard it too."

I glance down through my feet to see the shadowy lump Hudson pointed out earlier. It's moving on the floor below. My heart drops through my chest and my stomach like a brick.

I see an arm extend. The faintest suggestion of blond hair and a pale face turned up to the ceiling. Even from here, it's clear he's struggling to move. After falling like that, it's a miracle he's moving at all.

Clayton is still very much alive, but he's in bad shape. I take a breath to steady my nerves. He is not a threat to us in this condition. I just need to get to the alarm before he manages to find his gun.

RIVERVIEW THEATER LAWSUIT
SETTLED OUT OF COURT

Published 4:21 p.m. on September 4, 2023

The plaintiff and defendant in the well-publicized case have reached an agreement. PDG Development will pay the plaintiff damages in the amount of $415,000. Damages will benefit the Kohler-Price Foundation.

CHAPTER 38

THE SECOND HUDSON REACHES THE NEXT PLATFORM, I clap twice.

"What the he—"

I cut him off with my hand, my palm facing out in the universal signal to stop. Then I press my finger desperately to my lips. Please. Please understand.

It is hard to make out Hudson's face in this light, but he stays silent. He sees me well enough to read my expression. Let's hope that trend continues. I point straight down at the floor once. Twice. A third time to be sure he gets it.

Hudson's shoulders tense when he understands. There is more movement and another groan below, and I realize I am running out of time. I have no way of knowing how injured Clayton is. For all I know he managed to hold on to his gun and avoided breaking anything critical. If I'm going to make it across this walkway without drawing his attention or potentially getting shot, my best bet is to do it right now.

I pad along the walkway like a cat, my hands barely touching the handrails. With every step, I hear him moving below me. The drag of shoes across the concrete. The cry of pain when he moves in a way that hurts. I am halfway across when I dare to whisper at Hudson.

"Go! The stairs!"

He nods and starts toward them, shakes his head, and stretches out his hand. He's not going without me. I'm not sure if the relief I'm feeling shows on my face, but it should. I don't want to do this alone. And if we're together I can watch his back. For one moment, my gaze pauses on the door behind Hudson, the door that opens onto the platform. Is that another way into the mall? It's cracked open, and I'm afraid, wondering what might be hiding in the darkness.

But then I realize nothing is hiding. The only monster here is groaning and struggling three stories below. We're headed straight toward the only thing we need to fear.

The instant I reach the platform, I hear Clayton lumber to his feet. We all but hurl ourselves down the three flights of stairs, with Hudson in the lead. On the last flight, I'm stopped short by Hudson, who's struggling with a latch.

The last several stairs are folded up, chained to the platform above, probably to keep curious gamers from climbing into the rafters. Hudson finally unlatches the chain holding the stairs closed, and before I can warn him or help, it swings down, slamming into the concrete floor with a shocking bang.

We lock eyes, and I strain my ears, but there is no sound. No shuffling or footsteps or groans. Wherever Clayton is, he heard that. And he has gone completely and utterly quiet.

"What is it?" I ask.

"I don't see him," he says. He points at the area below the first platform—the area where I saw Clayton's body. "He was there, I swear it."

"I know," I say. But the spot is empty now, Clayton long gone. "Hurry. Just hurry."

I know this silence isn't good. We can't hear Clayton, but he sure as hell heard us. And if he still has his gun, that means we are back to exactly where we started. We are running for our lives.

"The alarm," I say.

We move for the closest red light, up a small platform about twenty yards away. There were ticket games up here once, little cranes that could collect tiny stuffed animals and rotating discs piled with tokens gamers could try to dislodge with a robotic arm. We make our way across the ratty carpet, tripping over loose electrical cords and moving around holes in the floor. We start up the five stairs that lead to the platform, and my foot slams through the flooring, scraping both sides of my ankle and calf.

I bite back a scream, and Hudson catches me by the elbows, hauls me up, and pulls me in. I feel the warm, wet trickle of blood inside my jeans. Pain blooms across my skin in throbbing waves, and I realize this is one of a dozen holes on the platform. Maybe more than that.

I shake my head. "We can't risk that happening five feet off the ground."

"Agreed," Hudson says, and then he points to a section of wall near the Putt-Putt course. Another light glows there. "Let's get that one."

I nod and we're off again, retracing our steps and heading to the alarm on the other side of the stairwell.

There's something unnerving about the silence. When Clayton was groaning, I knew where to find him, I knew how to triangulate the danger, but now he could be anywhere. We move through the miniature golf course, cutting across a hole with a giant trident spanning a small sea cave. Starfish bumpers create obstacles for a golfer's ball and present more shit to trip on in the dark.

We weave our way over the bumpers and across a small stone wall separating this hole from another. The next one slopes wildly downward and to the right. The alarm is straight ahead. The tall faux-reef walls tower up on either side of the green, creating a tunnel that leads right to the alarm.

It's like being inside the cubby all over again. I fight against memories of my father pushing me back, my knees bumping the safe as I crawled inside the cubby with Cara. I shake it off, ignoring the walls. We are almost there. We are almost—

Something moves at the top of the wall to our right.

I freeze for one moment, grabbing Hudson's arm. The shadow moves, lurking behind the faux coral ridge. My throat goes dry.

Clayton's up there. I don't know how. It makes no sense, but he's there. And if he jumps now, there will be nowhere to run.

"Hudson," my voice curls up at the end like a question.

Clayton leaps from the wall, and as he falls, I'm sure this is how it will end. But before the thought can even fully course through my mind, Clayton lands and instantly crumples, a howl of agony rising through the air. He rolls to the side, clutching a foot. His nose is bloody, and one cheek is bashed in, the skin around his eye bloody and grotesquely swollen.

He isn't the strongest man in the room anymore. He's the man who fell off the walkway three stories above. Just like Hannah fell. Except there's a big difference.

Hannah didn't deserve to die. And Clayton sure as hell doesn't deserve to live. But somehow he did, and turning our back on him feels dangerous.

"We can't leave him," I whisper.

"He's too messed up to hurt us," Hudson says.

We rush down the rest of the green, emerging a few feet from the back wall. I see the red glowing light of the fire alarm.

"Clayton's not on the ground! Jo! Jo, can you hear me?"

The voice is distant, coming from above us. I hear a steady thumping of light footsteps across the walkway. Naomi. She's made her way across the walkway and she's watching us from the platform. I wave my hands to quiet her. Once I have her attention, I press my finger to my lips and point behind us. Naomi nods her understanding.

In front of me, Hudson jabs the fire alarm button with more force than feels necessary. His expression tells me it might not be the first time he's tried to engage it, but there is no sound, no change in the light. My heart drops. Tell me it's working. It *has* to work.

"What's going on?" A panicky cold feeling rushes through me. "Is it not working?"

"It's just—what is this? Oh shit."

I force myself forward, try to look around him. The red light is lit. A smaller white light is slowly flashing. And there is something dark smeared on Hudson's fingers. More of it on the pale wall beside the alarm. My body goes cold.

"Is that blood?" I ask.

"Looks like." Hudson holds up his hands, and I see the stains on his fingers more clearly, the red unmistakable. My stomach flips over, my mouth gone sour.

"Something's not right," I say, feeling breathless. "That alarm should work. Clayton's already been here, but how could he have had time to disable—"

"Jo, get down!"

"Maybe it's just not working," I say.

Hudson's eyes go wide, and his face contorts. "Jo, get down!"

I whirl and see everything in slow motion: Clayton leaning against the side of the faux coral wall. Something dark dangles from his fingers. A needle of fear stabs through the base of my throat. He still has the gun, and he's trying to lift it.

A flash of movement darts in front of the stairs. Red hair and a golf club swinging. Hudson's arm hooks around my waist, and I feel myself moving backward even as the golf club slams into Clayton's hand. He drops the gun with a scream, lunging forward at his attacker.

There is a slow-moving commotion. A flurry of arms and legs batter each other weakly. Two voices cry out in pain. I try to make sense of it, but Hudson is still urging me back, pulling me to the Astroturf of a putting green. He pulls me back farther, until I am in a Putt-Putt cave that smells like chlorine and mildew.

In the tussle outside, someone stands. Long red hair swings. Summer. Summer is alive. My heart pounds as the slight figure stumbles and rights herself. Clayton can't quite manage standing and pushes himself to his knees beside her instead.

"Oh shit," Hudson says.

I move around Hudson in time to watch. Summer lifts the gun to Clayton's temple. And then Hudson's hands cover my eyes.

I have so much remorse about that day, but there's one thing I'll never regret.

I'm glad I pulled the trigger.

CHAPTER 39

ONCE UPON A TIME, I WOULD HAVE PREFERRED THIS—MY eyes covered, and my body hidden and still. Once upon a time, I believed this was what spared Cara from some part of the pain, but now I know the truth. What my imagination can conjure is even more horrifying than knowing what's true.

I wrench Hudson's hands away and move past him. We are out of the cave, out of the darkness. We are ten feet from the place where Summer has a gun pressed to Clayton's head.

What the hell is happening here?

Summer is crying without the slightest sound. Her shoulders shake up and down and the gun wobbles dangerously in her grip, trembling at Clayton's temple.

I try to step toward them, but Hudson's hand wraps around my arm.

"Baby."

My mind spins. Baby? Who the hell is—

"Baby, please." It's Clayton. His voice is soft and pleading. I cannot see his face, only the side of his head where Summer has the gun.

"No." Summer sobs. She shakes her head. "No."

Summer shifts under one of the emergency lights, and the sight of her is a horror. Her head is crusted in dried blood. She has one arm wrapped protectively across her stomach, and the other—the hand with the gun—shakes to the point of convulsing. She is beyond pale, her lips chalk white and eyes sunken.

But the expression on her face isn't made of fear. It's made of heartbreak.

My mind tries to wrap itself around the information unfurling before us. Clayton is slowly, gently reaching an arm toward her. "Please, Summer. I need you with me right now. Summer. Please."

Her name falls off his lips comfortably. Easily. His fingers brush her skirt, and she does not tense or mash the gun harder into his temple. She looks at him with a mix of emotions I'd never imagine her showing. Regret. Betrayal. Affection.

It's like a strange and terrible dream, but it's not. This is real. The tenderness between them—there is something here. Something sick and twisted that we all somehow missed.

How did we miss this?

Maybe we didn't all miss it.

Did Lexi know? Is that what happened in the locker room?

I think of Lexi's protective arm around Summer's shoulders earlier. The way she ushered her quickly from Ava's tirade. I think of Hannah, too, tearing after Clayton on the balcony. Summer is barely sixteen years old, and Clayton has to be thirty. This isn't a relationship—it's an outrage. No, it's more than that. It's criminal.

And if Lexi and Hannah found out? I think of Hannah's rage. *I know what you did!*

Hannah knew. They both knew and they confronted him. They did the right and decent thing and now they're dead.

"I thought I lost you, but you're here," Clayton says. "You're here to save us both, aren't you?"

Clayton tries to push himself up, but Summer shakes her head, jabbing the gun into him. "Stop." Her voice cracks into a splintered cry. "You killed them. You *killed* them."

"I didn't want to," he says. "I just want to be with you. Please, Summer. Let's go. It's what you want too, isn't it?" He beckons her with his words. His voice is so soft, but it is all lies. Silk sheets over shark teeth. "We can still be together. That's what you want. It's what we planned."

The church camp. There was no bus waiting to take Summer to a church camp. She lied to be with Clayton tonight. But Ava discovered something, and their twisted plans fell to pieces.

"It is what I wanted before," Summer whispers, and then a horrible, deafening alarm wails into the room—a shrill, insistent warning blaring the horror of this scene at the top of its lungs.

I whirl around, trying to figure out where the noise is coming from, but every alarm is lit now. Every emergency light is flashing steadily overhead.

Summer and Clayton are both crouching, looking around in shock at the sudden wail and flashing lights.

Hudson tugs me to the right, and I spot Naomi and Quincy slowly moving up behind Summer and Clayton. They must have hit another alarm! Quincy's right arm hangs limp at his side, and he's shuffling forward, his eyes fixed on something on the wall. They aren't even looking at Summer and Clayton. They can't be more than twenty feet from them, but it's like the scene unfolding before them is of no consequence.

Naomi marches forward with a tight, urgent pace. She flicks one glance at Summer and Clayton and moves closer to the wall, but whatever is happening with them does not distract her.

"What are they looking at?" I ask.

"The way out," Hudson says, and I see it then, four glowing letters over a black door. EXIT. It could be locked, but it's the first door we've seen without plywood nailed across it. Is it possible?

"Holy shit, they missed one," Hudson says over the wailing buzz of the alarm. The emergency lights are brighter now, casting strange blue shadows across the arcade. "They might get out. *We* might get out."

Naomi and Quincy pass dangerously close to Summer and Clayton on their way to the door. For one instant, the six of us are points on a triangle: Clayton and Summer at one junction, Quincy and Naomi at the second, and Hudson and I form the third point, tucked into the shadows of the Putt-Putt course.

Only Naomi and Quincy move. Summer and Clayton and

Hudson and I have slowed to a crawl. Clayton's shoulders slump. Summer's hand shakes around the gun. Hudson's arm tightens around me. And then, with no warning at all, Clayton explodes forward.

His fist jabs hard and fast—a direct hit to Summer's stomach. She is screaming before she even hits the floor, but Clayton shoves her to the side and searches the ground.

Summer's back arches, and I see the agony grip her. Her scream goes on and on as she falls. Something is wrong. This is more than the effect of one punch. She is in trouble.

I break into a run and see Clayton rise. The scene unfolds in bursts of strobing light. Clayton has the gun. He is aiming, but where? I search the room, spotting Naomi and Quincy. They've stopped near the door, turned by the sound of Summer's cry. Clayton's arm is unsteady, but he's lifting the gun toward them.

"Run!" I scream.

Hudson streaks past me, and then Naomi barrels forward. She's faster than I expected, and before I take another breath, she's slamming into Clayton's leg. He howls in pain, and Hudson leaps on his back. They are stopping a killer, and so I focus on trying to save a life.

Summer writhes and twitches, her face like parchment, her eyes rolling in anguish.

"Help me," I shout. "Something's wrong!"

I hear the gun skitter, and Clayton shouts in pain. I glance up to see his leg kick out and Naomi fly back. She shoves her palm out instinctively to brace her fall and I can see her arm jerk when the bones snap. Naomi curves in on herself with a howl, pulling her arm close to her chest. She rolls to the side with a low cry, and my chest tightens.

I see a vivid image of Naomi in our living room, her arms up with Cara's, dancing to some song too cool for me to know. Now her slim brown arm is bent where it should be straight. I take a step toward her, and then Summer gasps. She's gone completely gray, her lips milk pale in her face.

Dread rolls through me as I think of Naomi's words from all those weeks ago. *If you're going to be a doctor, you have to show them you're a person who can speak up and take action.*

But this time I don't know what action to take. Whatever is happening to Summer, it is invisible. And I'm beginning to fear it might be deadly. "Can you tell me what happened, Summer? Can you tell me where it hurts?"

Summer does not speak at all. Her breathing comes in unsteady rasps. A few feet from us, Hudson is holding Naomi's shoulders to the ground, keeping her still and safe as Quincy moves slowly closer to us all. I turn my attention to Summer, who still isn't speaking. Her back is arched. Her face is a mask of agony.

I touch her shoulder. "Where is it? Where does it hurt?"

Her next noise is a horrific gurgling groan. My stomach twists itself into a knot. This is the sound my father made. This is the glassy-eyed look he wore before he died. My hands flutter uselessly over her stomach.

"I'm sorry," she gurgles. "I told Lexi. I told her about me and Clay…"

"Don't talk," I say, but I don't know if that will help or if I just can't handle the anguish in her voice.

She ignores me, tears spilling out of the corners of her eyes, streaking through the blood on her face. "This is my fault. I told Lexi. I told Hannah. I did this to them."

"No," I say. I shake my head. "No, Summer, Clayton did this. It was Clayton."

"I tried to—" She swallows hard, wincing. "On the roof, I tried, but he shot me."

The smear of blood on the skylight. It *was* Summer. I have no idea how she got down those stairs, how she's here now.

"And then you came down here?" I prompt, trying to keep her talking. To keep her awake. "Were you trying to find us?"

She shakes her head. "The alarm. I came for the fire alarm, but it didn't work…"

She trails off in a hopeless sob. Can't she hear the alarm now? But, no. Her gaze is drifting, her eyes half-closed. She's too far gone now, and I don't know how to help.

With Quincy, I could stop the bleeding. With Hudson, I could protect his head. I am doing what I'm supposed to do—I am not frozen. I am trying. And I am still losing her.

I take her hand and blink back tears. "The alarm worked, Summer. You did it."

"I did?"

I force a warm smile. "You did."

In truth I think Naomi or Quincy hit it, but when a smile breaks through Summer's anguish, I know it doesn't matter. Just as quickly, a sob rips through her, and her body spasms in agony.

"Tell me what happened. Is there a wound? Did he shoot you?" I ask, because there's blood in her hair and down her neck, but when she turns her head, that injury doesn't look serious enough to be causing her this level of pain. Her hands are feathering over her stomach, but her dress is clean. Dread presses down on my chest. Summer's injury is internal.

She takes a stilted breath, and her hands flutter at her stomach again. Summer's color is getting worse. Now her lips have a bluish tinge. Panic sends little frissons of cold through my body.

Whatever is happening inside Summer isn't just hurting her. It's killing her.

"I'm sorry," she says to me. "Please tell my mom and dad to pray for my forgiveness."

"Summer, hold on," I say, squeezing her fingers.

Her next breath sticks somewhere halfway in.

"What's happening?" Quincy asks. His voice is small and frightened. He is right behind me, and he is ghost pale. "Summer? Are you okay?"

He drops to his knees beside her, taking one of her small pale hands in his. "You're okay. You are okay." He says it sternly, like if he says it with enough force, it will be the truth. "Help is coming. You just need to hold on for a little bit."

Summer looks at him, and I can see her lips move. I can see her trying to respond. Trying to thank him, maybe. But then her mouth goes slack, and her chest deflates. I remember the spread of blood on dirty linoleum. The gurgle of his breath. I remember his eyes losing focus just like hers. That's what happened when my father died.

I try to move Summer's shoulders, because her chest isn't rising. She isn't breathing. I press my fingers to her neck, but there's no pulse. The insistent buzz of the alarm feels like a knife to my ears. A worthless assault of noise and sound that does not do the thing it should. Because there is no help for Summer. It's too late.

Quincy releases her hand, his face stony.

"She's not breathing," I say, pushing back my panic as I rise to my knees.

I position my hands to start CPR, and then Naomi's voice pierces the shriek of the alarm. "Stop him! Stop him! He's going to get out!"

I look up in time to see a sliver of light on the back wall. The sliver widens into a gap and I can see the parking lot beyond. The door under the EXIT sign is open. Clayton is at the door. Somehow, between Naomi getting injured and me helping Summer, he found his way out, slithering under our noses like the snake he is.

Quincy leaps to his feet, and Hudson bursts forward. But Clayton is already shouldering his way outside. He's leaning heavily to the left, probably keeping his weight off his ankle, but he is making his way through. Naomi is right. He's going to get out. He's going to—

Pop. Pop. Pop. Pop.

Clayton's body jerks with the impact of each bullet. My whole body is shocked into stillness as his body falls gracelessly, flopping sideways to wedge in the half-open door. Clayton does not move or twitch. His body is motionless, a lump of muscle and clothing blinking in and out under the emergency lights.

I turn in the stunned silence, looking at Hudson, searching for the gun he must have picked up. But Hudson's hands are empty. Naomi is still on the ground. And then I hear the gun clatter to the concrete floor. And I see the man standing above the dropped weapon.

"Quincy?" Hudson asks, his voice hollow with shock.

Quincy stares down at the gun. He is pale and shaking, tears welled in his eyes. "No," he whispers. Then he looks up, ferocity clear in his face. "No, he isn't getting out."

I'm glad I'm the one who killed him.

CHAPTER 40

THE LETTER ARRIVES THREE MONTHS LATER. QUINCY'S handwriting is neat and crisp on the envelope. It is addressed to all of us, and so it sits on our coffee table until everyone arrives.

Well. Until Hudson gets here from work. Naomi is already here. She's been here a lot since the incident, and not just with Cara. She's here with me and Mom too. Mom's still out a lot, but something snapped open in her when she met us at the hospital the morning we were rescued. I saw it in her eyes the way I saw the change in my own reflection after Dad. Some things change you in ways that will never change back.

Apparently almost losing me did that for Mom. She took three weeks off work—an unthinkable length of time for her before. She cooked giant vats of vegetable soup and huge trays of lasagna that Cara and Naomi and I ate for breakfast, lunch, and dinner. She even bought ice packs and special pillows to help Naomi feel comfortable at our house while she recovered from elbow surgery.

Displaced fractures of the radius and ulna. She's had two surgeries and a hell of a rough road that isn't done yet.

Mom rattles her keys, and it shakes me out of my thoughts. She's watching the three of us from the door, her eyes drifting to the letter on the table. "I could call in. Get someone to cover the flight. Or you could open it now and save me the worry."

"It's going to be fine," I say.

Cara nods. "I've got this, Mom. You know I'll call you in a second if this is bad."

"It won't be bad," Naomi says, adjusting her sling. "Quincy doesn't have a bad bone in his body."

"He might have written something that brings it all back," Mom says. "You've been through so much."

I stand and give my mom a hug. She is small and soft like Cara. "It never really went away."

Mom nods, her eyes briefly tearing up. Then she sniffs and straightens her shoulders. "My flight takes off in ninety minutes. If you need me, just call."

"We will," Cara says firmly. "Now go."

Cara's changed too. Her nightmares have slowed, and I think she's enjoyed being strong for Naomi and me. She force-feeds us smoothies and made me join her yoga class. It's funny seeing her like this, standing a little straighter, wearing her long hair in a sleek ponytail as she reminds me of my next step on the college-prep checklist. The internship starts in two weeks, and, thanks to Cara, I'm ready.

Mom pauses at the door, and when she sees me, a flicker of sadness moves through her face. I wonder if it's like the way I see her in Cara. I've always taken after my dad. Maybe every time she looks at me, she sees him too.

On the way out, Mom runs into Hudson. The streaks in his hair are gone. He keeps it shorter now, and he doesn't laugh as easily. But he's still Hudson, and for all his jittery endless motion, he has kept me steady these long weeks.

"Ms. Thomas," he says to my mom in greeting.

"Mr. Kumar," she replies with a smile.

He wishes her a safe flight before he steps inside, grabbing an apple off the table and handing Cara a box of Assam tea she asked him to pick up at the international market. And then he situates himself on the couch beside me, his leg bouncing in a crazed rhythm. I put my hand on his knee, and he takes it, lacing his fingers with mine. The bouncing resumes.

"So. We ready to do this?" he asks, nodding at the letter.

"Yeah, I'm ready," Naomi says. She moves her thick braids behind her shoulder with her good arm. "But wait. Did any of you hear back from him at all?"

We've all been writing Quincy since he entered the six-month program for psychiatric treatment. We've sent letters, cards, messages, and even emails. No one has heard a word back in return. My last memory of Quincy was him crumpled sobbing on the floor, the gun not twelve inches from his body.

I don't know what possessed him to pick up that gun. What

made him end it. But I'm afraid he'll never recover from it. That the regret of it will eat him alive.

I tilt my head back and forth. "I'm…" I search for the right words, but the truth is the only thing that makes sense. "I'm afraid he's upset with me. I couldn't save Summer. What if he hasn't written because of that?"

Naomi narrows her eyes. "Jo, Summer's spleen ruptured. Remember what the nurse told you at the hospital. Even a trained surgeon probably couldn't have saved her. It was too fast."

"I know that. But I could have gone after her when she ran away. When I saw her on the balcony. I could have—"

"And I could have not yelled at Hannah," Hudson says.

"The would-have, could-have game isn't going to help any of you," Cara says. She shakes her head. "I'm going to go make us lunch. And the three of you are going to read this letter, and then we're going to move forward with whatever he says, okay?"

We nod and watch my sister retreat to the kitchen.

"Your girlfriend is getting bossy," I say to Naomi.

She grins. "I know. I like it."

Hudson reaches for the envelope and hands it to me. I take a breath, and he swoops in with a brief tender kiss. "We do this when you're ready."

I peel back the envelope flap and unfold the letter. And then I begin to read.

Dear Hudson, Naomi, and Jo,

I spend a lot of time thinking how that night was supposed to go. We were going to thank the customers who watched the last movie. We would eat one last handful of popcorn and lock the doors for a final time. Then we'd caravan to the IHOP for pancakes and stories and memories.

Now I just want to forget.

Who'd want to remember the night half of us died?

I wonder every day if we should have known he was capable of this. If I had paid closer attention or taken all his outbursts more seriously, could I have changed what happened? Could I have stopped the killing before it started?

Maybe it wouldn't have mattered, but the wondering messes with me. The whole world is a set of dominoes— everything we say and do touches another domino, and they all tumble this way or that. Your choices might ripple out to someone who cures cancer. Maybe my recent choices opened a window of opportunity for a killer.

I know you know what happened that night, but there are things I should tell you. I had a secret I never shared. And I knew someone else's secret too—the secret that set this whole thing in motion.

The secret I knew is about the two of them. I had seen them a few weeks earlier in the locker room. They moved apart quickly, trying to hide what they were doing, but I knew. When you're quiet, you see lots of things people try to keep hidden.

If I had told someone that day, maybe he'd have been fired and everything would be different. If I'd pulled that secret out into the light, Clayton wouldn't have been there at all. And if he wasn't there, they'd all be alive.

I didn't tell because I was angry. And I was angry because my secret is that I was in love.

I can't believe you didn't see the look all over my face. I saw how bright and interesting she was every day, but I never told her. What I saw didn't change how I felt; it only made me sure my feelings didn't matter. So I held back and kept quiet, and now she's dead and I'll always have to live with wondering if I could have stopped it.

How do you believe in your own goodness when you know something like that? Maybe one day I'll learn to make peace with what I did. Maybe we all have to make peace with that night, with the fact we're here and they're gone.

I have so much remorse about that day, but there's one thing I'll never regret.

I'm glad I pulled the trigger.

I'm glad I'm the one who killed him. For all of us, really, but for Summer most of all. It was the only thing I could give her in the end.

Quincy

We sit with the letter for a long time. Cara and Naomi eventually retire to Cara's room for reruns of *This Old House*. And Hudson sits with me on the couch, his legs jumping and his fingers drumming. Even more than usual, if that's possible.

"He sounds like he's in bad shape," Hudson says.

But I shake my head. "That's not what I got."

"No? Then what did you get out of that?"

"I got the truth, I think. He blames himself because he was in love with Summer. And that's why he did it. It makes sense, I guess."

Hudson goes still then, his dark eyes fixing on some faraway spot. "I could have done it, you know. If I'd found that gun first…"

"I know," I admit. "I've thought the same thing a thousand times, and I hate it."

"You should hate it. We should all hate this shit," Hudson says. "None of us should be thinking about any of this."

"But we are," I say. "It's the hand we were dealt, so we've got to do what we can."

"And what's that?" Hudson asks.

I shrug and pull out another piece of notebook paper and my favorite pen. "We play the cards we've got. We keep moving forward."

Hudson's in motion again, scooting up on the couch, curling his arm around my waist. I feel the weight of his head on my shoulder and take a deep breath that smells like all things Hudson.

"Moving forward," he says. "I like it."

I put my pen down and decide my response to Quincy can wait. I breathe in the warm, familiar smell of a boy who helped me survive. I put my hands on his face and press my lips to his mouth. His hands still shake on my face when he kisses me back, like the whole world is still an exciting shock. Hudson is always moving. With him, it's easy to avoid standing still.

I hear Naomi laugh in the other room, and I smile. She's got scars on her arm that will never leave. We've all got scars from that night, but we survived.

I take a breath and relish the fact I'm still here. Still breathing.

"I thought you were writing Quincy back," he says.

"I will," I say. "But right now, I'm enjoying this moment."

"Not too shabby as far as moments go."

I laugh and feel the delight of that. Of the breath in my lungs and Hudson's hands on my face. I'm awed by every piece of this moment, by the sheer simple wonder of being alive.

ACKNOLWEDGMENTS

There are always so many people to thank and so little brain-power left in me to remember them all. Through the seemingly endless slog of the pandemic, my outstanding support network taped me back together and kept me going. This book wouldn't exist without them.

Enormous thanks goes to the brilliant, innovative New Leaf Team. Suzie, Sophia, Kendra, Pouya, and so many others. I feel lucky every single day to be a Leaf. You make this job easier at every turn. Where on earth would I be without you?

Some stories really find their feet in edits, and this book was definitely one of them. Thank you to Eliza and Wendy for helping me to find the heart of Jo's story. Your wisdom and guidance have been a true gift. And to Beth and Karen and the countless other Sourcebooks rock stars who make it all happen—I'm so grateful!

Writing has its moments, and I have many smart, talented, beautiful women who help me to keep my chin up when those moments stink. Margaret Petersen Haddix, Edith Patou, and Lisa Klein in particular have been amazing friends. And my books and life in general work a million times better with my ride-or-die, Jody Casella, involved. Jody, I'll never thank you enough for your friendship. Not ever.

Beyond the writing, there are people who make life a little sweeter. A special thanks to my friends Sharon, Lacey, Tiffany and Leigh Anne, and to Emily, Robin, and Sam for making my weekdays nicer. To my fellow bookworm Troy for awesome book recommendations, and Lori Ann and Monique for unexpected flowery surprises, and especially to Janet and Jen, who offered not only friendship, but also many happy reader messages, the kind that keep me going when I just don't wanna. And of course to the best pair of Bens I know—thank you for sound advice, making me laugh, and for always offering to help. You're the best in the business.

I also have an outstanding family to support me. Sheila, Debi, Angela, Murray, and Debbie (one Debi isn't enough!), thank you for not giving up on me when I was a scrawny little thing who didn't want to have her hair brushed. And to David, who has navigated huge transitions with so much kindness and generosity. Thank you.

But yes, every single acknowledgment page I write always winds back to the same three people. To Ian, Adrienne, and

Lydia, the light of my world and loves of my life. The lives you are building are my favorite stories of all time. I'm so lucky to be your mom.

ABOUT THE AUTHOR

 Natalie D. Richards is the *New York Times* bestselling author of many page-turning thrillers. She lives in Ohio with her three amazing kids and an oversized dog named Wookie.

FIREreads

§ #getbooklit

Your hub for the hottest young adult books!

Visit us online and sign up for our
newsletter at FIREreads.com

 @sourcebooksfire

 sourcebooksfire

 firereads.tumblr.com